THE AMERICANS OF ABERCROMBY SQUARE

JP MAXWELL

On this second time around for Harriet, it would be remiss not to appreciate the city and people of Liverpool, past and present. Their unbreakable bond with the places and stories of the city made the psychogeography of this book come to life, and I am proud to mention the ancestors – known and unknown from Mayo to West Africa – in this mix again.

I'd like to thank my wife, Katy McGunigle, for her love, wisdom, strength and determination. Early proofers and beta readers Christian Murray-Smith (encore!), Jeanne Colwell (the sister and NOLa aficionado), Shahnaz Ahmed and Wendy Hollington, all helped me to find the centre. To Jonathon Nimmons of WriteSeen.com for his tireless Tasmanian Devil energy, to my brilliant publisher James Lumsden-Cook at Bennion Kearny for yet another leap of faith and investment, and to Clare Coombes at Liverpool Literary Agency for her incredible support then and now.

To my departed brother Paul, who worked with docks and ships all of his adult life. He is loved and missed.

- JP Maxwell, October 2024

Also by JP Maxwell

For exclusive content and more, visit
https://jpmaxwellwriter.art.blog

If you enjoy this book, please be a superstar...
... a review would be great!

#1 – WATERLOO SUNSET

Marine Crescent, Liverpool, April 14th 1865

It is a chilly spring evening to be sitting out on the porch, but she does so every evening, come wind, rain or shine. The rickety wicker rocking chair creaks as she moves back and forth, aligning its motion with the brooding swell of the Irish Sea out there, beyond the sand hills of the Waterloo shore, to the North of town.

Nearby are Blucher Street, Wellington Street, East Street. All references to the place and moment old Bony succumbed nearly a lifetime ago, rubbing it into every Frenchman's face that will ever pass through here. The grand terrace of Georgian townhouses and mansions overlooking the bay stretches for half a mile, home to shipping magnates, merchants and captains, the famous and infamous. And then, at number 6, Marine Crescent, is the grand Georgian pile Harriet Farrell chose to make her home after she left 101 Canning Street to Padraig and Sarah. This is the haven she made after the horror, but ghosts – angels and demons - have followed her. How she misses dear Conté, craves the moment that she wakes up from a bad dream.

Did Lee really surrender at Appomattox like the newspaper said? Then perhaps now Louisiana will become a safer place for her child, but she knows how bitter reality tastes after the sweet dream. There is nothing left there for them but ghosts too.

A yellow and orange sorbet sunset melts into the horizon and Harriet Farrell watches it, letting the marmalade sky remind her of the West and how there is very little to stop her upping sticks and returning to America now… but to what? Will it really be Louisiana, or should she prospect to California? The latter sounds like just the place to make a new start, to forget everything and look ahead to the Western sky and an ocean of possibilities, but here she remains in this odd corner of England, never one to sit upon her hands yet having to do so. If she endeavours to stay busy, then she may never move at all and at least then they will bury her with her beloved when that day comes. Harriet Farrell likes her ghosts and she just doesn't want to forget, but the problem is that neither does someone else.

The 'guests' have gone to bed early, perhaps because having a real bed in which to sleep is such a novelty. They are single girls, young women, and what society calls fallen women, though 'dropped' might be more apt. They are waifs and strays who otherwise might end up in brothels or the workhouse, who sought out the strange and kind American lady on the basis of a whisper, only to find that she is stranger and kinder than they would ever imagine.

But now her safe house is full to the rafters and even good-hearted people bring diseases and past traumas with them, no matter how much time Harriet spends on a clean regime of mind and body. She must look after her child. Perhaps it is time to sell and go, not least because these last few months, someone has been watching her and she senses a malign spirit descending upon this hermitage, upon a woman who only wanted to stay hidden, anonymous. It's a pity, because up until then she had found a peace that she had never known in her young life.

The evensong of wild and migratory birds, the fluttering of dragonflies past her nose, the rustling of hedgehogs and the fresh brine and sweet flora of the shore all points to this place as an idyll, but she knows that this means nothing if her violent past is still out there, waiting and watching, quite probably with malevolent intent.

She waits, as she does every evening, for the watcher to either make his move or reveal himself. Her Colt .45 remains a reflex away, as ever. She sniffs the air and gazes into the long shadows across the garden wall, beyond into the sandhills and silhouettes. He likes to stalk in the dark, but he arrives at dusk. Tonight, she has had enough of waiting for him.

The birds stop singing, the breeze drops to stillness, the aromas vanish into a void and Harriet knows he is there, yards away.

'What in hell do you want from me?' she whispers, out of any earshot bar her own.

She gets up from her rocker and strides down the path, shale crunching under her boots. Through the gate at across the road where the gas lighters have already visited, the neat line of lamp posts denoting the frontier between the terrace and nature. Of course, a Mississippi girl would live so close to the wild and the water, transposing tropical for frigid. Now the long row of Georgian elegance is behind her and she is in the long grass, where a few cattle graze and moo. To her left there is a twitch of movement and she knows it is *his* turn to be nervous, as very well he should be when she gets hold of him.

So, Harriet has a good relationship with most of the neighbours, save those who look down their noses upon her guests. These sound, stout neighbours have an understanding with her about the land out front, how she likes to use it for shooting practice and the occasional bagging of ducks or geese for the Thanksgiving or Christmas table. She often brings game birds to those neighbours too, once her own household is catered for, rather like a friendly cat might bring a gift to a doting human.

Those ones like her, for all her strangeness. So when she mentions that they might want to avoid the undergrowth for a day or two, they understand. They don't ask questions because they probably wouldn't get a straight answer anyways. No skin off their noses and nothing much of interest out there anyway off the beaten track to the beach. A fine enough accord.

Snap.

'Aaaargh, Jaysus bollocks! Me leg! Me fuckin' leg!'

He doesn't sound like someone who would live around here. Ever the Choctaw, Harriet could smell him at a distance, knowing that he would be determined to keep out of plain sight in his snooping detail. The further she walks into the sandhills, the further he is pushed back into the undergrowth towards the collection of iron mantraps she has laid in the undergrowth, among the pretty wild flowers. There is not much difference to snaring vermin, when it comes down to it.

'Aaargh, please God, the pain! Aaaargh! Help! Someone! Anyone!'

If in doubt, follow the screaming. She strides through the swaying reeds and is aware of the natural sounds and smells again, augmented by the moaning lump of a man before her, characterised by any one of the gangs operating out of the town, travelled to this hinterland.

'Howyer,' says Harriet Farrell before the pathetic, twitching bastard before her, yelping and yapping. It's her best Irish accent, just to put the wind further up him.

'Miss, oh thank God. Jaysus, Mary and Joseph can ye get someone to release me from this trap, the gamekeeper or summat? Me leg's in a dreadful mess, so.'

'Gladly. Once you tell me who sent you to spy on me.'

'Oh miss. What are ye sayin', like? Please help me.'

'Right ho. I'll be off home then for supper. There are wild dogs out here. They'll catch the smell of blood mighty quickly I would guess.'

That puts the fear of God into him. 'Don't go miss. I didn't mean ye no harm so.'

By the looks of him, she very much doubts that. 'I'll need a bit more information, old chum. Your name, for starters.'

'Seamus.'

'Seamus what?'

'Seamus Roscommon.'

'Where are you from, Seamus?'

'Scottie Road.'

'No, originally.'

'Ireland.'

'County?'

'Roscommon.'

'Seamus Roscommon from Roscommon. Right.'

'Aye. This smarts awful, Miss.'

'You must think I was born with cotton for brains, Seamus Roscommon.'

'No, Miss.'

'So who sent you?'

'I works for meself, like. I was slipped some guineas in an envelope with a note. Watch you, record everything I see,' he taps his temple, gasping and sweating, 'up there and await further instructions.'

'Do you have the note?'

'It said to burn it. Now please let me out of this thing. Tis a cruel fate so you're wishing on me.'

'I could put you out of your misery.'

'No miss, I beg you. I have seven nips so. Beautiful babies, aye.'

'Why now? After all this time?'

'What?'

Seamus Roscommon from Roscommon really does have no idea what she is talking about. Harriet has met good liars and terrible liars before, she would like to think that she falls into the former category herself. Seamus here is telling the truth, as any normal man under such duress would, save divulging his own name, which is immaterial. She could and probably should put him out of his misery, just to send a message to the scumbag who commissioned him, but that's just cheap murder and she's vowed away from that since the dirty business of '63.

This little incident has made her mind up about something, though. She pulls her gun.

'Oh dear God, no. I've told ye everything.'

'Shut up.'

She jams the barrel into the spring mechanism and the trap snaps open. He pulls his lame leg free, wincing.

'Oh, thank the lord.'

'I'd use some of that cash they gave you to pay a physician, before infection sets in and you lose the leg. Or worse.'

A high-pitched whine and drawl emanate from him. 'Worse? Wh-what?'

'You should get going, but not before I give you a message for them, Seamus Roscommon from Roscommon. If I can't shoot you in the head it will have to be something else.'

He struggles up on his good leg, tears of pain running down his ruddy cheeks. 'Miss?'

'You tell them that Harriet Farrell is retired. You tell them that she is going somewhere they'll never find her and if they try to follow her, the next spy or his manager in the enterprise won't get off so lightly. Can you do that?'

'Surely. When I hear from them, Miss.'

She picks up a long piece of driftwood, ideal for a crutch. He gladly accepts it. 'So you'd better beat it, Seamus Roscommon. Those wild dogs will start mooching soon. They'll awful nasty fangs, so they have.'

'Aye, Miss. Don't need a second invitation. Aaargh, jaysus, me leg.'

'Good man yourself.'

And he's off, hobbling away back towards the long crescent to find his pony and trap. Just another idiot and how she tires of them in this world.

Something is going down and this is only the start of it. She can sniff it like she sniffed Seamus Roscommon from Roscommon. She'd be a liar to say she hadn't been considering it for a while, in spite of her desire to stay for the sake of a dead beloved, a memory that can never be struck. Time to get their things in order, time to bail from this backwater like she should have done two years ago. A lonely grave meaning nothing to anyone but a handful of people kept her here, but now Harriet must break the past before it comes back and breaks her. Why did she ever think that it wouldn't?

She begins springing the traps, her last task before home, bed and a sleepless night. There's a heap of arranging to do.

#2 – FORD'S THEATRE

Washington D.C., April 14th 1865

Bang.

Dang.

Got him. Actually. Got him. Almost as dammit square in the back of his head. The slug thudded into his brain and there ain't a man alive who might survive that, twitch, groan and splutter as he may. What fools they were, letting JWB get so close, but that must be thanks to good old Maj. Gen. Butler and his string-pulling. Some officer in blue had tried to intervene, but the promising young buck of an actor was primed for some resistance. If the fella hadn't made a move to defend himself, he would have seen his jugular ripped, too, but the shoulder slash was enough to get him out of the way. Too bad, as it would have been one less blue bastard. That was the sum total of the security retinue around Lincoln, so it was a turkey shoot. For that moment, time slowed. Not that dashing Young JWB is hanging around up here to admire his work, for there's a bow to take below, where his adoring fans wait in stunned silence. Back to normal speed now. He leaps. Crack.

Now he is on the stage, at last gleaning the full attention of an audience who are not sure about whether or not they've just seen a very weird stunt or the actual assassination of their President. Well, lookee, a rapt crowd, about goddamn time too. That stunned silence is like a blanket over 'em, pregnant gasps and a few agonised tears are all he gets by way of a curtain call, but everyone knows that JWB has stolen the show this evening. His ankle is throbbing and he may well have bust it in the jump down from the box, but he is so pumped right now that it just don't matter. He's used to treading the boards in this city, with their po-faced take on just about everything and their fawning, false love of his sissy, pacifist brother, but this is *his* show now. At last, JWB has his moment, and *what* a moment – one that will resound through history.

There ya go, JWB. Showed them what yas are made of. All of 'em. Bang, dang. Glory, glory, hallelujah.

John Wilkes Booth will be a name remembered long after his brother or father, fellow thespians and Yankee stooges alike. He will die more of a hero than they'll ever be, once the South rises again. All of his world is a stage and he just wishes that he could stay longer to milk it. This here is real theatre. Time to take his bow and his exit.

'Sic semper tyrannos!' he cries in his rehearsed exclamation, the battle cry of Virginia, then under his breath as he drinks the attention, 'The South is avenged.' The fulsome end.

Still, no one makes to stop him. He saunters off into the wings, past Miss Keene, an English ham in the lead role who shall now be known forever in a bit part to the greatest entrance ever made. She recoils in fright, her best performance all night, all goddamn season, all her career. What a curtain call.

'Bravo,' he mutters and vanishes into the backstage labyrinth. JWB, for one night only.

#3 – CODA

St James Cemetery, Liverpool, April 26th 1865

Conté Marie-Louise Louverture, 9th May 1841 to 24th June 1863.
Eternal Rest Grant Upon Her o Lord
and Let Perpetual Light Shine Upon Her
- Her Friend, Harriet.

'Hello again.'

A fresh morning, for April. Surrounding the sunken, limestone bowl of a former quarry, now a necropolis for a metropolis; oaks, beeches and sycamores gyrate in the seaside air like Polovtsian dancers, protecting the dead from the worst of the biting elements. As for the living, Harriet and Baba Farrell, a nineteen-month-old cannonball of energy, are quite comfortable in this place among rich and poor, slaves and slavers, come fair or foul winds. It is where an essential piece of them remains, and no dirty Liverpool squall will ever put them off seeing their beloved Conté. Only the forthcoming distance of their move a world away can achieve that feat.

'Da-da, da-da,' babbles Baba, stomping and splashing upon the wet earth on the grave, part toddler, part amphibian. She falls backwards with a splat and chuckles, grabbing a handful of delicious, moist soil and eating it. This breaks Harriet's trance, and she picks up her child, wiping and muttering.

'There are worms and cholera and all sorts in that, Baba. What kind of mother will people think I am? Look at you. Filthy child. Spit it out, I say.'

'Aw, mama.'

Baba is not prone to tantrums, which is a blessing. She just gets on with being a rambunctious infant, but Harriet is quite sure that her progeny understands more about her mother than is immediately obvious. That trait runs in the family, as does being an excellent swimmer, even in shallow mud. One day soon, her daughter will swim in the Pacific.

Snap. From the cinder path behind them. Is this another spy? Harriet trains her Colt upon the interloper.

'Harry love, you'll shoot me balls off one day. Like you did that devil man you called a husband.'

Harriet lowers the piece and curls a lip. 'Then don't go creeping up on us, Pat. You should know better.'

'*You* said to meet you here. I'm not for doing no creeping so. And I know what creeping is; I did it for a living once.'

'And very good you were.'

'Ooh, thanks.'

'Sarcasm is the lowest form of wit, Padraig.'

Pat looks around himself and shivers. 'I don't like this place too much, girls. Your Uncle Pat gets the collywobbles, so he does.' He tickles Baba's belly, and she squeaks gibberish back at him. 'Small pig.'

'She's the only person who makes any sense out of you.'

'Aye, so. Smart girl.'

'Have you made the arrangements?'

'Everything is in crates, ready to stow on the passage. We're going to miss youse two. But…'

He hesitates.

Padraig McCartney is the picture of an Irish country gentleman in his tweeds, clutching a brolly and a newspaper, which Harriet knows he can't read. This appearance is a little bit of a surprise, for he rarely takes a day off from his business of cleaning windows up and down Dale Street, Castle Street, and Water Street, which has an endless demand. Pat used to break such windows; now he polishes them, and there is no better man for the job in town. He often goes up without even taking his ladders, famed for his daily, death-defying act as much as for his speed and efficiency. Right now, though, his words seem to be stuck in his throat.

'Pat, what is the matter?'

He wafts the broadsheet in front of her nose. 'See for yourself.'

She takes the copy of the Liverpool Mercury off him as Baba coos and reaches out a chubby arm for her Uncle Pat. Then, an invisible fist punches Harriet Farrell in the guts, forcing her to gasp as she scans the headline.

'Oh my Dear God, no.'

Here they are, back in the US Consulate back-office on Paradise Street, the most appropriate place to go after receiving such awful news. She confines her audiences with Mr Thomas Haines Dudley, United States Consul to the Borough of Liverpool, to rarer, special occasions these days. Dudley has had plenty of business fighting the increasingly organised and aggressive presence of the Confederacy, which she thought, like the vast majority of others, would be destined to end in the light of Robert E. Lee's capitulation. Harriet's only business of late has been keeping a good house up on the sands of Waterloo. Up until an hour ago, leaving that place was all she had in mind.

'I am truly sorry to hear about your friend, Thomas.'

Dudley's eyes are red, wet, and raw. Perhaps from too little sleep and too many court cases, but more likely as a result of a particular communiqué from Washington, which would have reached him at the same time that it found its way to the news desks, straight off the steamer. His is a very personal grief. Lincoln's serene portrait stares down at them both. Harriet has lost a president, but Thomas has lost his pal. The shock is palpable.

'I heartily appreciate the visit, Harriet. No others in this town would understand. Not even my loyal staff.'

Dudley strokes Baba's face as the toddler clumps around his bureau, bouncing off the furniture. Harriet doesn't really know what else to say as it won't get past the lump in her gullet or the rocks in her belly. She settles for practicalities. 'Is there anything I can help you with?'

Harriet curses the offer coming from her lips, for there isn't much she should do, really. A steamer will depart for New York this evening and all she should consider is being on it with her child. Dudley looks worn out, a little jaundiced even. 'The shooter didn't act alone. I can't believe he got past the Pinkertons so easily. Something stinks.'

'The war's won and our work here is finished, Thomas.' She didn't mean it to come out so crass and uncaring, but this has been burning away at Harriet since she read the headline. No more, no more.

Dudley twitches. She's never seen him so agitated, not even when the Rebs were taking over the town with promises of cotton. 'I want a drink. Would you like a drink? Yes, of course you would, Harriet.'

All the carafes and decanters in the cabinet are drained. She never took Dudley for a boozer, although she is all too aware of how some hide it better than others. 'Now lookee, you're not setting a good example, supping with the young widow of a Southern Commander in your own office.'

'Good point, Mrs Dunwoody.'

'No. It's Farrell. Never that name please Thomas, not even in jest.'

Dudley sifts through the rest of the cupboard, finding only dust. 'And it appears that I am bone dry. We shall go to the Athenaeum. Dammit, yes, we shall.'

'They don't let women in there. Are you drunk already, Thomas?'

'They permit wives and daughters on Wednesdays. For sherry and backgammon.'

'I am neither. Unless you are proposing to a merry widow, you old goat?'

A weak smile invades his face for the first time. 'No, but you'll pass for family. My niece. I'm still the Consul to this damn borough, you know. I can swing the lead when I have cause.'

'Like when getting drunk.'

'Never a more appropriate moment. Please, I need the company.'

'What about Pat?'

Dudley squirms in his shoes, but Pat covers him quickly enough, fidgeting with the cap in his hands. 'Yes, thanks for the offer, Mr Dudley.'

The Consul flinches a little, being the gentleman that he is. 'Don't be like that, Pat. Yes, they may tolerate a female, but never an Irishman. I hope you understand.'

'Pfft. Don't fuckin' drink anyway. And even if I did, it wouldn't be with all ye posh nobs, like. So, no thank you, for nothin'.'

Harriet glances at her pocket watch. 'My boat leaves in four hours.'

'Then you have time,' says Dudley. Harriet emits a long breath. Should she explain why she is leaving? The straw that broke the camel's back? The interloper in the sandhills?

Baba drools all over his Chesterfield sofa. 'The baby?'

'Let my staff mind her.'

'I'm not sure. No offence, but she never leaves my side.'

'She will be fine. This building is officially United States territory and the safest spot in the entire town, nay the entire country. Please, Harriet. I need this. You are the only person left in town who will understand.'

'I'll take her,' says Pat.

'No, Mr Dudley is right. You've done enough, Pat,' she says, 'Look, I am afraid I can't, Thomas. Today of all days. This visit was to say goodbye and to thank you.' Again, she debates with herself whether or not to tell him about the watcher in the long grass, but the Consul clearly has enough on his plate.

'You must, Harriet. Please. I am a shell of a man, and I sorely need an hour of your company and wisdom.' Dudley has gone grey, not just in his hair but in his pallor. Something has scared the bejesus out of him. Perhaps she needs to know. Perhaps she should just get out of town.

Baba couldn't care less. Is this not the high time that she shook off her own anvil of grief for Conté and set her soulmate free? That Creole ghost has admonished Harriet for her self-imposed exile over the past score of months. Harriet should not become Queen Victoria, a weeping widow mourning for years on end. 'When I drink, I mean business, Thomas. Just a caveat.'

'Which makes you the ideal foil for me. You do nothing by half measures.' Dudley offers his arm to link. How can she refuse him at this sad moment?

'You're buying, Consul.'

One drink. What harm can it do?

Church Street is an outlier in the borough, a drag dedicated to couture for the growing artisan class with spectacular arcades hidden within tidy alleys and grand boutiques for those with a discerning and wealthy footfall. The impressive crown of thorns

13

tower of St Peter's Church welcomes wealthy promenaders and shoppers up and down the wide pavements and adjacent is the Athenaeum and library. Hidden in plain sight, the plain entrance to the club is found at an ornate but narrow doorway cloistered between a haberdashery and a tobacconist. This place is not meant to be noticed by passers-by, for the comfort and discretion of its gentlemen members.

Dudley shuts the door behind them, and they head upstairs, feet clacking on the marble steps. Harriet wonders why she agreed to come here just for the sake of a drink, a place where the same combination of rich tobacco stink and expensive cologne as her dead husband lingers, cloying all the way up the nostrils, dominating the sensibility. Banastre Xavier Dunwoody lives on in these very walls. She never cares to think about that bastard, even about his fulsome comeuppance, but some places have a way of summoning the dead, however much the dead themselves are redacted from the memory. Still, being here makes Harriet feel like she matters again, even if it is just to temporarily salve poor Dudley's grief. The most important American in Liverpool is in a sad state, and he needs the company of the only person in the borough who understands his acute pain. Further, it has been a long, long time since she let her hair down, dubious venue that the Athenaeum is. They climb the marble steps.

The attendant looks like he's trying to swallow a lump of coal when he sets eyes upon her.

'Ah, Halls. This is my sister's daughter. Visiting from Louisiana.'

'Yes sir, but strictly speaking, we cannot...'

'Set us up in my usual spot with a bottle of the best.'

'But...'

'Are you going to make a show of me in front of my favourite niece, Halls?'

'Of course not, sir.'

'Then hop to it.'

'Yes sir. Very good, sir. And for the lady?'

'Just another glass,' she says. Halls emits a curt bow and a thinly-disguised sneer.

The attendant doesn't look too convinced, but Dudley's presence carries more weight than most in this town. How long the Consul will remain in post after the news that just rolled off that steamer is another question. Everyone watches America in this town, North and South. They are led across the grand smoking room towards a snug booth in the corner, which affords a full view of the floor without being in earshot of any of the other patrons. Fortunately, only two others occupy the space at the other end.

'Place is like a morgue,' mutters Dudley.

'Replete with ghosts. Nasty ones, too.'

'It's not normally this quiet.'

'I'm not au fait with such things, Thomas.'

'Gentlemen's clubs are a place for dirty secrets to be discussed and hairbrained scheming to be concocted. Not much else.'

Brandy arrives. 'Thank you, my good man,' says Harriet, in an exaggerated male pitch. Halls looks like she's just shot his dog as she displays her swagger and confidence. 'I'll serve.' She waves him away and pours. 'To the 16th President of the United States.'

'The President. Good old Abe.'

This gets the attention of the two nosy parkers at the other side of the floor. 'Aye. Sláinte, Abe.'

'Down the hatch.' They drink. Dudley's face begins to drop as he notices the men himself. Harriet doesn't recognise the characters, but their style is instantly familiar. 'Oh Harriet. Can I not get a moment's peace from them?'

'What is it, Thomas? Who are they?'

Dudley hauls himself to his feet to greet the men as they approach. One of them sports a spectacular set of sideburns and a bald pate. He holds his back ramrod straight and is clearly the military type. Harriet's nouse hasn't diminished. She knows a Johnny Reb when she sees one. They're like an infestation in this town. Some are even living up in Waterloo, but she avoids them like she avoids cholera.

'Jeepers, James Bulloch. What are you doing here? I'd have thought you would have been on the first boat home. What's the word? Redundant?' says Dudley, trying to maintain a stiff wit. His veneer is painfully thin.

The man with lambchop sideburns titters. 'I don't think so, Thomas. Your boys would have me up before a court martial quicker than a rat up a sewer pipe.' He offers a bow to Harriet. 'Pardon the base likeness, ma'am. But you are in a gentleman's club.'

What's that drawl? Georgia? Savannah? The circles around Dudley's eyes grow blacker again. 'So, Commander Bulloch here still believes that he is a gentleman.'

Bulloch's companion, a squat, oily man with a rich but awful taste in fashion, won't stop leering at her. He *knows* her, of course. The Commander seizes her attention by kissing her hand. 'Charmed I am though in the rare presence of a Southern lady, ma'am.'

A shiver races up her spine and she is already regretting her presence here. This day gets even more bizarre. Have they come here to gloat? The name Bulloch only means one thing, and she has successfully dodged these two oafs since they landed here in her late husband's wake, which has been no mean feat given their gravitas in the borough and hubris in the war effort. He is Commander James D. Bulloch of the Confederate Navy, a Navy this man helped to build right here in Liverpool with the financial assistance of his crony, a certain cotton broker called Charles Prioleau, the aforesaid oily bastard. She considers how much physical damage she could get away with doing to these two carpet baggers in this fine establishment without copping a night in the Bridewell and scuppering her pending exit. Maybe it is worth it as a tiny recompense for Lincoln, for there will be other boats. The hairs stand up on the back of her neck as she figures that Conté is coursing through her right now. We are the sum of people we know, especially those we have lost. But what could these two pompous asses have to do with Lincoln, aside from their thinly-disguised celebration? Their race is run, as has Dudley's.

Patience. Humour. Dignity. Deportment. But how she hates putting on an act for the sake of a pair of Reb oafs putting on the airs and graces. The myth of the Southern Gentleman is a stodgy one to digest. Conté's ghost suggests that she stabs one and shoots the other in the ass.

'You have come here to toast Abraham's demise, I trust?' says Dudley, breaking her sweet, violent fantasy.

"You do me a disservice, sir. Mr Lincoln was a good man by some – if not all – accounts. It is not the right time to discuss the pond life who served him, or vouched as much. Or the atrocities committed in his name.'

Dudley cuts across him. 'And yet you just did, James.'

'Remember, Atlanta burned. Sherman gloated and his President acquiesced.'

An awkward pause. Prioleau pipes up. 'We have business, so we must be on our way.'

'Oh. What business is that?' asks Dudley.

'That's for us to know and for you to discover,' hisses Prioleau. 'If you still have the gumption and the mandate. Both, I suspect, are in short order.'

Prioleau tips his hat to her and Bulloch follows suit. They saunter out, clearly still amused with themselves. Dudley's face returns to cracked stone. 'Thomas, what in hell was that all about?'

'You curse too readily.'

'I am done playing roles or biting my tongue. Quit that back in '63. It took all my strength to refrain from speaking my mind just then. Why are you even consorting with those two Devil Dogs?'

'Leave it, Harriet. I am so tired of it all. This is ruining me.'

'They tried to commission an entire fleet from under your nose. Petitioned Napoleon and Palmerston directly.'

'That's war for you.'

'They are as bad as Banastre and that is coming from me.'

'No one is as bad as Banastre, my dear.' He grabs the bottle and tops them up. 'Come on, let's drink to the President.'

'I need to go, Thomas.'

'Please, Harriet. Take one more drink with me.'

'You shot him in the balls. You shot your dear old husband in the balls. That put the mayor in Rainhill Asylum. Did you know that? The flame-haired old windbag lost his marbles completely. Now he's eating his own shit.'

'Yes, Thomas. Pipe down about it.'

'But you said don't bite your tongue, did you not, dear?'

'I know but …'

'You. Harriet Dunwoody…'

'Farrell.'

'Shot him. Banastre Dunwoody. In. The balls. I love you, Harriet. You are the true American Heroine for our times.'

'Shush. Hush now.'

The smoking room has filled up in the past hour. Worryingly, as more members arrived for their spot of dinner, Dudley has gotten increasingly tanked up on brandy, to the extent that he polished off that decanter, and then started hitting the port, continuing the trend that she spotted earlier with his empty drinks cabinet. Harriet stopped keeping up with him when she realised that this little afternoon sojourn and wake for Abraham has become a rescue mission. The man is a wreck foundering on the rocks of grief and drowning in a sea of liquor, mumbling about conspiracies. This is abject shock being anesthetised in plain sight, and it is all too familiar to her. Lincoln is dearer to him than she ever could have countenanced.

'She shot him in the balls, everyone! Deserved it, too. He used to pay gangs to rub turds all over my front door. Every day, I had to clean that dirty, brown slurry up. Every goddamn day, without complaint. Scrubbing on my hands and knees while they laughed. So, she shot Commander Dixie in his big balls, ha.'

'Sir, since you insist on behaving in this manner with your… woman… we must ask you both to leave.'

Halls is probably right. They should leave. Before Dudley starts blabbing state secrets out. This is not drunken tittle-tattle that sounds too outrageous to believe; it has substance to damage, and the chattering classes of this borough will relay it into common knowledge faster than the speed of thought. Although, why should Harriet care? She's going to California.

'Dear Uncle, I think the fellow is correct. You have had enough. Let us get you home, eh? Halls, is it?'

'Yes. Miss.'

'A Hansom cab if you please.'

Halls looks like a wasp just stung him. He's not used to women in the club, never mind getting orders from one.

Every eye is upon them, which only winds Dudley up further. 'I am the Official Consul to this borough from the United States Government.'

'I know who you are, sir.'

'And she. Shot her husband in the balls.' Cue a chorus of gruff harrumphs.

'Sir, that is quite enough. I'll take that.'

Halls removes the bottle from Dudley's grip. The Consul gets up and shoves his face right into the attendant, nose-to-nose with him. Statesmanship and reason be damned.

'That is a declaration of war. President Lincoln shall hear about this.'

An impudent smirk crosses Halls' face. 'President Lincoln is dead, sir. Have you not heard the news?'

The place erupts into laughter. Everyone in this room knows that Dudley's days are numbered in Liverpool. He looks finally beaten, even if the Union have won the war. After all these years of fighting in the courts to stop blockade runners and gunships being built under a loophole, appointing spies and private detectives to undermine at first Banastre Dunwoody and then Bulloch and Prioleau, Thomas Haines Dudley is finally done. The latter men were able to operate in plain sight and independently from Banastre, petitioning and damn nearly succeeding in getting the Confederate States recognised as a sovereign power. They outlasted their comrade by being altogether more circumspect and canny. They ground him down, not with guns and gangs but with cotton bonds and expensive lawyers. He was right about Banastre; they weren't as bad as him. They were worse. These are moribund days, and coming to this nest of vipers this afternoon was a mistake.

The only blessing is that the enemy are no longer here to witness this humiliation at his own hands. Harriet will take Baba to California, and that will be the end of it.

Dudley punches Halls square on the chin, dropping him with a Yale Boxing Society uppercut. Halls sprawls over the Afghan weave.

'Who's laughing now?'

'Oh, Thomas. Why did you have to go and do that?'

'She left me.' His face crumples into wailing tears.

'Who?'

'Emaline.'

'But you are Quakers. You don't just leave each other. That is preposterous.'

'Everything is preposterous, dear.'

As Halls clambers back to his feet, there is a knock on the window. Pat waves at Harriet. Incredulous eyes turn to him. She approaches and pulls up the sash.

'Pat, I'm a little busy. The American Consul is about to end up in the clink.'

Dudley has built up another froth as staff and fellow Athenians try to cajole him out. 'Away to fuck with all of you. Damned borough, up its own ass, I say. Harriet! Emaline!'

'Harry, you must come,' says Pat.

'And what are you doing climbing up here? I'll end up with the pair of you sharing a cell like a pair of hobos. Between you and him today, man. I swear to God, do you not know I've got a boat to catch?'

'Harry, Harriet, listen…'

But Harriet won't listen. 'Pat, go and fetch the Consulate chief of staff. Tell him to bring a few able fellas down here to rescue Mr Dudley. It's high time I got Baba and we headed for the Landing Stage.'

'Harry, I've just *come* from the Consulate.'

His face is ashen. She should have read it immediately but was so taken up by Dudley's oafish, sozzled grief. 'What is it?'

'Harry, I'm sorry. I have no idea how the hell they got in there. I told you to let me look after her.'

'What? Who's *they*? Where?'

'Harry, I'm so sorry, love.'

Dudley's making an almighty racket behind them, but her focus is now completely upon Pat. Her stomach churns.

'Stop saying sorry. What? Who?' For the second time today, the ground has shaken beneath her. But while the earlier news was a tremor, this is a cataclysmic earthquake.

'Harry…'

'What? Baba Conté? My baby?'

'I am so sorry, love. She's gone.'

#4 – THE TOBACCO SILO

Garrett's Farm, Virginia. April 26th, 1865

'Eleven full days, General sir. Eleven pitiless days I spent hiding up a tree out in that Maryland swamp waiting for you to come. Eleven days of squatting in a bush, wiping my ass on maple leaves and keeping Dixie for Yankees chasing my bounty. That was just not the arrangement, Major General, sir. No sir at all, I say.'

Major General Benjamin Franklin Butler claps JWB on the shoulder and winks at young Herold, Booth's slightly younger and distinctly less garrulous pharmacist pal, a kid who came along for the ride and ended up staying the whole way. 'Credit is due, sunshine. I'll admit that you have had a rough rodeo.'

The rich and heady aroma of stored, moist, cured tobacco emanates around the silo. Booth sits cross-legged up in the loft, rubbing his torn-up ankle with witch hazel. It smarts real bad now. Herold is next to Butler below, hanging on his every word.

JWB stiffens. 'We need more than credit, Major General, sir. I am to be a hero, and I must be placed thus in the pantheon. We must never feel those boots upon our necks again. We must never surrender.'

'Fine words, well delivered.'

Booth emits a neat salute, happy for even a small audience. 'Thank you.'

'Now, how's the leg?'

'Dr Mudd set it for me, but I am not disposed to scrambling around the bush while the Yankees chase me.'

'Of course not, you poor fellow.'

'So where is the support you promised? Why am I still here with chafing on my asshole and a bust ankle?'

Christ. Will the complaining ever cease? Butler came some distance to watch Booth's melodramatic epilogue, but knowing that it was only ever about a long-term itch for fame rather than anything approaching political acumen, the remainder of this game must be played out promptly in order for the next phase of the project to begin. Nevertheless, it is irksome.

Alas, for this fellow, he cannot tell the difference between real life and drama, so give him what he expects. 'You will have your tickets to Liverpool. I can guarantee you a haven there until the dust is settled, and you'll know that it is a good theatre town.' As lies go, it comes straight out of Butler's lower drawer of stock bullshit. Many Southerners are aware of the sympathies expressed over in England, so it is prudent to use it in order to placate the boy, even tantalise him with the prospect of escape and sanctuary, even an opportunity to bask in his infamy, which he clearly cannot distinguish from fame. Butler turns to Herold, who continues to pitch and scrape. 'If only your friends had held their nerve, too.'

Then President Johnson would be a dead Vice-President, as would Secretary of State Seward and the path to high office would be altogether less stodgy. A decimated high command would have been ripe for a new Presidential candidate. What a result that would have been, but woulda coulda shoulda, you can't have everything. Time may come, but at least that lanky, stove pipe prick is taken care of.

'I want top billing. My name on the play script, too.'

'We'll get your name in lights, bigger and better than ever before, Mr Booth. Who knows, the West End may beckon.'

Herold twitches, looking far younger than his 23 years. 'I'll still be permitted to travel with Johnny, won't I, sir? Won't I? I can be his stage manager.'

JWB looks askance at Herold, who cramps his style. 'Hush, Davey. You speak when you are spoken to. I told you.'

Butler smiles and strokes the back of Herold's neck. Oh, these impressionable young boys and their crushes for famous actors. 'I would not begrudge the brave young man anything in this hour.'

A yell from outside, followed by an order. 'Booth! Herold! Come out with your hands above your heads!' Not before time.

JWB is stirred fast, like a scalded cat. He shuffles towards the ladder and slides down, wincing all the way, peashooting Derringer .44 in hand, regarding Butler with tears in his eyes. 'You promised us, Major General sir. This was safe territory, you said. We were going to Liverpool, you said. Theatre, you said.'

'Oh, dear Lord. I had no idea, lads. I am so sorry,' replies Butler, unable to muster too much effect in his voice. Booth is no better judge of acting than he is an actor himself. No matter. Play along all the way through. Herold looks fair ready to mess his trousers. Booth looks fair ready to fight on and extend his legend. That's the difference between the two of them. Booth will take fame over life, whereas Herold had no idea what he was getting himself into. They say that love is blind, but stupidity has a million different faces.

Booth glances out through a crack in the slats of the barn to see what Butler expected them to see: a detachment from the 16th New York Cavalry regiment and a pair of detectives in leather frock coats, including Butler's very own fine man, Luther Baker. JWB yells, impervious to the idea that one bullet could readily penetrate the woodwork and his dense skull. This is why an actor makes for a good assassin but a lousy schemer. 'Identify yourselves!'

Butler chants into his ear. "Isn't it obvious, son?"

'No,' growls Booth, then to the group outside. 'Identify yourselves now!'

Baker knows what to say. It's Butler's script, after all. 'It don't make any difference who we are. We know who you are, and we want you. We want to take you prisoners.'

Booth nods like he's just discovered some sort of elixir. 'I am a cripple. I have got but one leg. If you will withdraw your men in line, a hundred yards from the door, I will come out and fight you.'

'John Boy, just come out. We ain't here for a fight.'

'Don't you go calling me John Boy. Mister Booth to you, I say. Famous actor. Fifty, I say. All I need is fifty yards.' Judging by the smell, brave Herold really has messed himself now. The boy runs out of the door, hands aloft, squealing like a runt pig. Booth is incredulous. 'You little maggot. Damned coward. Making a show of me.'

Butler stands at his shoulder. 'I think we should give ourselves up, son. High time.' High time for boiled beef and potatoes, another good reason to wrap this up promptly. His belly gurgles.

Booth flinches and fidgets. Now his moment has arrived; it isn't how he saw it. This isn't the West End, or even the Liverpool stage. There are no adoring English folks to witness it, just blue-bottle bastards everywhere. 'You've got smarts. You're a lawyer. You can talk your way out of anything, Major General, sir. Not me. All I have left is a hero's death.'

Really? 'No, John. Not this one. I'm as damned as you are.' Butler really is growing tired of this charade, his own lazy lies that Booth swallows every time.

Baker pipes up again from outside the barn. 'Come now, Mister Booth.'

Booth grabs his long knife and a carbine, ready for action. Now he can do some damage. 'Well, my brave boys. Prepare a stretcher for me. I'm coming then. I will not hang.'

Butler draws his own pistol – 'Do spare us any more, son' – and empties a round into the back of Booth's head, about the same spot as the actor popped into Lincoln, and he drops. John Wilkes Booth's work in this project is complete. 'Strong as an ox, crazy as a shithouse rat, dumb as pigshit. We're ready for you, Luther. Luther? I say, get in here pronto.'

'Sir!'

Baker and his men file into the barn. Herold is already trussed and ready for export to the pen. His face crumples when he sees Butler all palsy-walsy with Luther. 'Judas! Traitor! I knew we shouldn't never have trusted you!'

'Don't lie, son. You had no idea.'

'That there's the real killer of Abraham Lincoln, and I'll tattle-tale I will.'

'You'll swing boy, and no sane person will ever believe such a cockamamie tale,' says Luther, a little too eager to impress his boss. Well, you can't be too eager in that respect. Butler kicks Booth's corpse to make sure that he's expired, and it's all over bar the farting.

'I thought you wanted the showpiece hanging, sir?'

'I did, Luther. But I had plain enough of his wittering. We'll still get our fanfare, rest assured.' Butler holsters up his smoking, warm gun. 'What about the loose end? Any news?'

'No. But we're following it up, sir.'

Even the whiff of ineptitude can presage a disaster. 'No, Luther. *I'm* following it up. Got that? Booth should never have made it out of that theatre on two feet, never mind with a broken ankle.'

'Yes sir. Sorry about that, sir.'

'Butler, you fat bastard! Did you hear me?! I'll tell all, I shall!' A burly Sergeant piledrives his ham hock fist into Herold's guts, knocking the idiot out of him.

'If you want a good job doing, you've got to do it yourself. Never mind, move it on, Lucas.'

'Sir, yes sir. You heard him, lads!'

Butler replaces his cap upon his bald pate and heads for his horse. JWB twitches one last time and then is still.

#5 – ROLLING ON THE RIVER

New Orleans, July 4th, 1858, nearly seven years earlier

A sweet and sultry morning in the city. Bits of masonry, splinters of wood and roof tiles scattered about the ground indicate that a big blow has just passed. It has freshened up the air just about enough to make it tolerable for the two young ladies who alight the *Proud Mary* riverboat at the landing jetty, off the dawn crossing from Baton Rouge. In normal circumstances, extra caution and the cover of night or disguise would be required in order to safely traverse the bustle of dock rabble moonlighting as lumber boys here, but on this day, it is entirely necessary for Harriet and Conté to arrive in their full finery, to be as noticed as they are notable.

For this is just what the stiff-necked, taciturn, roly-poly of a fellow Monsieur Leconte expected as managing director of the Consolidated Association of Planters Bank. And this youthful, pretty pair have long since learned not to disappoint a gentleman's expectations of them. That tool has proven to be as handy as a beavertail sap ever since they started their 'business' in the city and environs, playing upon social mores for the advantage of the tribe. Who would guess that such an exquisite young lady with perfect deportment and her maid would be capable of rifling a pocket or two? But today, their game has been raised several notches.

'Mademoiselle Blanc. Enchanté,' he mews as they alight the gangplank, like he really doesn't like pitching and scraping but has to do so anyway. He studies Harriet, not giving the Creole a second glance. It is difficult to hide their lack of years, for all their wiles in disguise, but the perceived innocence of youth factors in their favour this morning. Nevertheless, Harriet is playing a character only a few years her senior. Thus, it is important to get the details of her movements and mannerisms just right, as if she is a product of a Swiss finishing school rather than the deep, dank and dirty swamp.

'It is Madame, not Mademoiselle,' grunts Conté, keen to stamp her presence down immediately with the over-familiar little fellow.

In a protocol that has quickly been established, Leconte doesn't even look at Conté as they head towards his carriage. 'Of course. May I offer my sincere condolences, *Madame* Blanc. So unfortunate to lose one's husband at such a young age. Typhus is so mean, ain't it just.'

On this cue, Harriet coughs into a handkerchief and fakes a slight swoon. Conté rolls her eyes and takes up the rear as they board Leconte's carriage. A woman of colour in finery is a rare but not a unique sight in this town as New Orleans is an enclave port where former slaves and indentured servants have more freedom of status than the rest of the South, or indeed the North, but Conté has no inclination to mimic Harriet's role of delicate, bereaved fleur. Harriet wishes again that her friend would make a better fist of hiding her disdain for the likes of men like Leconte, however much such fellows buy into their act.

They ride, and the recently widowed Mme Blanche Blanc of Baton Rouge looks suitably upset at inheriting a vast fortune from her husband, as much as Monsieur Jerome Leconte of La Nouvelle-Orléans barely suppresses his glee at being able to deposit said fortune in his bank, situated but a mile to the west of the docks, in the more genteel end of town. This deal is bigger to him than the Louisiana Purchase, if the figures involved are to be verified.

Harriet weeps like a stranded kitten, verging upon a sob. Conté eyeballs her long enough to remind her friend about laying it on too thick. A swift glance back reveals that Harriet knows that laying it on too thick doesn't exist with men like Jerome Leconte.

'There, there, Madame. You will surely feel better once you know that your money is safe in our hands.'

'Is it, though?' coughs Harriet through her tears as the carriage galumphs along the cinder track and up into Canal Street, the long boulevard that is becoming its own version of the Parisian Belle Époque. 'My sweet Manu's last words before the sickness took him were to seek you out, Monsieur Leconte, but just how will I know that I can trust my future with you, sir? I am a woman alone, you see. Vulnerable to man and beast.'

'And beastly men,' says Conté, chewing her lower lip. This is worse than a Molière farce.

The cover story: Mme Blanc's beloved husband Emmanuel Blanc married her as a lonely, childless and entirely fictional widower; an 88-year-old saddle bag of wrinkles wedded to this pristine Southern debutante of 17. He promptly fell off the perch, leaving her as little older than a child with a vast fortune in cotton fields, estates and monies. It is highly plausible, backed up with documentation forged by their own fair hands back at River Haven. Such a sweet honey pot, indeed.

Leconte chances holding Harriet's hand. 'Oh belle, this will pass, as must all things. We possess the best vault in Louisiana. I dare say the safest this side of New York City. When you find a kind gentleman of good stock to remarry you, you can make a new family with the full peace of mind that your money and investments are secure in the hands of The Consolidated.'

'I so wish that I could be thus reassured, sir. Forgive me.'

'Well, lady. In your grief, I can well understand. But we will look after you in every way, shape and form. No hoodlum has ever got the better of The Consolidated, nor ever will they. You have come to the right bank, young ma'am.'

Harriet nods, sucking up her tears, ether solution kicking the back of her throat. It stings a little but does the job. 'Merci, Monsieur.'

'You know, I will have to introduce you to my nephew, if I may be so bold? He is a fine boy.'

'Why, I shall think upon it, sir.'

'You do that.'

Great. Now they're practically family.

The carriage approaches the branch, situated in a faux-Venetian façade upon this vivacious drag, next door to the sumptuous edifice of a neighbouring hotel. No lollygaggers or scallywags to be seen, aside from a few Irish navvies engaged in the endless construction industry in this town. Three such men block the entrance to the bank right now with their wagon of lumber and bricks, much to the purple-faced chagrin of Monsieur Leconte as he hops from the cabin. Oh, this won't do at all.

'I say you, Paddy Whack! Get this contraption away from my entrance hall. Immediately, I say. Oi!'

All three men are clearly not used to the heat of Louisiana. The leader's face is nearly as red as his hair, flakes of sunburn and streams of sweat coursing his cheeks. Currently, such fellows are commonplace in this town, coming over in droves to meet the huge demand for skilled workers on the building sites, levees, canals and docks. This one clutches a printed requisition and scratches his pate. 'My apologies boss, but this is where we were told to deliver, like.'

'Like?' grunts Leconte. 'Like what? Speak English.'

'Right so.'

Leconte is about ready to spit feathers. Conté and Harriet remain within the carriage. 'Go round the back, you imbecile. How many times do you idiots need to be told? We have appearances to maintain.'

'Oh. Round the back, is it?'

'Are you a fucking macaw or something? Yes, that is what I just said. Right now, pronto and quick about it,' bellows Leconte, with a rage befitting his status. 'Irish ass.' Conté hovers at the door of the carriage. She clears her throat to get his attention. Leconte glances back at Mme Blanc and flinches. 'Oh Mademoiselle, erm sorry Madame, I do apologise for the coarse vocabulary. These chappies only understand this way of speaking.'

Conté leers at him. 'My mistress should not be kept waiting, sir.'

Leconte tilts his chin, every part of his expression betraying how he wants to whip the impudent Creole cur for addressing him in that tone, but Madame follows her maid off the carriage and onto the sidewalk, and the bank manager plays chameleon again, pitching and toadying. Harriet wonders if his nephew is just as impressive a specimen as he is. 'Of course, very good Madame Blanc. This way. If you please.'

Leconte links Harriet, and they head into the Italianate foyer, shoes clacking against the cool marble. The impossible, arrogant wealth of the place is an immediate assault on the senses. Imported fittings from Milan, Amazonian hardwoods, gold finials up the grand staircase. Is this a bank or a palace?

Conté would readily gasp at the opulence, as would her 'Mistress'. That is, had they not already cased the building only last week.

Two giant men in faux-military uniforms guard either side of an elevator door like a pair of sequoias, clearly not the bellboys. Conté steals another glance at Harriet. This had better work, but then how many options do they have left? The discreet services of Oisín, Terence and Sean out there in the road didn't come cheap, and they exhausted the last of the tribal coffers in making a down payment to them in lieu of what they make today. Just like Monsieur Leconte, they are not entirely sure whether or not the Irishmen can be trusted to carry out their commission, but both women know that this is the last chance. The virtue of being white and Creole is that this cannot be traced back to the Choctaw, but after this gig, the tribe that adopted them and made them part of their own is clean out of funds and options.

Do this, or we'll lose the lands. Forever.

Do this or die.

Now or never.

Leconte pulls back the iron railings and unlocks the plush, red leather-bound door to the elevator with a mortice key attached to a bunch that is chained to his waist. He's keen to display the ingenuity of their scrupulous security, but not half as keen as they are to get the job done and leave this place.

'I am gratified that a gentleman such as yourself creates such great pains to accommodate and protect a young and vulnerable widow who is alone in your city, sir.' Yes, it's a mouthful, but the act must endure for the full length of the play.

Leconte tips his hat, smiles and jabs a button with his thumb. The elevator shunts and moves down into the bowels of the building. The two tree-men rise above into shadows before disappearing. 'We must discuss the transfer procedure, of course. In detail. Where are your funds presently, Madame?'

Oh, he's all about business now he has them in his lair, isn't he just? 'In the cellars beneath our house on the plantation, sir,' says Harriet, gentle as a mouse.

'Heavens above. Oh, that will not do. Not do at all. What if some Indian savage, escaped negro, or bushwhacker got wind of such information? Lawks ma'am, I shudder to think. You did not come here before time, I must tell you. You poor young thing. So innocent, so vulnerable to predation.' So *easy*.

Conté looks like she wants to vomit. More tears and fretful shaking from Harriet, on cue as the elevator shudders to a stop, but Leconte isn't too interested now he has this young Madame just where he wants her. They follow him down a plain passage where a solid iron door awaits them. 'So then, we have a dozen deadbolt steel rods with a solid iron housing, forged in the Siemens-Martin process, controlled by multiple locking mechanisms.' More jangling of keys and unlocking of mortices before Leconte's pièce de résistance, a combination dial turned back and forth with dazzling speed. Of course, he is right. No hoodlum could ever break into his vault.

With a smug grin and a delicate push, Leconte teases the door open and turns to his hideously wealthy customer, only for his expression to slip away into absolute dread like wet manure from a shovel. 'Monsieur Leconte. You will do exactly as we say,' whispers Conté. He's looking her in the eye now, alright, in between viewing the two sawn-off shotguns being aimed point-blank at his gaping maw. Leconte dry gulps like a camel and his eyes bulge. Right now, Harriet and Conté hope to sweet baby Jesus that Oisín, Terence and Sean up there have got their timing right and successfully taken care of the security detail, for it's a long way back to Baton Rouge. Hopefully, they'll fit all of the gold onto the back of their wagon.

#6 – GREEDY MCCREEDY

River Haven, Louisiana, July 20th, 1858

'Not many of youse left, is there? Seemed it was teeming with you scarlet skins last time I came to your little camp. Scarlet skins! Listen to me would ye. You'd pass for white, and I can't see why you would choose not to for the life of me. As would your pretty daughter here. As for her …' He jabs a thumb in the direction of Conté, 'Well, as for her, I've not the foggiest so I haven't …'

McCreedy spits on the rug and chuckles before examining some papers before him: deeds and contracts. Well, he can read then, but Harriet has seen his kind before, time and again, at either end of a gun barrel. She shoots one and, like some sideshow gallery, another appears immediately, lured here to the shores of the Mississippi with the promise of rich pickings at the expense of the dumb natives. They're like breeding rats, minus the sophistication.

'I believe the most direct translation into English would be 'village' rather than 'camp', Mr McCreedy.' The other native sits at the other end of the long table, smoking a clay pipe. He belies every idea in McCreedy's dense head of what a Choctaw is. Peter Pitchlynn is some years past forty with long black hair, an aquiline nose, broad cheekbones, a sunburnt complexion, and bright, piercing eyes. He is the elder of elders, possessed of a degree, speaks several native and European tongues, and is the son of Major John Pitchlynn, a man of Scots descent himself raised from childhood by the Choctaw after the death of his father, a detail not lost on the two foundlings who sit awkwardly in the middle of the table, much to McCreedy's bemusement and amusement. This man would never be capable of fathoming such a story, and there is no point in trying to explain it to him.

'Ain't much more than a pissant. Most of youse have had the good sense to get gone. Time you joined them.'

'You are Irish, sir?' says Peter.

'American.' That could mean anything, but his accent says Antrim.

'Surely you can see the issue from our perspective? Being displaced from our lands. Is it not what the English did to you? The Ulster Plantation, I gather?'

McCreedy emits something between a laugh, a sneer, and the mating call of a randy cane toad. 'Couldn't be less arsed. I heard about that money your people up in Oklahoma gave when them daft micks ran outta spuds. What was it, a few pathetic bucks? Fat lot of fucking use that was, in the end. Don't know why you people have to make such a big deal out of such things.' McCreedy taps the side of his head with a dirty forefinger. 'Mad, so ye are. This is just why I'm an American now. Sentimental bollocks, so it is, and I'm well shut of it.' He returns to the papers in front of him.

Harriet keeps her counsel in spite of wanting to swot this journeyman ingrate into next week. Her innards boil. Peter glances at her, but he knows that she will remain unmoved, no matter what McCreedy says to provoke them. Ever since European settlers arrived in these lands, the Choctaw have been taking in orphans and refugees. Now, a descendent of those settlers is Principal Chief of a tribal nation of refugees. For all of Peter's grace, stature, superior intellect and cultured manners, McCreedy knows who has the whip hand here. He finishes reading, leans back, and puts a muddy boot up on the table. Conté's knuckles whiten and her jaw tightens, making no effort to hide her disdain. Harriet knows that it wouldn't take much at all, would it? One slit and he is history, but others just like him would arrive presently, and they would arrive with guns and bombs.

'Well, Mr McCreedy?' says Peter Pitchlynn, retaining more of his poise and patience than either of his young charges could ever muster in front of such flagrant, malodourous, bushwhacker scum. They know and learn from the hidden strength beneath their leader's gentle countenance, but all McCreedy sees is a soft target.

'Ways I figure it, you haven't got no legal claim to these lands. We done checked with lawyers and lawmakers. Our offer to assist in the, ah, relocation of your peoples to Oklahoma is more than generous, ol' Pete.'

'And if we refuse to leave?'

McCreedy chuckles and spits again. 'Ah, come on now. You scarlet skins are going in your droves, on your say-so or not. They know the game is up, they know the wood from the trees. That's sensible, so it is. What do you think is going to happen if you don't follow suit, um? The few of you remaining will duke it out with us, the US Marshals? High time you wised up like your cousins. Take the offer, Big Chief Balls. Have done with it and live out the rest of your days in peace. I'm calling you a fool if you don't, and I'm one of the good fellas.'

His badge gleams on his chest, incongruous with the rest of his scruffy, unkempt exterior. The man carries an uneasy reek of old cheese only masked by booze and stale, encrusted urine. It has long since stopped being a shock that they recruit criminals into official positions. Doubtless, one day, such an oaf will become President. Harriet glances at Conté, who gently kicks at a chest beneath the table. Peter nods to them and they lift it up onto the tabletop.

'If the covenant of the lands is not settled in your law …' McCreedy's eyes follow the chest and he licks his lips. No mystery to what he's thinking, then. 'Then we propose to buy our lands from the United States Government. To make it legal.'

Not that it is the US Government's land to sell, but the argument has long become moot. 'What? Really, old Red? You're shitting me, so you are. I don't like it when fellas go shitting me either.' Harriet pulls open the chest to reveal a horde of minted gold coins. McCreedy gasps like he's just found Blackbeard's loot. 'Jesus fucking Christ … How in hell did you daft sods get hold of that? Is that real? Oh my.'

That changed his attitude in a heartbeat. Peter makes his play. 'We are a resourceful people. Hard-working, scrimping and saving. And part of our agreement will be that you don't ask questions.'

McCreedy approaches the loot, carrying his reek closer. Harriet feels the hairs on the back of her neck stand up and her nostrils flinch at his proximity, but he's paying no heed to anyone or anything but the loot now. 'That's a nice chunk of change, alright. But you'll need to tell me that there's more.'

'There is more.'

McCreedy massages his stubble, working up a lather of sweat, his beady imagination figuring it out. 'I see. Well, that does seem to put a different complexion on matters, I'll venture.'

'Glad that you think so, Mr McCreedy,' says Peter, chuffing his pipe. He's remaining calm amid a cauldron of desperation among his people, knowing that this is their last shot to keep their roots in the Mississippi, to fend off the Europeans by buying their own lands off them. Using stolen money, albeit, but that detail mustn't factor into these negotiations. McCreedy here is a Government-sponsored racketeer, grifter and bounty hunter. He roams the plains between towns and cities, so the hope is that he doesn't care much for recent local news about a spectacular heist on Canal Street. This is all about risk versus benefit in the bleakest of times.

Peter Pitchlynn leans forward. 'Take it. All yours.'

McCreedy still can't believe his luck. 'What? Really?'

'Yes. As a down payment. Come back with those deeds signed by the Governor of Louisiana and a Federal order to the effect that we own the territories and you will get the rest. The full amount is written on the back of the deed.'

The 'territories' are negligible compared to the original Choctaw lands, which have long been swallowed up with settlements, plantations, farms and other arable tracts sold by white men to white men, but they represent permanence, a last hope of retaining their ancient home next to the sacred river.

McCreedy studies the back of the deed and grinds his jaw. He pockets it and returns to the chest. 'No questions, no papers? If you want me to sign summat, I will sign it. I am a legitimate fellow.'

'Nothing to sign today. We trust you. Don't we, girls?' Neither of them nod; just stare.

The Marshal's face reddens with glee. Whatever he does with it is up to him, but there is little or no chance of this particular trove ending up in State or Federal coffers and they are counting upon that. Over two score multiples of this amount sits in a cave along the riverside, waiting for this filthy devil to come back with signed papers from his equally corrupt Governor. They're counting upon his dishonesty and base avarice to push the deal through.

McCreedy grins, spits on his palm, and offers it to Peter Pitchlynn. Peter stares back up at him, unmoving. The Marshal wipes his palm, grabs the chest and heaves it off the table, struggling with the weight. He came here alone, probably because he doesn't like others to see how he does his business.

'Good job I brought the pony and trap.'

'Hmm. Do you need help with that?'

'I'll manage, so I will.'

'Fine, Marshal McCreedy.'

McCreedy nods at Peter, then to Harriet and Conté. 'Ladies. Be seeing you.'

And he's out of the door and away. They listen to the silence, as if letting the spirits give their approval. Then to the sound of McCreedy giddying his horse and his trap trundling off down the dirt track out of River Haven.

'Well done, you two,' says Peter, all the guarded propriety dropping, brow low and furrowed.

Harriet throws her head back, relieved that the man's rancid stink and malign presence has departed like an ill wind blows over. 'We can only hope now.'

Of course, he was never comfortable with the plan, but it was this or Oklahoma. 'Your necks are on the block directly now. I shall never forgive myself if this goes wrong.'

The two childhood friends have spent more time lately in the city – working pockets in the banks, casinos, and drinking dens and building their covers – than they have back at this small stead that occupies a natural clearing in the bush. River Haven is set back just far enough away from the river and paths to attract the immediate attention of criminals and prospectors. Well, that's how it *used* to work, at least. Once, it really was a haven, but now their location is common knowledge and their numbers too few to fend off a sustained attack. Money got them into this and only money can get them out.

The sweet incense of aromatic pipe tobacco laced with oils lingers from the night before, when the two convened cross-legged in silence, reading the latest Dickens tomes stolen from the public library at Baton Rouge. Since they were rescued by the Choctaw as children, they have led this double life. Educated in English ways but raised by the river spirit. They stir at the same time, their living patterns synchronised from dawn until dusk, like sisters except more so. *Much* more so, but the Choctaw understands and accepts who they really are more than any European could fathom or articulate. Harriet contemplates this dangerous world as she does every day upon the blessing of waking up, checks her guns, and wonders how either one would ever cope without the other by their side. Chances are, in their line of work, that scenario will come true at any moment.

She fixes coffee on the hot stove and serves it up to Conté in her trusty, dented pewter mug. For the last three days, they've not been assigned a detail by Peter or any of the elders. For the first time since they could remember, they've been instructed to stay put: hear, see, speak no evil. It's maddening. River Haven used to be the safest place upon the endless banks of the Mississippi for a couple of foundlings invested into the Choctaw nation, but now it is probably one of the most dangerous places on earth, a place where Hell awaits.

And what else is there to do but check guns and read Charles Dickens? Watch and wait, watch and wait. The English scribe has the knack of evoking the faraway city of London, but he can't transport them away from the feeling that their world may come crashing down. Harriet sips. Conté sips. Without a mark or a plan of action, conversation runs rather dry and easily descends into bickering. Silence is always golden.

How will the enemy arrive? With a retinue and a charabanc of pressmen, celebrating the 'purchase' of lands? Or with a platoon of blue uniforms or hired guns, intent upon massacre or clearance, whichever is more expedient? Will McCreedy just attempt to strongarm the rest of the loot out of them? Harriet and Conté can agree on one thing: to expect the worst and hope for the best, but it is out of their hands now.

A knock on the cabin door. They glance at each other. It is not in Choctaw culture to knock. Wooden cabins with doors are a new thing, and the concept of knocking has yet to be instilled in River Haven. Harriet primes her Derringer. Conté pulls the net curtain aside and looks out, her hard, beavertail sap in hand as the best weapon for close combat. She frowns at the waiting visitors. Harriet needs more than that. 'Who is it, Conté? Don't keep me in suspense.'

'Hmm.'

'Hmm? What's hmm?'

Another knock. Peter Pitchlynn has joined the strange female visitor waiting at the door. The woman clutches a carpet bag and holds herself with a stiff, straight-backed posture, like some sort of deranged English nanny. Conté concludes that it might be a good idea to answer. Harriet takes a look out of the window and gasps as her friend opens the door. Blue uniforms swarm around River Haven, appearing and vanishing like St Elmo's Fire. They've arrived here with stealth, as if they'd been expected. They could run amok at any moment and no one would stop them.

'Shit, not good,' mutters Harriet.

Peter trails behind the woman as she enters, sturdy boots clacking against the bare wooden floor. She is clad in a buffalo hide poncho, trousers and chaps, a loose blouse dominated by a gunbelt, and a blue US Cavalry cap over her plaited, burnt orange hair. She is an odd sort indeed.

'Sit down, ladies,' she instructs, her voice soft but her manner firm, like the schoolteacher they never had. Harriet glances at Peter, who nods. Whatever has happened, he looks deflated, defeated. They have known him for as long as they can remember and he has never carried such a wan face.

'Shit,' Harriet repeats.

'Cursing so is not becoming of a young lady,' the woman says, as much to assert control as to instruct. Who in hell is this?

'Peter, please explain.' Peter nods at Harriet again and they return to the edge of the bed they share. She eyes the weapons on the woman's waist and contemplates how she might take her down.

'I am Katherine Warne,' she says, her nose turned up at the messy, cramped quarters. 'Harriet and Conté, you've made quite an impression with your brash ingenuity and wit. I like your substance, even if your style could do with refinement.' She runs a finger along the windowsill, scooping up dirt and dust. 'As could your basic housekeeping skills.'

Warne dusts her hands off and smiles. Conté wades in first. 'Have you come to see us swing from a rope, Miss?'

'Warne. Ms.'

'Yes, Miss, Mrs, Ms. Well, have you? You should have sent your men in first if so, for we won't go without a fight, and you're a fool if you think that you can take both of us by yourself.'

Harriet has her Derringer trained upon the visitor's heart. It makes no impression upon Warne. 'Perhaps I didn't need to bring my irons today, girls. They're just for show, I assure you. There will be no trouble, unless you instigate it.'

'Harriet, just put the piece down,' says Peter, fatigue and resignation in his voice. This vexes her far more than the presence of this odd female. Nevertheless, she has been in this woman's company for a minute and already she can't stand the sight of her.

'Peter, please tell us what is going on. Before I plant a slug in her fat ass.'

Warne laughs hard, only adding to their discombobulation. Peter continues to look at the floor. Just *why* is he so cowed? 'Let her say her piece. Put down the gun first and listen, please.'

'Her piece?' says Harriet, 'What piece?'

'Disengage, both of you,' says Peter, more of an order this time. Harriet clips up her pistol and Conté pockets her sap.

'Excellent. Altogether more cordial.' Katherine Warne smiles again and places the bag on the table. 'I am a firm believer in showing rather than telling, girls. It saves that most precious of commodities. Time. You may approach me.'

What the hell is this? Sit down, get up. Dance to her tune? Harriet has a bellyful of butterflies.

'Do come on over,' adds Warne, 'I won't bite.'

She is in her early thirties. Perhaps. But hard-bitten at closer inspection, her every movement steady as a rock. Peter continues to stare at the floor as Katherine Warne opens the carpet bag and flies escape. There is that familiar odour of cheese and booze, with the added, heady, noxious aroma of rotting flesh. Harriet looks into the bag and looks upon the face of Mr McCreedy, who is staring back up at her. The bone of his skull is stripped bare and he has clearly been scalped. Her stomach dips again as she notices Warne's buffalo skin poncho, which is perhaps not made from that animal after all.

'Shit.'

'Thrice is a charm.' Katherine Warne snaps the bag shut. 'There you have it. Now you can get rid of it.'

Conté's face crumples in disgust.

'So what now?' says Harriet, McCreedy's dead face still imprinted on her eyes.

'Your choice. Our client who commissioned us to locate the missing gold and bring the culprits to justice, Monsieur Leconte of the Consolidated Bank, would gleefully see you both dangle. Of course he would, because men like him have a complete lack of imagination. And *The Agency* would see such a scenario as a clear waste of raw talent.'

'The what?' asks Harriet.

'I will brief you.'

Conté steps up to Warne, slapping her sap into her palm. 'And if we told you to go to hell and take that flea-infested head with you?'

Warne studies her. 'How very cute you two specimens are. You shall need training of course. Sassy black women aren't tolerated by many, just about anywhere.'

'Ever been to Haiti?' says Conté.

Peter pipes up. 'Take her offer. No sense in you two perishing in this mess.'

'No,' says Harriet, at Conté's side now, 'You're on our land. How dare you. I think you should go to hell, lady. You and whoever controls you.'

Warne chuckles. 'Go there all the time. Perk of the job.'

Conté looks to Peter, but his eyes are fixed on the floor. '*Ishahli Hatak*, Peter, I beg you. Say something other than just go with her. We are the same spirit.'

'I have failed you, *Ulla* daughter. Go with her.'

'What about you? The *okla?*'

'We must see out our time here, however long the river spirit decrees, and then follow the trail to our kin. Que sera.'

Despair battles with raw anger. Conté clutches her sap, ever ready to use it. Warne stacks her pipe and looks at her pocket

43

watch. 'Time's a-wasting, my dashing new recruits. So what is it to be?'

#7 – THE BALTIMORE PLOT

Camden Street Depot, Baltimore, February 15th, 1861

'*He shall not pass.*'

'What in hell is that supposed to mean?'

'You're looking at me as if I've got the answers, Harry.'

'Do you think they're serious? They look serious.'

'Yes, they look serious.'

'What has that bitch gotten us into now?'

Chanting. '*He shall not pass. He Shall Not Pass.* HE SHALL NOT PASS.'

The President-Elect shall not pass. Abraham Lincoln shall not pass. President-Elect Abraham Lincoln shall die in a very public fashion and a full coup will be underway before he even reaches Washington, takes the oath and offends the South even more with his repressive taxes and laws, before he sends Dixie into a bottomless chasm. A deep-laid conspiracy is afoot to capture the Capitol, destroy all the avenues leading to it from the North, East, and West, and thus prevent the inauguration of Mr Lincoln. It is a de facto coup, evidenced by the frothing throng present here today at Baltimore: this critical junction between the Northern and Southern states. Every manjack and his wife in this House of God want that man dead, save these two young women. The chanting reaches a frenzy, verging upon ritual sacrifice. They don't care who knows this heinous, treasonous act is about to unfold. The fear and loathing is palpable, irresistible to all bar Harriet and Conté.

'Man alive,' mutters Conté, 'They'll tear him to shreds.'

The gallery in the church is reserved for female spectators as the men below debate. Stout men, Baltimore men and hard, Carolinian men of the Palmetto Regiment, past and current, land privateers and the most feared military mob in the South, modern conquistadors of Mexico. The armed guard at the doors to this packed venue evidences just how much Harriet and Conté had to use all their wiles of disguise to take their place this evening among the righteous and the bold. That distressed, Southern military belle widow and her maid old trick works pretty much every time, thankfully. None of Pinkerton's men would dare try to infiltrate this mob, having neither the wiles nor the looks.

He shall not pass. A sibilant hiss emits from the double 's' on pass, snaking around the floor and back to the podium in a thunderous, rhythmic bootstomp, where stands one Otis K. Hillard, a bull of a man in austere dress, acting out like the preacher, a Cromwell of the South. The stomping chant dies down as Hillard raises his hands, for he has more to say. He's the kind that always has more to say.

'Gentlemen, gentlewomen.' He consults his pocket watch. 'We have reached the hour. He. Shall not. Pass.'

Their eardrums could burst with the noise this prompts. On cue, the double doors are pulled open and the congregation spills out into a much, much bigger throng in the grounds and out into the square of the depot.

'Jesus lord,' says Conté as the biting cold air and the smell of winter hits them, 'Most of Maryland is out there.'

They wade into the throng and push against the tide, like salmon swimming upriver. It turns out that Mr Pinkerton's intelligence about how the square in front of Camden Station and the interior concourse would be cleared and ready for Lincoln's cavalcade is quite cataclysmically wrong. Thus, it turns out that Mr Pinkerton and Miss Warne are accompanying Mr President-Elect, their number one client, to his and their impending death by stampede. The God-fearing, righteous people of Baltimore, stoked by the likes of Hillard and guarded against armed suppression by the Palmetto Troops, are determined to tear Lincoln and all of his reformist ideals limb from limb, quite literally. Mr Lincoln shall pass indeed, but only through the pearly gates. If they succeed, this country will go to a hell from which there is no return. Or so Conté has told Harriet as she reads about these things, but Harriet will trust her over what their employers say a million-fold.

They push and squirm through the human traffic, seeking the steps down into the crypt, from where they can exit the rear of the building, circumvent the mob, and try to intercept the Pinkerton convoy before it is too late. Harriet cleaves a way through in Conté's wake. 'Who in hell told them that he was taking the train to Washington?'

46

'You thinking what I'm thinking?'

Pinkerton has a snitch in his ranks, someone who shares the Palmetto Brigade's ideal of Lincoln not seeing the White House ever again, if not the cause of the South itself.

Whoops and cheers from inside and outside the church. Scythes, swords, pitchforks and machetes are brandished by the frothing mob. Hillard is carried upon the shoulders of burly Palmetto boys, already the conquering hero. The crowd parts to let them through.

They make it to the steps, down and through an oak door. The crypt is pitch black save for a shaft of light at the far end that is a beacon for their exit. Heavy, acrid, ancient dust pollutes the air as the footsteps from up above thud along, to the extent that the ceiling could buckle and the whole story would end, new dead joining the long dead. Their unease is equally palpable down here, as if even the corpses want a piece of the action. They scramble to the exit and pull open the iron door. Light bursts in, but so does a voluminous shadow.

'What in hell are you two doing here?' says the rotund, moustachioed chap looking down at them from the boneyard out back. He should be a friendly, familiar face. Familiar Mr Benjamin Franklin Butler is indeed, friendly he is never.

'We have to locate the cavalcade,' says Harriet, making to push past him. Butler raises a sturdy cane to block her path. Snow falls in thick gobbets.

'And lead these crazies directly to the President-Elect? Are you out of your own tiny fucking minds?'

'Mr Butler,' replies Conté, 'Please remove yourself from our path.'

'Major General Butler to you. I am commissioned, you know.'

The man looks like a Vaudeville caricature of a soldier, but Harriet plays along. '*Major General* Butler, we have intelligence that Mr Lincoln is in grave peril. We need to divert that convoy now.'

Butler's crook holds firm. 'It is in hand. You can stand down.'

'No,' replies Conté. Butler sneers at her impertinence.

'No?'

'Sir, we only take orders from our employer. Not you. With respect.'

'Well, I cannot allow you to proceed further.'

'With respect, Major General,' Harriet parrots Conté, unfazed by his stubborn posture. At a glance around them, she can see that he is on his own. 'We have our orders.'

'You are my subordinates.'

'We are private detectives, sir. You do not have the jurisdiction to command us.'

Butler draws a revolver. He trains it on them.

'You are a pair of meddlesome fillies. Know your place or I'll empty this and no further questions shall be asked, you can be assured.'

Harriet looks him in the eye. 'Can I ask what *you* are doing here, Major General?'

Butler frowns, as if a bubble of genius has appeared in his mind. He answers a question with a question. 'Perhaps I might interest you in a job? Both of you, efficient girls.'

What? Where in hell did that come from? 'There is a matter at hand, General.'

He considers Harriet's quick rebuttal for a moment, unfazed by their need for alacrity.

'No? Ah well. Shame.' He pulls back the hammer and nuzzles the gun's barrel against her forehead, pushing her back. 'Get back down there and do not reappear until I tell you to. This is United States Government business. That is all you need to know.' Harriet smiles gently at him. Butler is unaware that she is holding two fingers and folded thumb behind her back to the watching Conté, who knows precisely what to do. 'I'm rather fond of old Pinkerton's racket, after a fashion, so I'd prefer not to put a slug in a perfectly useful young female agent's head. But you do need to know your place, my dear.'

Thud. The short, folded steel blade has embedded itself in Butler's right shin. This gets his attention.

'We have not got time to debate this, Major General sir,' replies Harriet, moving out of his way as he begins to lose balance.

'Cunts. Sheer cuntishness.' Butler wobbles and his leg gives way underneath him. His gun reports, but the bullet pings off the masonry. He collapses down the steps and rolls inside the mausoleum like a deflated medicine ball. Conté assists his momentum with a swift kick and then pulls the heavy door shut after him. She pulls the deadbolts.

'Someone will be back later for you, sir,' says Harriet. Conté stifles a chuckle. 'Major General? Can you hear me?'

Muffled, from behind the door. 'Cunts, I say!'

'Thank you, sir.'

'Good riddance,' says Conté. 'Come on, Harry.'

'Righto.'

They run to their horses and mount. There is not a second further to waste.

'You did good, girls.'

Pinkerton's mousey, receded hair and beard are exactly the same length. Save for his piercing green eyes, pasty complexion and chevron nose, he could be the complete human simian. If he had anything approaching a normal face, a smile might crack it.

Conté and Harriet exchange glances. *Did good? They saved Mr Lincoln's bacon, ergo the United States of America.* Of course, they know that against Pinkerton's gruff, dour, Glaswegian temperament, his statement should count as a glowing tribute.

'We should brief you about Major General Butler, sir. His behaviour was odd, to say the least. You know that ...'

'I am aware.' He holds his palm up to stop Harriet in her attempt to create some flow. The train rattles along in a rhythmic 4:4 beat. Pinkerton pours two scotches and gives one to Miss Warne. When she is in his company, Warne prefers to say nothing at all. She glowers at them like a bitch pit bull. He sips his booze and rattles the liquor cabinet with his fingertips. She sips Pinkerton's booze and copies him, like the psycho sycophant that she is.

In the adjacent room, Abraham and Mrs Lincoln are resting after the short ordeal of earlier today, when upon they were diverted in the nick of time into another carriage while the decoy continued to Camden Station. Their train was halted at the preceding junction by Pinkerton operatives and Mr Lincoln, clad in the disguise of a scotch cap and long cloak, boarded a cattle car to the rear with his wife Mary, taking the inconvenience and danger with their customary grace and good humour. They swapped cows' asses for the more salubrious luxury of this executive carriage once the train was clear of the Maryland Mob, but the future of the nation owes his very existence to these two rookie female operatives. Is the President-Elect aware of this? Not that either Conté or Harriet should expect even a curt acknowledgement, let alone a medal. Warne smokes her pipe, keeps her arms folded and her face tight, sour as ever. Her boss sips more whisky and tops himself up.

'You will alight the train at the next stop and return to your post to await orders. I will take care of Butler. That is all.'

And just how will he do that? From their limited experience of the 'Major General', Harriet can see that he has his own agenda. Boston lawyer by day, bloated subhuman demagogue by night. He is already using the lobbies to undermine Lincoln's every move in both Congress and the Senate, which is not exactly a state secret. If Pinkerton really is acting in his client's best interests, he should send them back to that Baltimore crypt to finish the job. But Pinkerton remains vaguely deferential to the man, as if the infamous Boston Blob has something on him. Perhaps that is not a stone they want or need to turn over.

'Yes sir.'

Do not ask questions. It is the Pinkerton way, and they need not be reminded how lucky they are to be in his service. It was this or the noose, after all.

Except they do. Need to be reminded. Every day.

'Dismissed.'

Pony Express, Baton Rouge on the post mark. Paid for out of Pinkerton's budget, one of a few discreet misdemeanours in exchange for their loyalty and their souls.

Choctaw Chief Peter Pitchlynn says that they are holding firm in Louisiana, which has to be some kind of miracle. Either that or their people have aligned themselves with some bad lots in order to keep River Haven. The sap is rising in the South and there are deals to be done, but they need to be mighty careful about who they do business with. As ordered, they jumped the train before it reached Washington, bought a pair of horses and headed way out West to their garret in Chicago, another town built by navvies and populated by a swarm of Irish who fled the Hunger back home. No potato blight or British dominion here, but plenty of slums, dysentery and cholera to remind Harriet of where she came from.

God knows why Pinkerton chose to station them here, save for this being near the place where he founded The Agency alongside his cooperage, in a Scottish enclave of Illinois called Dundee Township. They sit and wait in their bare-floored and freezing-cold safe house upon a terrace on Dearborn, with enough of a bankroll at their disposal to live in a palace but with strict orders to remain discreet and austere. The terrace was raised up on two hundred jackscrews to evade the pathogenic water, recently identified as the source of many Chicago cholera outbreaks. Harriet's long-lost countrymen and women are still waiting to be redeemed from the slurry on the banks of Lake Michigan.

How long before they can return to their people? Will it be Louisiana or Oklahoma?

Harriet fumbles with a clay pipe as Conté perches on a rocking chair away from the draught of the windows, next to a crackling fire, reading as per usual. Damn this incessant winter cold that invades every crack and exposed pore, unimaginable where they come from. It has been two years now and still they haven't acclimatised.

'Are you going to smoke that or use it as an ornament?' says Conté without looking up from her tome.

'Maybe I will take up smoking. Seems like a fun pastime.'

'You know my feelings about it. And you'll do it outside if that is your choice.'

'You imbibe the tribal pipe.'

'That is not the same thing and you know it, Harry.'

'Hrmph.'

'Hrmph yourself.'

A knock on the front door. Harriet climbs to her feet like a sulking child, not wanting to let in the cold air again. 'Please let that be a job for us.'

'Please let it not. I'm quite happy here.'

'Be like that, Conté. You can stay and keep the cold company, then.'

Harriet opens the door. A boy in a neat trench coat and cap stands to attention. He passes her a docket and she scratches out the signature of one of her alias names in pencil before shutting the door in his face and jamming the draft excluder up to the crack.

'What is it?'

'I won't know until I open it, will I?'

'Well open it.'

'I will.'

Harriet breaks the US Government seal. 'Well?' says Conté, eyes still fixed on her book. 'A job? Say it isn't so. I was just getting comfortable.'

Her friend smiles and peruses the letter. 'Nope. Not a job.'

'Then what?'

Harriet tosses the paper into Conté's lap and raises her hands up in thanks to the Lord.

'We're going home, Conté.'

There's no such thing as an uneventful journey when going across the big country. Travel by coach or railroad, and you're at the mercy of robbers and bandits; that's just your fellow passengers. Travel on horseback, and you're at the mercy of every louse who sees a couple of females as an easy target. Once the louse is shown the contrary and eats lead, it is too late and too troublesome for a moratorium. Then some John Q. Law shows up asking questions and a sharp exit must be made. Repeat ad infinitum and ad nauseam until some bandit gets lucky. It is a hazardous, tiresome business. Horseback it is, though. Both women prefer control over their own destiny and there are only half a dozen attempted ransacks this time on the 900-mile trek from Chicago to River Haven. Some going, but it isn't a journey either of them cares to repeat soon. They pray that they might be able to stay, to nurture some roots here, but there is a growing menace crossing into New France, one that has tailed them all the way down here, getting more fearsome and febrile the further south they travel. It feels like a tornado is upon them, stalking their ride all the way home.

Sobering as they finally approach River Haven is how the lands have been pared back even further since '58, with yet more plantations and homesteads appearing along the banks of the river and more woodland cleared. Every familiar landmark along the trail, from a particular tree stump or stream to a gully or frond is going, going, going as white picket modernity encroaches. Farms, plantations and entire towns have sprung up en masse. The Englishman is everywhere.

They ride into River Haven along the Southern pass, the only way accessible by horse. A timber fortification has been erected to deter the varmints who feel that raiding the Choctaw village is as free and easy as fishing for salmon, but it won't keep US Marshals or even a small platoon of troops out, if and when it ever comes to that. Peter Pitchlynn has an accord with the Pinkertons, but this is thinner than the paper it was written upon and Harriet's guts tell her that the citadel could fall at any minute and for any reason. Menace is in the very air they breathe, corrupting its sweet Mississippi lilt.

Peter waits for them at the gate. His scouts must have told him that they were imminent. At least something still works around here. They dismount, thighs and asses sore from long saddle hours.

'What chance of a bath, Peter?' asks Conté, reading Harriet's mind. 'Or at least a soak in the stream?'

'Welcome back, you two. You have been missed.'

Harriet checks the fortification. A keen effort, but nothing more than a symbolic stronghold. 'It isn't right that we copy them. It isn't right that you… *we* are holed up in here like rabbits in a boobytrapped warren.'

'You have been party to the full range of solutions, child. This is what remains of the *okla*.'

Harriet strokes his face. Such a dear, sweet, bright man. He seems to have aged another decade since they last spoke. 'I am sorry, Peter. For you, for us.'

Perhaps there is bathing and food waiting. Maybe even a celebration of sorts. It can't all be doom and gloom, can it?

'A guest has arrived for you. He waits in your cabin.'

'Oh. Great.' Of course. There had to be a reason that the Pinkertons were summoning them home.

It seems that their miserable existence up North followed them down here so well that it arrived before them. Conté ties up her horse and shakes her head, striding past without acknowledging Peter. Harriet follows in her wake, trying to apologise for her friend, but he can't even look her in the eye. What now? Who now?

A main street of sorts has developed up the slight incline of a pathway through the fronds, indicative of just how much the wings of the Choctaw have been clipped and just how hemmed in they are nowadays. Soon, nature will vanish and the ancestors will scream their last, then the river spirit will die too. This used to be a movable camp among many others; now, it is a bastion prison posing as a village. They approach the cabin and step inside. A musty, musky, male aroma is immediately upon them, like a hock of ham left out in the sun too long. It is familiar and unwelcome.

'Mister Butler. What brings you to Louisiana?'

'Major General Butler to you, Miss Farrell. You forget so readily.'

Butler is in full, blue uniform. He appears alone, but it is a dime to a dollar he has come with a full garrison waiting for his order or signal, close at hand. Conté checks out back but it is futile. There's no hiding from him this time; he would have made damn sure.

'I'd offer you our hospitality, but as you can see we have just finished a long ride, sir.'

'Um.'

His considerable, formidable ass adorns Conté's favourite chair. It creaks beneath the voluminous bulk. Harriet stands over him. 'So, sir. Major General. We are in the service of a private company and that is the only detail I can divulge to you, as per our conversation in Baltimore.'

'Huh,' Butler pulls out a docket and tosses it to Harriet's feet. 'Well, consider yourselves relieved of duty from the Pinkertons. You two are now property of the United States Government. Congratulations. You work for me.'

Property? Just as Conté returns, Harriet rips the folder open and finds a printed requisition order signed by Pinkerton himself, the Secretary of State, and Butler.

'Military assignments to Secret Service detail,' says Conté, 'Pieces of meat traded for what, Butler?'

'If you were meat, I might have you for dinner. I prefer to use the term 'assets'.'

'Wh-'

'-Your chief out there, dour fellow with the weird, mongrel face. He's agreed to it. Not that he has a pot to piss in, mind. Any deal is a good deal for his sorry red ass.'

'And what exactly is that deal?' asks Conté. Harriet notices Butler's walking stick. Perhaps Conté is thinking about doing his other leg and making a matching pair.

'Read it and don't waste my time with banal and obvious questions. I rate you. Both of you. I like using women and negros, they are easier to control and they can get into places that regular men cannot or will not go. No one likes a smart woman, but better still no one expects one.'

Harriet is only able to respond to the corpulent, condescending bastard with her own brand of bristling sarcasm. 'I appreciate the compliment, sir. What a refreshing stance you have.'

'It isn't a social standpoint, just expedient and strategic, so put a cap on the attitude, young lady.'

'Right.'

'You should be grateful to be getting this opportunity.'

How did he engineer this? Did he simply buy them off Allan Pinkerton? Did Pinkerton lose them in a game of cards? What in hell is happening right now?

'What does this opportunity entail, sir?'

'The South. Ructions and factions. Dangerous ideas and machinations. You have already had a brush with the Palmetto Brigade in Baltimore, so you will be cognisant.'

'And we stopped them from murdering our elected President. No thanks to you,' chirps Conté, altogether more direct, as usual.

'You understand nothing, back in Maryland or right now. But, fortunately, I haven't commissioned you two for your political acumen. Since when will two girls of dubious stock have an opinion that matters? No, I need you for a special detail, to infiltrate this secessionist cabal, to use your considerable skills of acting bluff in the service of your country.'

Conté nods at Harriet and faces Butler. 'You mean this war that we have got coming?'

'Yes. The Palmettos aren't a fraction of it. Richmond has recruited entire battalions, defected from us and freshly signed up. Fighting Tigers here in Louisiana, previously unitary brigades across the South and mid-West are now joined in a common cause. Country boys with big guns. Strapping, angry bastards, extremely fit and adept. They've ordered conscription for men with less than twenty slaves. A raft of some of our best-commissioned officers and our finest Generals and strategists from Beauregard to Lee have defected. They have ready supplies of the best artillery and ordinance. They have sharp shooters in their droves. They've even got their own White House in Richmond with Jeff Davis as President, God help us. They're pissed about mostly everything to do with Washington, taxes being their main gripe and Lincoln is the very devil to them, the single point I have sympathy with them on. This has been a long time coming. So, yes, war.'

'And what do we get in return? For fighting your war?' says Conté. Yes, why should it be their problem?

'This is everyone's war, girl.'

'Not ours. Not the Choctaw's.'

'You should train her to shut her mouth and follow orders, Miss Farrell. You will need to keep up appearances on this brief. Her subservience is top of the list.'

Harriet stands shoulder to shoulder with Conté. 'It was a valid question, sir. You clearly want our hearts, our minds, our souls. Give us something.'

'How pithy.'

'If you say so.'

'Emancipation. Freedom for all slaves.'

Conté seethes. 'Pull the other one. Are you using that line to recruit all the strong negro boys, then? Just how desperate are you?'

Butler smiles or winces. It is difficult to tell which. 'You get to tell Mr Pitchlynn that he can keep his village.'

'Not *his*. *Ours*. And it is a settlement.'

'Semantics. It's a postage stamp. Look around you to see the changes.'

Conté replies, 'Will we have a legal debenture? Enshrined in Federal Statute? And a commitment of money? You are buying us, after all.'

'The Federal Government will honour the Pinkerton agreement. That's all you'll get and be happy with it. I requisitioned you from Allan Pinkerton, not the Redskins.'

'We can refuse. Not cooperate.'

'Then, Miss Louverture, we will clear the Choctaws out once and for all, right this very moment. Shouldn't take much, they're hardly Apache or Cheyenne in a scrap, I'll vouch. I thought you would be a few steps further than that, dear.'

'What a keen value you must place in us, Major General sir,' says Harriet, less able to stem her disgust at the betrayal of the Pinkertons with every second in his company.

'I need trained operatives ready to go. New Orleans must be controlled by us or the port will become a stronghold for a potential Rebel Navy. And…'

Conté, as ever, refuses to be left out of the conversation. 'And what?'

'Overtures are being made. To the British, the French. Russians and Prussians even. Plenty of admirers for the Palmetto cause from afar. We Yankees are a veritable threat it seems, too powerful altogether in the Americas. Of course, the imperial powers know how to sniff a land grab, as they always do.' He rubs his thumb and forefingers together. 'Money, molasses, cotton. There, you're in my confidence already. How does it feel to be aboard?'

Any periodical imported from Europe would tell them as much, stripped of his bias and bluster. The round-faced buffoon must think that they don't read. 'I see.'

'No, you do not see, Miss Farrell. But we will brief you with exactly the right amount of intelligence for your roles.'

Butler groans as he uses his stick to climb to his feet. 'Just how is the leg, then?' asks Conté, purposely seeking to provoke him.

'My surgeon expects a full recovery. I'll be clear that there is no personal grudge. You will come to know that is how I work. It was a deft move, I'll grant you.'

Harriet exchanges a quick look with Conté, long enough to declare bullshit. Men like Butler take *everything* personally. 'Yes.'

'Yes what?'

'Yes. Sir.'

Butler narrows his eyes. 'Although try those antics again and I will slit both your throats and burn down every Choctaw shack here and in Oklahoma. The next time that you will touch me will be to kiss my ass in gratitude, Miss Louverture.'

Conté flinches. 'Ugh.'

And there it is. Butler stands on no further ceremony. He hobbles out. 'Stand fast and await orders.'

And with that, the door slams shut and he's gone.

'Damn,' says Harriet, 'That's us told.'

#8 – THE FRIEND OF THE SOUTH

Washington D.C., 14th April 1865

All the boys are here tonight at her boarding house on the eve of the deed. Captain Tom Conrad, Danny Cloud, Tippie Ruggles, Georgie Atzerodt, Davey Herold, Louie Powell, JWB and her brave, beautiful son, John Junior. Young men but veterans still, heroes all. They shall deliver; they shall smash this foul injustice, for they are strong, god-fearing boys. No, not boys, but men. Handsome men, too, perhaps with the exception of little Davey and that silver spoon fool Ruggles. And Conrad, she don't like the look of him much either, all high and mighty in his tight collar and military stripes, strutting round like he owns the place when *she* owns the place. But the rest of them are fine young gentlemen. Praise be.

Why, then, does she continue to harbour a god-awful feeling about all of this? Why does she want to yell "stop!" at the very top of her lungs and send them all home to their wives and their mommas? Because this damn plan stinks to high heaven, that's why.

Said boys play five card stud for matchsticks, as all the preparation is done for the Great Revolutionary Event, the operation that will turn the tide. Some might say it is too late for this, that Lee has surrendered and that President Davis is on the brink of penal servitude, but the boys say that it is the optimum time to strike and that they have God on their side. God and a certain fellow who is running late tonight for a final inspection. An older, fatter chap altogether conspicuous by his absence and the font of her unease, as he has been for nearly two years now since he came into the lives of the Surratt family. He makes her skin crawl and her belly quake, but all the boys think he is just the bees' knees, not least her John Jr. Oh, John Jr!

'Dammit, Butler. You Yankee weasel,' mutters Mary Surratt as she serves cookies to her boys. John Jr eyes her askance. He is winning the game, as usual. No one else notices her cussing.

'Momma, quit fretting. Have faith. He is a friend of the South. Bona fide, proven. His neck is on the line as much as ours, more so even.' He chuffs on his crème cigar and clutches her hand. This warms her heart. He makes the soul of his dearly departed Daddy John Sr glow with pride with his actions, the youngest of the bunch at 21 but surely the wiliest, bravest and certainly the most handsome. Well, with the exception of Lewis Powell, but that boy could make any lady flutter at a thousand paces. Good, true, brave boys as they are, they would surely flounder on the rocks of perdition were it not for her golden son. Their leader in all but name. That makes it all the harder for her, as Mary knows that the one thing he lacks she has in abundance: intuition.

'But where in hell is that man, Johnnie?' she mutters. He placates her by eating another cookie.

There's more cigar smoke, swigging of whiskey and munching of her baked goods. These boys need their moment of distraction, for they all know that they are waiting for their orders. Perhaps her presence isn't wanted or needed up here in the garret of her boarding house in the District of Columbia, a Northern capital in a Southern setting, but she will not rest and darn and sew until the day after tomorrow, when she knows that this game will really be done.

'Momma?'

'Yes, John?'

'Quit twitching, and go check the shooting irons, please.'

'We checked them earlier. You and I did so.'

'Go check them again, Momma. These boys are done wound tight. They need to unwind. You ain't helping with your fidgeting.'

'Are you saying that I'm making them all anxious, John?'

'I'm saying to go check the shooting irons, Momma.'

Mary harrumphs and galumphs out of the garret and down the narrow staircase, then down again past the rooms she keeps for respectable young men lately demobilised from the war and down, down, down into the bowel basement, into the kitchen and the pantry where the rifles and pistols are kept behind the vats of flour, churned butter, syrup and cinnamon she uses to bake her excellent cookies. She hears footsteps in the kitchen, grabs a pistol and stalks through.

'Miss Mary?'

It's that negro owned by Ruggles. The door that leads through to the backyard hangs open. Sweat glistens on the boy's brow. Only by a quirk of fate has she run into him right now.

'What have you got there, William?'

William holds his hands behind his back, eyes furtive. 'Something direct for Captain Conrad, Miss Mary.'

'Give it here. I shall make sure he gets it.'

'No, Miss Mary.'

'No?' She strokes the pistol. 'Give it here, boy. Less of your impertinence.'

'Aw, Miss Mary.'

'Give.'

'Aw.'

He clutches a sealed envelope in his huge hands. Mary snatches it off him and swats his ear with the butt of the gun, drawing blood. This might be her basement, and he might be Tippie Ruggles' property, but she will never trust a black boy since one of his ilk set fire to her old homestead a few score moons back. They're all aggrieved and stirred by the fighting over emancipation. High time that they all went back to their place, for their own good and for the general peace of the world.

'What did I say about you coming directly to me?'

'Sorry, Miss Mary.'

'You will be.'

A pot of stew bubbles on the hot range for the boys' supper. She adjusts the lid, and some steam escapes, allowing her to open the envelope without revealing her tamper. Upon perusing it, her blood runs cold.

BURN AFTER READING.

Confirmation of plan. Mr Surratt to handle Lincoln alone. Mr Booth and Mr Atzerodt to handle Johnson, Mr Powell to handle Seward. Security will be lax tomorrow, as per my instructions. You will not see me again.

God speed,

BFB.

So, this is the news that they've all been waiting for. 'Damn you, Butler. I knew you'd pull something on us.'

After all, she kinda saw it coming. Her instincts had never failed her. Butler had resolved to give the exact details of the plan tonight, at the last possible moment. He gives himself away not by the content of the message but by the method of its delivery. A feeling that has been gurgling in Mary Surratt's guts since her blessed boy was recruited now bubbles away like that tasty stew on the stove. Lincoln was supposed to be kidnapped, not assassinated. And killing Vice President Johnson and Secretary of State Seward has only just become a prerogative. Why? Don't ask questions, says the almighty Butler. Jump in the fire, says the almighty Butler. Well, screw the almighty Butler. This deal is altogether too sour for her liking. She will not have it.

So what to do? Let it be or pull the plug? God has gifted her the power of a sacred intervention. She must hold true, even though her son and his friends will not like it an iota. None of this will do, but she must act quickly and cutely with an attic full of young guns not disposed to listening to a middle-aged lady. They have no idea that they are rats in a trap.

The Pterotype machine, built by Jonathan Pratt of Centre, Alabama, sits proudly on the kitchen table. Mary has become a dab hand at using it to write coded missives for John Jr, so that his own hand cannot be identified in the event of an arrest. She cracks her knuckles and sits down. Major General Butler's absence this evening speaks volumes. Time to bake something up that they'll all swallow fast.

'Your dumbass act doesn't fool me,' she drawls as she types.

'Beg pardon, Miss Mary?' says William, shuffling on his feet, ear smarting.

'Your daddy was your master. I know all about your roots, boy.'

'What? My master is Mr Ruggles. His son.'

'And your brother, yes. But I know you work for Butler, boy. His note proves it.'

'No, Miss Mary. Where does it say that?'

'Yes, Miss Mary. And it don't have to say nothing. I know. And you'll tell me everything you know, or I'll see to it that your momma and your whole family are strung up from trees. You know what we're capable of, boy.' Mary finishes typing, folds the message and replaces it in the envelope before resealing it. She pockets it, climbs to her feet, and grabs a set of darning pins and heats them up on the stove. William gulps. 'Now, time's a-spoiling, so you better get talking.'

'Miss Mary I …'

John Jr rips open the envelope and laughs even though what he reads is not remotely amusing.

BURN AFTER READING.

Change of plan. Mr Booth to handle Lincoln alone. Mr Surratt and Mr Atzerodt to handle Johnson, Mr Powell to handle Seward. Tell Booth to use the same lines given to Surratt. Security will be lax tomorrow, as per my instructions. You will not see me again.

God speed,

BFB.

For a group of young men on the receiving end of instructions for a suicide mission, the atmosphere among them remains upbeat, almost jovial. John Jr is the exception. His face is morose like he has just been cheated. Conrad, the senior of the bunch according to rank, snatches the paper and reads. 'JWB on his ownsome. Well, well.'

'Wow,' mews Booth, excitement rising, his eyes blazing, 'Lemme see. Wowwee.'

Conrad holds it up to Booth's face. 'I suppose it makes sense to have an actor do the deed. It being a theatre and all.'

'No wonder you lost just about every fight in the war, Tommy,' grunts John Jr, 'Booth can't shoot for shit. I'm the trained agent. He's a fucking actor. This is plain foolish.'

'Hey, I resent that. I'm a dab hand at stage combat. Mind your language in front of your lady momma, too.'

'Hear hear,' agrees Conrad.

'Jesus fucking …' John Jr catches Mary's stern glance, 'Forgive me for cussing, Momma, but the Major General didn't even have the courtesy to tell me to my face. Two goddamn years of hard training, of waiting for this opportunity. It makes no sense.'

Mary nods with extra vigour. 'I say we all cut and run. You cannot trust this man. I told you all, time and again. Let us regroup and return stronger.'

Conrad intervenes. 'Mrs Surratt, there will never be another opportunity like this ever again. Now, all of us appreciate the kind support that you have lent us, but leave the figuring to the men, please.'

Her hands are on her hips now. 'Benjamin Butler's a Yankee, and we should never trust one of them. I say we cut.' Conrad deems this serious enough to put out his cigar. 'There are funds we can use to get to Mexico. Or Canada. Regroup and return. We don't need him.'

'Ma'am, on the contrary,' says Conrad, trying to retain composure, 'We very much do. He has influence in places that we would never be able to get. He has plans that I cannot divulge, but they are magnificent. Revolutionary in every way.'

'Take the wool out of your eyes, Tom Conrad. I am sorry if this upsets you young fellas, but you need to listen to this momma. Butler is leading you to the gallows for his own ends. Why can none of you see it?' Mary is aware that she is letting her mouth run, but she has kept quiet for far too long.

'Surratt, maybe your mother should stick to baking cookies?' says Ruggles, the toffee-nosed little pest.

Cruel chuckles. Mary steps into Ruggles' face, to his surprise. John Jr whistles and gets in between them. 'Momma, orders are orders. I don't like it any more than you do, but he must have his reasons.' Mary wouldn't relent for any other man in the room other than her John Jr. JWB looks like the cat that got the cream, for it might well be his name going down in history. Provided he can shoot straight and not fluff his lines, but this is about so much more than killing Lincoln. 'Momma, you know too much already. Please, don't get caught up in all of this. Let it be, I say.'

Mary nods, turns on her heel and leaves the boys to play. They are not her responsibility, but her son is a different matter. She knew damned well her protests would be fruitless, which is why she switched the names on Butler's memo.

Conrad relights his cigar and burns the message on the tip. 'Let's get back to the game. Never mind the lady. She's going through the change; I know about these things. Makes them crazy. No offence, Surratt.'

Mary listens through the door. Yes, they can all go to hell, but they sure ain't taking her boy with them.

The very next day.

'Momma, you had no right meddling.'

'Junior, as God is my witness, that man is up to no good.'

'Atzerodt is weak. He hasn't the guts or wiles to kill a varmint, never mind the Vice President. What have you done, leaving him alone to do the job?'

'I have saved you, son. From some heinous conspiracy.'

'Momma, you have damned us all.'

Tears of loathing well in John Jr's eyes, brimming on anger as he raises his fist to strike his mother. 'Do it, Junior. Hit me as hard as you can, just like your Daddy did. Take your pistol and kill me, but I know what I did was right. You are still a boy, and you do not understand men like Benjamin Butler. I do.'

John Jr punches the stone wall, bloodying his knuckles. He steps back into the shadows of the chapel of St Peter, a Catholic pocket in an Anglican city and one of the few safe places in the District of Columbia where this fugitive can hide. He prowls back and forth. 'You sap my soul, Momma. I hate you.'

'I understand, Junior. I can only love you.'

They're round the corner from the Kirkwood House, where Vice President Andrew Johnson is presently residing quite comfortably, having not had a bullet put in him by her son. Government men are currently swarming the lobby and John Jr would have been walking into a trap laid by Butler, for all of the assurances about lax security. He would have been allowed to do the deed and then been caught red-handed doing a job meant for JWB; only Mary was finally wise to Butler's meddling, complex plan. Of course, John Jr's mother was waiting for him in the lobby, before he drew the attention of the G Men. She couldn't stop the others, but she could stop him. He collapses to his knees and hugs her legs, perhaps looking to crawl back into her womb. He would be welcome if that is what will keep him safe.

'Momma, what am I to do?'

Mary takes his face in her palms. 'Run, John. Run far away.'

'What will become of you? Of the South?'

'This scheme was nothing to do with the South and all to do with Benjamin Butler. I had my suspicions all along. That slave boy confirmed it after I threatened his family and jabbed him a few times with a hot needle.'

'Come with me, Momma.'

'I cannot. I must not. You will be much faster on your own, and they will be looking for you soon.'

All of a sudden, there is much yelling and caterwauling in the street outside. She can't make it out, but surely – by this hour – JWB's appointment has been and gone. All the more urgency then, whatever the outcome.

She kisses his forehead and places Butler's original communique in his clammy grip. 'Go to Canada, St Liboire. Find Father Boucher and he'll arrange passage to England for you. We have friends there. I will stay here and throw them off the scent a while. Give Butler a taste of his own vittles. Instructions and some cash are in your satchel. Yours is a holy mission now.'

'What will they do to you?'

'They won't hang a woman. Maybe they won't do anything.'

'I don't believe you, momma.'

John Jr remains angry and confused, which is another reason why he must haul his ass out of Washington D.C. immediately. His ability to think straight is shot under the pressure, which is a trait he inherited from his father, alas. Again, Mary curses herself for going along with the plan at all and for listening to Butler's lies about offering a dividend to the South when he gets to the Oval Office. All highfalutin', snake talk. Lincoln may or may not have died, but Andrew Johnson won't, so the fat man's big idea sticks in his craw. For now.

Mary Surratt gently guides her son John to his feet. 'Go, Junior. Go now.'

It turns out that John Wilkes Booth could shoot just fine. He even managed an escape, such was the extent of the deliberately inept security on the night. What tore it for Mary is that Butler didn't show up when he was supposed to, that and the presence of his spy of a slave in her house. That man's reputation as Governor of New Orleans, sullying good Southern ladies as prostitutes, meant she never trusted him like her boy John Jr did, or his pals. Her conscience is salved and clear, her place at the right-hand side of God assured.

Now Booth and Herold are in her kitchen, grabbing carbines, binoculars and a hemp sack of Mrs Surratt's famous freshly-baked cookies. They're going on a journey that Mary knows is entirely pointless and doomed. She is staying right here until they come for her and then? Well, then may God have mercy upon her, but at least her boy is headed somewhere they can't get to him.

#9 – BIRTHDAY GIRL

Liverpool, June 25th, 1865

Constable Payton Ake closes his hands around Conté's throat, black leather gloves stretching and creaking as he throttles her into an early grave. All of her power and ferocity are reduced to nothing by this man mountain of hate.

Harriet tries to come between them, to prise Ake off her, but they are ghosts occupying a different moment in time and she can only swipe at the gloopy air, trying to connect with something solid.

Harriett looks him in the eye and finds only a seemingly bottomless pit. Then, travelling down, down, down into what was once a noble and gentle Igbo soul, she gets a fleeting glimpse of his wellspring of hope in spite of the cruel world that he had to abet. But it dissolves into ash, replaced by a damned, slain leviathan right at the bottom of the pit, condemned for eternity. Harriet returns back to the surface at sickening speed to find the victim and her killer are frozen in still relief, like some awful living sculpture depicting a single moment of absolute terror. Harriet sidesteps and walks to the rear of Ake, gazing into Conté's agonised glare. Then, her beloved shuts her eyes forever. Again.

She presses her Colt .45 to the back of Ake's skull. 'Let her be.' But Ake squeezes harder, until Conté vanishes herself into ash, and now Baba is in his crushing hands. Harriet grinds her jaw and lets him have it, bone and brain spraying over the gravestone of her beloved. White light engulfs everything and the dream becomes the requiem.

She kicks dirt over the unmarked grave where she knows that he lies, only a few feet away from Conté in vengeance's last laugh. 'Happy Birthday,' she whispers to her baby girl, before holstering her gun and striding back up the track towards her ride, ready to continue the search. She will never find peace here again until she is reunited with their daughter. Goodbye for now, ghosts.

69

Pat takes a mighty swig from his hipflask, the rough Paddy Whiskey slipping down his throat and into his belly, offering immediate succour. He dips his rag into the bucket, which is balanced precariously on the ledge of the upper floor of Martins Bank on Water Street, his first and only job of the day. Clients have been going over to other fellas who have moved onto his patch since he stopped turning up on time, but with a drop of whiskey and his sinewy grip on the side of the building, he's convinced that he can restore his business. All those other fellas have to use ladders, whereas Pat can climb like no other. Pat's the quickest and the best. He'll get his patch back in no time and bring home the bacon to Sarah. No fear. *He* hangs off the ledge with one hand, thumb smarting a bit, but it's easy enough. He slaps the sopping wet rag onto the glass of the sash window and sings an old country song.

There's a tear in your eye and I'm wondering why that it ever should be there at all

… With such power in your smile, sure a stone you'd beguile and there's never a teardrop should fall

… When your sweet lilting laughter's like some fairy song and your eyes sparkle bright as can be

… Oh then laugh all the while and all other times smile and then smile a smile for me.'

'What is that infernal dirge?' The voice rises up from the floor below. Pat glances down to see the bank manager leering back up at him, head sticking out of the window, round-rimmed spectacles steaming up with indignation.

'Good morning, Mr Rollo. I shall be finished presently. Another hot day, I reckon, eh? I am sweating already, so I am.'

Rollo inspects the glass, running a finger along the still-wet surface. 'Have you done this one? There are streaks. And that one.'

Pat holds up his rag. It drips down into Rollo's face. 'Aye, Mr Rollo. Suds with extra shine, sir. Them streaks will dry so. They will gleam, so they will.'

'Good God, man.' Rollo wipes himself with his sleeve and then squints back up at Pat. 'This is filthy and you are pissed as a newt.'

'I might have had a few small nips.'

'If you fall and break your neck, that's your problem, but a corpse on the pavement will disturb my clients. Now bugger off and do not come back. I will not tell you again.'

Pat's face drops. He was relying upon the bit of change from this job for a few in the Crown later and a bit of supper for the family. 'Ah, come on now, Mr Rollo! I can do it again. Easy and quick so. Watch me.'

'No. I said, bugger off!'

'There you go. You did tell me again.'

'I will call a constable to remove you!'

'Ah, alright then.' Pat makes a grab for his bucket but it topples off the ledge and whacks Rollo square on his pate, showering him with grime, seagull shit and dirty water. 'Oh, sorry sir.'

'You nearly brained me! Off! Now! Irish cretin!'

'I'll clean it up. I'll do the whole front and back for free this week. No, a month.'

'No. Off with you!'

Rollo retreats back into his office like an angry mole. Pat kicks the wall in frustration and nearly drops to fulfil Rollo's prophesy. He steadies himself and then climbs back down.

'Friggin' posh knobs. Hate the lot of them I do. Don't fuckin' need this. Sarah will marmalise me.'

A faint round of applause in the ballroom of The Washington Hotel on Lime Street, another venue run by the underworld, trying and failing to offer a veneer of respectability, as if the management of this establishment would ever know what that meant. The singing girl, Mademoiselle Foufou, as advertised in the poster, has a sweet if mousey voice but the woman on the piano, Madame de Pomfrette, sounds like a foghorn giving out a distress call. The pair are done up like a couple of French fancies but are about as Gallic as a pan of lobscouse.

'Ladies and gentlemen, we will return after a short intermission. Please feel free to order drinks and food from the dining staff who will attend your tables,' announces the senior of the two, and then they skittle away.

More half-hearted clapping. 'Thank God for that,' grunts Dudley, 'Where has he got to this time?'

Harriet shrugs. She makes eye contact with the girl as she shimmies off stage, ogled by the middle-aged and older gentlemen who make up the majority of the small throng of an audience. This place reeks of dirty cash and bad form. Nothing unique there.

Dudley glances at his pocket watch and sips more tea. 'Bloody imposition, it is.'

'You sound more and more like a limey with every day, Thomas.'

Dudley checks himself and chuckles, but he is the only one of the two who finds it amusing. 'I guess, Harriet.' He eyes the staff serving the tables, looking for anyone who might be able to help them. 'Perhaps we should ask them ourselves? What harm could it do?'

'No. Pat might be Pat, but he knows every door and who runs every door in this borough. Stick with the brief, Thomas.'

'Of course, Harriet. Just that I… Just that I cannot abide what has happened to you and your child.' Dudley stops himself, unable to look at her or continue the same spiel that he has spouted since that dreadful day.

Once upon a time, Harriet might have comforted him. He remains wracked with guilt, but she can't see past this search or her own desperation. 'We wait.'

Dudley checks the same watch he checked a moment ago. 'I have a call of nature.' He gets up and walks across the ballroom towards the gentlemen's toilet. Harriet eyes the entrance, looking for activity. It has become standard procedure since they began systematically checking every venue in Liverpool, putting Pat's nouse and contacts to good use, but drawing a blank every time. On first impressions, she doesn't have high hopes for this place, but she is alert to anything and everything.

'Say, you're a sturdy one. A fine figure of a woman.'

Randy drunk at twelve o'clock, here for the matinee performance and convinced that any unaccompanied female is fair game. He is in her face and wants to be in much more. 'I am with a gentleman, sir.'

The drunk looks around himself. 'Are you? I do not see him?'

'Just because you do not see him does not mean that he is not here.'

'American, eh? Or are you putting the accent on for us boys?'

'No.'

'Well, I don't see this mysterious fellow and possession is nine-tenths of the law.'

'Go away.'

'Are you giving me the brush off, young lady? I paid good money for a good time.'

No sign of Dudley. He must have gone to do solids. Harriet emits a long breath and stands up. The flushed gentleman grins back at her and takes a hefty snort of snuff. He offers it to her. 'And just who did you pay your good money to, sir?'

'The concierge, hic.'

'Of course.' If Pat doesn't show, they could always check with the front of house. Dudley could pretend to be a paying guest, although he is rather too well-known in this borough for it to be a reliable cover. It's all a mess, really. More clutched straws, more bad dreams. At times like this, it really does feel like her daughter has vanished off the face of the Earth, which is a thought that leaves her with far more dread than this pest hovering around her.

As the clockwork cogs whirr in her head, the drunk decides to move in directly. 'I want some comfort right now. A nice bit of rump... oooofff!' Her knee connects firmly between his legs, and he collapses against her.

He freezes like stunned prey. Harriet manoeuvres his weight back into a seat. 'There you go. Watch the rest of the show like a good boy and keep nice and quiet. You dirty old prick.'

'Ha, fine work,' says Pat, worse for wear himself.

Harriet scans him up and down. 'Had an urgent appointment in The Crown did we, Padraig?'

'Just needed one. To settle me nerves.'

'Bullshit. You need to lay off the sauce. You are becoming a liability.' It feels a little cruel, but it also feels redundant. Much like Dudley, Harriet is in no position to save Pat from himself.

'Ah, put a cork in it, will ye? I'm sorry about your baby and all but it's not my fault. If Mr Dudley had ...'

'If Mr Dudley what?' says Dudley, returning. 'Spit it out, Pat.'

'Oh sweet baby Jesus, stop it, you two.'

'If Mr Dudley had better staff, we wouldn't be chasing our tails all over the town like fuckin' eejits so. There it is. I said it.' What is it with drunks repeating themselves?

'The baby was in a secure room in the Consulate. No one saw it coming; we have been through this ...'

Harriet holds a palm across Dudley's chest and shakes her head. She's not in the mood for any of it. Not now, not ever again. 'Pat, will you take us to the management or not?'

Pat straightens up his braces. 'Aye, square go. Wait there. Both of yers. Please, like.'

He saunters off in the direction of the bar. Dudley sneers as he watches him. 'Not a word, Thomas,' says Harriet, keen to avoid further bellyaching, angst and repetition. Is she just humouring these two? Would she work better alone? She's long known the answer to both of those questions.

'Harridan,' grunts the drunk, reanimated after his little shock. He smashes a bottle on the table and goes for Harriet.

Dudley steps in front of him. 'You will put that down, sir.'

'She has dish- dish- dishonoured me, sir,' he moans.

'She is with me. You oaf. You dishonour me.'

The fellow eyes Harriet and then Dudley. He tosses the bottle on the table and staggers off. Harriet delivers a slow handclap. 'Oh, my hero.'

'No need to be glib. My intentions were ...'

'Honourable? That's all I ever hear. Next time, leave the pricks to me. If there is a next time.' Harriet lights a clay pipe, gleaning the unwanted attention of other patrons. How unseemly to see a woman in here and one who smokes. 'What are you looking at?'

Back at the bar, she spots the randy drunk being accosted by two burly lads who have appeared from nowhere. At last, the true face of this establishment appears. No doubt they are taking the troublemaker out back for a little correction. Passing them is Pat with a formidable, brick shithouse of a man eating a juicy pear. His arms and chest are huge, bursting out of his shirt and waistcoat. His neck and head merge into one solid slab. He fair looks like he could take down a raging bull in an alley.

'He must be Tierney,' says Dudley.

'He must be.' Dudley places his small valise on the table. 'You do the talking,' she adds. 'As ever.'

'I'm sorry, Harriet. It is the way of the world.'

'Shut up and get on with it.'

'Alright, dear. As you say.'

Tierney hovers with Pat. He devours the fruit whole, core, stem and all. 'Mr Dudley, this is Aston Tierney. Owner of this fine place.'

Tierney shakes Dudley's hand and refines Pat's description. 'Proprietor of The Washington Hotel. I hope you are both being looked after. Miss?'

'This is Mrs Dunwoody.' Even mention of that name makes her stomach twitch. Don't lay it on thick, Thomas.

'Ah, the famous Lady from Louisiana. I am charmed.' The reference connects with Tierney, who clearly possesses a sharp mind to belie the initial impression of big, bad and dumb. 'My family have business interests in New Orleans. In the building trade.'

Harriet nods but still refrains from answering, allowing Dudley to continue the protocol. 'She has not returned for two years, I gather.'

'Their loss is our gain,' says Tierney. He knows money when he sees it. Pat is a non-entity to him. 'So how can I help you good people?'

'Can we go somewhere more private?' asks Dudley. Pat, behind Tierney, shakes his head. Dudley frowns.

'You are in my office now, Mr Consul.' Mr Consul, is it? No flies on him. What has he got to hide? As much as any common Irishman who landed here off the boat and found himself head of the most notorious gang in the borough and owner of a string of establishments *for the discerning gentleman*, this one included. It might not look like a brothel, but that is part of its appeal to clientele fresh off the trains, here for a little business and a little pleasure.

Dudley unhooks the clasp on his valise and opens it. Tierney doesn't even look inside, maintaining his dubiously welcoming posture. 'We are seeking information leading to the whereabouts of Mrs Dunwoody's baby daughter, missing for some ten weeks now.'

'Oh?' says Tierney. 'That is just awful so.'

'Most distressing for her as you can see. I gather that you and your… erm… associates have excellent connections about the town?'

Tierney closes the case with his giant hand, a little too much into Dudley's personal space. 'Consider it a service, Mr Dudley. Gratis, of course. Nothing so vulgar as a bit of cash, is there?'

It snaps shut. 'I apologise if I have insulted you, sir.'

'No, no surely you haven't, Mr Consul. It would be a privilege to assist this fine Southern Belle in her search. It must be just terrible desperate and bleak for you, dear?' Harriet nods, but she's not giving him much else. 'I've a large family myself. Sons and daughters all loved little cherubs so. I can't say how much they mean to me.'

'Thank you, Mr Tierney.'

'I love the United States, so I do. One day, we might move over there with a fair wind. Rejoin the kin.'

'I would be delighted to facilitate that process.'

Tierney smiles and shakes Dudley's hand again. 'Then we have ourselves a bargain. Leave it with me.'

'Very good.'

Tierney offers a curt nod to Harriet and wanders off back in the direction he came from. The two singers return to the stage to a ripple of applause and a few wolf whistles. 'Oh Lord, not them again. Shall we, Harriet?' says Dudley.

Harriet has already started making for the exit, Dudley and Pat trail in her wake.

She strides towards her horse. Grace attends with Rosalinda.

'That went well. I think we have ourselves an ally,' mews Dudley.

'Sometimes you are so naïve for such a learned man, Thomas.'

'Explain yourself, Harriet.'

Harriet mounts, looking down at the pair of them. 'No. I am too tired to do that, Thomas.'

Pat chips in. 'Ah, come on now, Harry. Aston's a right nasty twat, so he is, but he's in our corner. That's a tidy little result, I'd say.'

'At what price? Yet another hoodlum holding a debt over us. Just what we need.'

'Steady on, Harriet,' says Dudley, 'Pat has got a point. We will need a network to find her. If she is still in town.'

'She's still here.' Harriet is itching to giddy Rosalinda. She wants to get away from these two, and that episode in the hotel just sealed the idea.

'Oi, we're trying our fuckin' best here, yanno,' says Pat. He looks like he hasn't washed in weeks, food and bodily fluids caked into his tatty shirt, braces twisted, trousers filthy and at half-mast.

'She hasn't forgiven us, Pat,' says Dudley, lurching back into his morose countenance.

'Stop making this about you, Thomas.'

'Harriet, I was not...'

'Enough. Really. Enough. The pair of you need to go and help yourselves. Look after your families and fucking leave me alone. Neither of you are helping.'

Pat pipes up. 'Oh that's charming so 'tis.'

'Enough.' Harriet giddies and gallops away. Grace follows upon one of her colts.

Dudley and Pat watch them thunder down Lime Street, overtaking omnibuses and traps, vanishing out of their sight.

'I cannot believe that woman,' grunts Pat.

Dudley leers at him. 'If you weren't such a mess, perhaps she would feel a little better.'

'What are you blaming me for? Jaysus, I only got the pair of youse a parlay with the biggest cheese in Liverpool so. That's the fuckin' thanks I get.'

Dudley shakes his head. 'We've just lost her.'

'Two minutes ago, you was bleating on about Aston being the great white hope? There's no pleasing you, maudlin git.'

Dudley looks at his watch. 'We will see.'

'Aye, we will so.'

The Consul reaches into his pocket and flips Pat a coin. He catches it. 'Three o'clock. The Crown is open. Go fill your boots,

McCartney.' Then Dudley strides off in the direction of Paradise Street.

'Oh, some right charming bollocks that is, so it is,' says Pat, 'I don't want your fucking money, so. Posh prick. Yers can all fuck right off, so ye can.' Pat is talking to thin air now. He looks at Dudley's coin in his palm, then towards The Crown where Diarmuid is opening up the front shutters. 'Ah well, just the one, suppose.'

#10 – AT THE SCAFFOLD

Arsenal Penitentiary, Fort McNair, Washington D.C., July 7th 1865

'She stuck me with red hot darning pins, Ben. It was surprisingly hard not to spill the beans.'

'I'm impressed with your restraint. I'd have swotted her smack dab for that alone.' Butler is amused by his own turn of phrase. The subject of their conversation is being led up onto the scaffold at this very moment, along with the three other conspirators.

'Alas. If that devious old crone had only stuck to the plan, I'd have cleared the path. Drained the swamp.'

William nods to the scaffold. 'They would still be there, and we would still be here.'

'But that idiot Johnson wouldn't be swinging the lead, nor would his lackey Seward. It's embarrassing. The pair of them make Lincoln look good. They will lose the war after it was won.'

Despite the easy rapport in their small talk, Benjamin Butler and William Ruggles – erstwhile known as Achike within his Igbo mother's roots, or as Willy only to Ben – are all about the business today. Willy scribbles shorthand with a pencil to document the event for the official record, edits it to Butler's whim, and simultaneously makes the aforesaid small talk. His master's family took him into the house from the age of three, and he accompanied his de facto half-sister, Miss Lily, everywhere until she got to 15. No great childhood friendship transpired as Miss Lily always knew who he was, and Willy knew vice versa; their places set for life. A disguised benefit was that he took to the best homeschooling the master of a plantation could buy in a far more enthusiastic manner than the intended pupil. He quickly grasped everything that was offered by virtue of being the living, black doll of the Master's daughter. By the age of 15, young Lily Ruggles grew distracted by the expectations of a young lady of her status now elevated to the sister of Tiddie, the new master of the estate, and it was made plain that William had served out his usefulness in the household. He received the short, sharp shock of having to go back into the fields and to return to a darker-skinned family he didn't know or particularly like. Fortunately, Major General Benjamin Butler had a long reach into the South, and one of the first places he would go talent spotting would be the plantations. He recruited Willy's master, Tiddie Ruggles, into the bargain. Ben prefers negros and women to white men in his employ, but he prefers the former again in order of priority. Far more appreciative and loyal, hence this unusually familiar manner of exchange.

William, of course, is a cut above in Butler's inner circle, as he has exceptional talents, first among them being a honed ability to see and do several things at once. Two hundred hand-picked soldiers and dignitaries are in the crowd today, selected by Butler personally for their allegiance and discretion after the military tribunal committed Mary Surratt and her co-conspirators to the gallows. Mary and Lewis Powell, by far the handsomest of the three men, cut the prouder figures. She asked for a Catholic priest and got one. As the Padre babbles his catechisms and prayers, Mary leers through Butler, who has a front row seat with Willy.

'Looky here. Ain't you two a cosy pair? See you showed up this time,' she spits and yells, holy water spraying her eyes and face.

'Strike that, Willy.' Willy obliges, striking through the statement.

Mrs Surratt had been taken ill during her trial, which was either a ruse for sympathy or genuine, but it makes no difference now. The verdict was always going to be just so. They truss her feet together as she sits on a chair. 'Boys, I got the cramps bad. Go easy on those tethers.'

'So you keep saying,' says one of her guards.

'Strike the last two lines,' says Butler. William redacts.

'My arms hurt.'

'Well, they won't hurt long, ma'am,' says the preparing officer. 'Please stand.'

'Mrs Surratt is innocent. She doesn't deserve to die with the rest of us,' says Powell. How noble.

'Keep those. They're good,' says Butler, 'Dramatic.'

'Yes, Ben.'

Mary Surratt, Lewis Powell, George Atzerodt and David Herold all climb to their feet, the nooses are positioned, and white bags are fitted over their heads. Suddenly, there is a quiver in Mary's voice. 'You'll never find him, Butler.'

'Oh, we will, dear. Canada and then Liverpool, was it? I will have my best operative assigned to him. Rest assured, you will be reunited soon.'

'How? Oh my dear God, no.'

Her guard guides her towards the dropping ledge. 'Strike that exchange, Willy.'

'Done.'

'Butler is a traitor!' she yells at the top of her voice, 'He set this up! He killed Lincoln!'

Butler laughs. 'What with? The power of my mind?' Then, into William's ear, 'Strike that.'

There is muffled weeping beneath the cloth. 'Please don't let me fall.'

'Keep that line. That works. Dramatic.'

'Sure.'

'For God and the South, I shall see you in Hell, Butler.'

'Strike.'

'Yes, Ben.'

Four soldiers of Company F of the 14th Veteran Reserves knock out the supports holding the ledge in place, and the condemned fall. Mary's slender neck snaps easily and she jerks, then in moments she is still. Atzerodt's stomach heaves and he lurches, then hangs like a side of beef. Powell and Herold do the hempen jig, choking. The fall failed to break their necks, so they will have to dangle and strangle for as long as it takes their sorry lives to eke away.

Is that a hint of rain? Butler alights his perch and William copies him. 'Good show.'

'Yes, Ben.'

'T-bone steak, onions, sauerkraut, potatoes. Plum pudding with cream for afters. How about it, Willy? My treat, as usual.'

'Yes, Ben.'

'Then we'll write this ripping yarn up and get it over to the press.'

'For sure, Ben.'

'Good show all around, then. Well done, boys. Come then, Willy. I've worked up quite an appetite.'

The two make their way out of the compound, pushing past a rather sallow, sombre Allan Pinkerton and Kate Warne without a single acknowledgement. Powell and Herold continue to dance from the gibbet like the worst marionette show in the county fair.

'Oh, and Willy?'

'Yes Ben?'

'I know Miss Mary extracted the information from you. So don't play brave with me.'

'Yes, Ben.'

The big wheel churns up its own surf as the steamer powers across a calm ocean, a miracle of transportation. John Surratt Jr observes his recently-grown pencil moustache in his mother's compact mirror, one of the few items she stowed in his satchel on that fateful day, like a proud momma packing some goodies for her precious boy's summer camp.

Not for the first time even today, Surratt chokes those big old salty tears back. Nothing his fellow passengers would notice as they promenade and take in the balmy, briny September air, but decorum must be maintained. Who would vouch that there was a fugitive in their midst, the only one at large after the earth-shattering assassination of the President of the United States? Who would know that it was all a gambit from one dirty bastard of a Boston lawyer with his own designs upon power?

He examines Butler's original telegram for the umpteenth time and wonders how and when he can use it to exact his satisfaction over him. Perhaps these gentlemen in Liverpool might offer some ideas and assistance? Momma was wrong, of course. Not about Butler, for she could not be more right about him, and he can see that now the fog has lifted, but about how they would never hang a woman. Momma, despite her entreaties, swung along with Powell, Herold and the gutless Atzerodt. No doubt she sang like a canary about Butler right to the end, but he would have made damn sure no one listened.

He wants to crush that note and toss it into the swell, but Surratt knows that it is probably the only piece of evidence that exists about Benjamin Franklin Butler's plot to assassinate President Abraham Lincoln, Vice-President Andrew Johnson, and Secretary of State William Seward. The bona fide watermark proves when, where, and from whom the message was sent.

John Surratt Jr sure can't wait to arrive in Liverpool. Maybe then he can do something about this accursed, gnawing shame that wracks his brain, body and soul. He sure hopes that she died quickly on that awful scaffold. His grief and guilt are such that he can't even begin to contemplate the fate of his friends in addition. He must have confession and absolution.

'Sorry, Momma. I am so sorry,' he tells the surf, which just laps back at him in response.

#11 – FIGHT AND FLIGHT AT NIGHT

Liverpool, October 9th 1865

Another day, another church, although this seems to be just another lame lead. Harriet kneels in the confession booth of Holy Cross on Tithebarn Street – a hop, skip and jump away from Rumford Place, the centre of her dear, departed husband's racket 20 months ago. It is a new parish that serves the Irish slums around here and to the North on Scotland Road as one of the main fonts of piety, and she knows Father Jovliet well by reputation, which is not to say she particularly likes the fellow.

The faith has never meant much to Harriet, aside from some very dim memories of attending church in Clontarf before she sailed to America with her Daddy. Not much call for the Holy See in Choctaw lands, but it is all powerful in this end of town, and this is exactly what draws her to Jovliet and his big flock. She can play the role of pious widow as well as any other if it means unlocking something, anything about the whereabouts of her daughter.

Harriet affects her accent to Irish. 'Forgive me, Father, for I have sinned.'

'Tell me, my child.'

'I will, father. I will,' she says, choking back tears, 'Nearly two years ago, my dear husband departed this Earth ...'

Jovliet watches his parishioners like a hawk, which is rather fitting as he looks just like one, right down to sharp eyes and beak of a nose. Harriet knows about his connections directly with the Vatican, having been tasked with one of the highest Catholic populations in Great Britain as part of a Québecois mission. He is a de facto Bishop here and a man worth knowing, but you have to play his game, engage on his terms. Few of his peers in the Diocese sanctify themselves quite as much as Jovliet does, with his lofty ambitions in the direction of Rome. There is a local yarn that St Patrick himself stopped at this very spot in AD632 and consecrated it as holy ground, a story she suspects was started by the parish priest here to enthral the swollen immigrant Irish congregation.

'… I have been searching for my child in every unseemly place in town, bringing me into contact with prostitutes and thieves. I have seen things that no good woman should have to see. Oh, I feel ashamed, I do, to be telling you…'

She can hear his breath quicken from behind the curtain. 'My child, do tell me about these places and events. Tell me about how it made you feel. Did you do things to yourself, thinking about these places? God sees every detail.'

Well, he doesn't hang around, does he? She perseveres, pretending that she didn't notice that pass upon who he perceives to be a vulnerable young widow. If God sees every detail, then why does she need to tell him? 'Father, I must find my baby. A mulatto child. She has a U-shaped birthmark on the back of her neck.'

'*Mulatto?* And you confess to this, do you?'

'Yes, I admit to it, but it is not my confession. She was born from love.'

'That is not for you to decide. That is shameful, my child.'

'Can you help me? Please, any information you can give me would be a service to God.'

Jovliet hisses on the other side of the booth. 'This is a confessional, child. You do the confessing, not me. Repent, or you and your child will go to hell, I assure you.'

'I will repent, Father. But how?'

'You will visit the presbytery at 8 pm this evening and ask for me personally. I will give you direct instruction.'

Of course he will. She hasn't got time for this. 'So you are not aware of a mulatto child of two years in your congregation? Or in this end of town? Please, I would be most grateful. I could donate money …'

'Did you not listen to what I just said, jezebel? Are you half-witted as well as heretical?'

It was a nice try, but she isn't getting too far with him today. Harriet makes the sign of the cross and gets up. 'Three Hail Marys and an Our Father, then.'

'What? What are you doing? I did not say we were finished.'

'God bless you, Father. No one else will.'

It wouldn't be appropriate to take out all this frustration on a priest, would it? Even this pervert? What can he really know?

This is all just clutching at straws, and there's more chance of God Himself intervening and finding Baba than getting this dirty old bastard to help her.

'You impudent ... What is your name? You will go to *hell*. I have a personal friendship with the Holy Father, and I will make sure of it. Hell, I say!'

No, it is not worth it. She'd sure like to pistol whip him, though. For *his* sins. But if she starts, she will not stop, and a trail of blood across town will not get her any closer to her baby. This might be a church, but how she wishes that one spirit would talk to her right now. She's seen a thousand faces just like his in her search for Baba Conté, and it only confirms again her worst fears about the nature of humanity.

'I am already there, Father.'

'How dare you come into my church ...'

'Oh, *your* church, is it?' Harriet rips down the curtain and glares at Jovliet. He cowers and crosses himself. He reaches for a knife secreted beneath his cowl.

'Be gone,' he hisses, as if exorcising a demon. It seems it is Father Jovliet who needs exorcising, but Harriet isn't the one to do it today. She slips out of the booth, and the cue for penance and absolution moves along.

'So, too, when England wants to set the heel of her power more firmly in the quivering heart of old Ireland, the Celts are an "inferior race". So, too, the Negro, when he is to be robbed of any right which is justly his, is an "inferior man". It is said that we are ignorant; I admit it. But if we know enough to be hung, we know enough to vote.'

'It's hanged, not hung! Jesus, I should know.'

'I beg your pardon?'

'Fine words so. Fine words, Mister. Save it all for me arse, though, cos it'll never happen, aye. Hic.'

The fellow with the fine words on the podium is one Frederick Douglass. He is considerably more famous than his sozzled Irish heckler, who is immediately being removed from this grand little Doric theatre, Hope Hall on Hope Street.

Douglass is a beautiful man of West African descent, lost in the sands of the forced migration of his forebears. He is arguably the most efficacious orator on either side of the Atlantic, a former slave who emancipated and educated himself, confidante of presidents, abolitionist and proponent of women's suffrage. Handsome, courageous, erudite and the most photographed human in America, more so than even his late, great friend, Abraham Lincoln. Pat is from Cavan, and he is very drunk indeed.

'Be gentle with him,' asks the orator above the hubbub. It's clear that he doesn't wholly approve of the manhandling of the chap, even if the poor individual is possessed with the demon drink. One of Mr Douglass' other campaigns is for temperance, and the drunk who is being ushered out of the auditorium by the burly retinue employed by his London publisher is a perfect illustration of the need for it. 'Oh dear, what a poor soul. Be kind, people. I shall continue, I guess.'

And continue he will. Changing hearts and minds in this town and the next. Continue Pat will, too, through the grand doors to the theatre, rolling into a heap on the cobbles of Hope Street. 'Jaysus fucker,' he grunts as he slips and struggles on the hard, wet york stone, up onto his feet before barrelling down Mount Pleasant in search of the more earthy delights of an ale house.

Long and heavy shadows, everywhere you look and go, day or night. Salthouse Dock. Negative. George's Dock, negative.

Canning, King's, Queen's, Clarence, Bramley Moore, Brunswick, Waterloo, Victoria, Trafalgar, Coburg, Harrington, Albert, Salisbury, Collingwood, Stanley, Nelson, Wellington, Sandon, Huskisson, Canada, Canada Half, Toxteth Dock. All negative. Long, heavy, immobile, sinister shadows, demons in the dark.

Seven excruciating months looking for her child have passed, and those same shadows are deep inside her. No sleep, only waking dreams of how she will slake her vengeance when she gets hold of the bastard that took her Baba. She pulls the hammer back on her pistol as the warehouse foreman talks in broken biscuits, sobbing uncontrollably, tragicomic in his terror. She knows this man, like she knows all of his kind. Willing to turn a blind eye to the droves of people being smuggled back and forth out of the port, penned up in his cellars at the behest of the gangs who control a filthy, inhuman trade. The Dead Rabbits, the Hibernians, the Lemon Streeters; all emerged from Irish immigrants and now preying upon their own kind, vultures akin to those in government, or that ghastly pervert of a priest at Holy Cross, albeit uncouth and unrefined. The cellars of these warehouses are cholera pits and those who survive arrive into forced labour, prostitution, the workhouse or death by another, circuitous route, the last of which is probably the best outcome. Hordes of human cattle continue to arrive daily and are bought and sold. Her daughter can and must not be among their number.

'Please, Miss.'

This one is an arch-lackey of the gangs. Paid quadruple his wages in commission, just for opening a gate and keeping his whiskey hole shut. She almost prefers to be in the company of that lecherous priest. Harriet could, and probably should, pull the trigger, and do the world a favour. No peeler or court would be interested in his murder, but there will be another along in quick order to take his place as gaoler of this red brick hell underneath Stanley Dock, right in the sinister shadows of the biggest warehouses in the world. It is the second time today that she feels like an avenging angel, like she should swoop down and reap away all this evil, but it would take an eternity to clear this town. Once she starts, she will not stop.

She replaces the hammer and lowers the gun. For the second time today, and the thousandth time since her child vanished, she has stopped short of murder. 'You shall communicate with my house directly should you find the child that matches my description.'

'Muh-muh-muh-'

'What? Spit it out.'

'Mulatto?'

'Yes. Distinctive. Remember the birthmark on her shoulder. And she was plump and cute, at least in comparison to the poor souls you trap down there. Although I doubt that she will be plump now. Or cute.'

'Miss, I will let you know. I promise.'

'See to it.'

'I will, Miss. I promise, Miss.'

'Aren't you just full of promises?'

'Yes, Miss.'

'And those people down there? In the vault deep below?'

'What people? What vault?'

'Do not try my patience.'

'Ah, *those* people, right. Aye. Yes, Miss.'

'Release them. And return their money to them, with some extra for their hardship.'

'Ah, come on, Miss. The Rabbits will string me up by me bollocks so.'

She massages the barrel of her shooter. 'Well, at least you won't feel that with a lead slug in your thick skull.'

He mutters and moans, which amounts to agreement. Threats mean just about the same currency as money around this part of the docks. Harriet has found out the names and addresses of every bent customs officer, warehouseman and hoodlum from Garston to Bootle in order to be able to either harangue or bribe them directly, in some cases both. No stone has been, or will be, left unturned, but the same look in every eye has told her that no one knows anything in this savage underworld, for there is a type of honesty to be had in the expression of the common criminal that cannot be found in richer men when their lives are threatened, or there is the opportunity to make a quick, small fortune.

Can she look elsewhere, apart from the docks? In the pubs and seraglios? In the coffee houses or the rooms above them? Even in the banks and exchanges? Not with any success, for everything about this town begins and ends in the docks, from a purloined case of rum to a missing child. Liverpool, docks or otherwise, is too easy a place to go missing. Harriet climbs up the stone steps that take her up a narrow, dank passageway. The mossy walls seem like they might close in upon her – to end her anguish – for there is no finding her baby, and she is chronically exhausted. No matter about her, she'll trawl the nine circles of hell personally, and she will never stop until she prevails.

Princess Grace, her African friend who continues to run a good, honest business in a foul, dishonest town, attends her in the narrow alley, clutching the reigns to Rosalinda, Conté's favourite filly and now Harriet's ride all the way back to the homestead in Waterloo. Pain is etched on Grace's face, almost as much as her own. She doesn't need to ask if the latest instalment of Harriet's mission was a success. They mount and head out into the endless Dock Road that spans the newly-emerged berths north of the borough. Harriet could have taken a Hansom cab, but the business should always go to her friend, especially since she doesn't seem to have many of them left in this town right now.

'Will I accompany you, Harriet?' asks Grace as they canter. 'I can stable Rosalinda for you, so you can easily go and rest. I have some horses to collect up that end, so it is no imposition.'

'No thank you, Grace.'

'It is no trouble, really.'

'It is seven miles out of your way. It will be midnight before you get home to West Derby.' Living out in the sticks has its drawbacks, but it is a worthy price for getting out of a fetid, diseased town.

'I can look after myself, ma'am.'

'I won't hear another word of it. I will return Rosalinda to you tomorrow morning. 6 am. As agreed.'

'Get some sleep, Harriet.'

'Go home, Grace.'

A horse-drawn tram passes between them, stopping to let passengers alight from the open rear platform. When it leaves, Grace is gone, but another familiar figure has replaced her. She stands alone on the narrow pavement in a shawl, shivering in the cool evening. Harriet can immediately tell that some cruel misfortune has visited her. She didn't get off that tram; rather, she has clearly walked here.

'Sarah?'

Yes, Sarah McCarthy, or McCartney, as it was misspelt in the Liverpool Census records of '61. Another careless statistic. Suffering wife of the pathetic lush Padraig McCarthy-McCartney, whose business has gone to ruin along with his sense of responsibility and propriety, all now pickled in poitín. For all of Thomas Haines Dudley's grand promises (once he had sobered up that day), the two men are now the same: pathetic, useless, self-absorbed, weak, broken, drunk wretches. And Harriet has neither the time nor the means to fix or forgive either of them, as much as this may conflict her with the help they gave her only two years ago. Seeing Sarah like this only infuriates her to a further extent again, just when she thought that she could not get any more livid.

'I know you have your own grief, and I would never have dared to intrude upon that, but I had to find you as this affects both our households, Mrs Dunwoody.'

Sarah is probably the only person alive that Harriet will permit to call her by that name. 'You are always welcome, Sarah. What vexes you?'

'The bailiffs arrived. They have removed us from your house on Canning Street.'

What? How? Why? 'That is *your* house now. And that is impossible, Sarah. I signed it over: lock, stock and barrel. Even the covenant is yours. Someone has tricked you.'

Sarah either can't or won't register Harriet's logic. 'Ma'am, the bailiffs brought peelers and papers, which I couldn't read. I had to ask our Finn to look them over as he's my brightest boy with the most schooling. It said that the house is property of the United States Government. A sais asson.'

'A what?'

'A sais asson. French, I think.'

'Not French. What in hell is that? A sais what?'

'A sais asson. I dunno. Our Finn doesn't speak French. Or German, like. Or American. Just English and a bit of Irish.'

Much like the earth-shattering news on that day back in April, she has a feeling *who* and *what* this points back to. Dudley might well be in her bad books, but he would never sanction a requisition order on their houses. Something is afoot.

'Sarah? Are your children safe?'

'They left the stable door unlocked. Finn is keeping an eye on them in there.'

So much happened in that stable when Harriet lived there. That is not good. 'You were right to come find me.' She reaches down a hand. 'Are you fit to ride with me?'

'I have never ridden a horse.'

'Climb up and hold on tight to my waist. I will do the rest.'

Sarah nods. Harriet pulls her up on the stirrup and she clings on. They kick into a fast gallop north.

On an evening such as this, the view from Waterloo to the north of Liverpool Bay, of the Wirral Peninsular and Welsh Mountains jutting out into the Irish Sea, is painterly and gorgeous upon the eye. This particular dusk is much like the night, months ago, when she decided to return to America and venture West with her daughter. The inhabitants of Waterloo think they are a cut above Liverpool riff-raff, but Harriet knows that this – spiritually, if not geographically – is the end of the world.

6 Marine Crescent is no longer the haven. Wooden boards have been nailed across the windows in the time that she has been outdoors, and the front door has been shored up with timber and a padlock bigger than her head. Were Padraig compos mentis and available, he might climb up and get them access via the loft, but Pat has become part of the problem since his marbles rolled off a cliff and into a frothy sea of booze. Pat, as Sarah informed him on the ride here, has given up on his family, his business, the Fenian cause and even himself. His family cannot go down with him, not after this. Did he gamble their house away? No, because Harriet would still have her own home, but even though this instance cannot be laid at his feet, the fact remains that his family is now destitute and broken.

Harriet could, of course, gain access to the house herself, but what would she find that hasn't already been ransacked? Only trinkets and keepsakes that would slow her down, and right now, she needs to be as light on her feet as possible. It chokes her, for the last of Conté is in there, as it was in cargo crates before her world disintegrated over one stupid decision to humour an old, drunken sot. The grief for her beloved and for their missing baby threatens to wash over her like the angry swell out there on the shore.

She studies the front one last time and climbs back up on Rosalinda, offering Sarah her hand. 'What will you do, Sarah?'

'I've family in America. New York. They would send money for passage, but we'll starve by the time it gets here. I can't afford the stamp for a letter to them and I can't even write that letter. I could ask my son, if you'll spare us a penny.'

'Men are rats. The lot of them. Even the ones you think are honourable. With the exception of your son, of course.'

'Aye, Mrs Dunwoody.'

'Wait a moment. What's that?'

'Beg pardon?'

A few items are strewn across the lawn. Bits of clothes, mainly, save for a single object not native to these shores. It is black, harder than rock and fits neatly into the palm of one's hand. It is that final relic of Conté, her beavertail sap, the sturdiest and sneakiest of Choctaw weapons. Harriet could jump for joy and weep rivers at once. She chooses neither, just to climb down and slip it into her petticoat.

'You'll never make it to New York, Sarah. Letter or no letter.'

Sarah swallows any response, maintaining her uncomfortable deference to Harriet, perceived due to her finery and upper-class manners that are as much an old habit as a complete act. Harriet glances at her pocket watch. Now she knows how she can help. It means hurting a once loyal friend, but it is a stark choice between this and seeing his wife and family starve and resort to the workhouse. So many never come out of that place, so better that the pain comes to Pat in this way as he is in no fit state to help himself or his loved ones. She climbs back up, they canter and then gallop back south, towards town, away from that glorious Waterloo sunset one last time.

#12 – ROLLING ROLLO
Liverpool, October 9th 1865

A sonorous groan and clang of the iron door, one of the thousands in this town behind which sit vast, secret fortunes and information that must remain hidden, sometimes even people that must remain hidden. Water Street is never deserted, but it is a little more funereal than usual tonight. Even the drunks are keeping their counsel, although in this part of town, those drunks are likely to be rich traders, merchants, bankers or aldermen, fresh out of the public houses or tired from gaming or dipping their syphilitic wicks in the upstairs seraglios dotted around the intersection with Castle Street.

This door glides open. It is made of the same impenetrable, folded compound that is used to make the safes in the vault of this building – Martin's Bank. It is long out of business hours, except for the most discerning clients.

Mr Rollo, the manager who never seems to leave this place or take time away, treats her as if she is a regular midday caller, although his face hardens upon looking at her poorer companion. 'Two houses repossessed, Mr Rollo. All the deeds put them as my property until I had you personally arrange the conveyance to Mr and Mrs McCartney.'

Rollo glances at Sarah above his pince-nez. 'And just where is Mr McCartney this evening, ma'am? He is the signatory.'

Sarah looks spooked at Rollo, unaccustomed to dealing with such men, money men. Harriet never has that problem. 'Never you mind, Rollo. To the business of those properties and the black magician who made our ownership vanish.'

'Yes, ma'am.'

'Yes what? Will you spit it out?'

'No, ma'am.'

'No? Why?'

'As a customer of this bank, you will be fully aware of the extent of our discretion. High it is, ma'am. I cannot divulge.'

'But-'

'Only that aforesaid properties are no longer in your ownership.'

'Yes, I know that.'

'Very good, ma'am.'

Harriet's stomach is doing spectacular vaults, but she cannot show this to Sarah, or anyone, least of all Rollo here. 'And the money? The assets?' she asks.

'Seized.'

'Sais asson,' mutters Harriet, 'Seized assets.'

'Yes,' says Sarah, eyes darting between them. 'That's what they said.'

'What is the game, Rollo?'

'I cannot yet divulge.'

'*Yet?*'

Rollo offers the thinnest of smiles and shuffles on his feet. Yet, he answered the door and welcomed her in his customary stiff, starchy way, which means that in some way, shape or form, Harriet must remain a valued client of Martin's. All rather fishy, but she is reluctant to ask too many questions in front of Sarah, who must remain innocent to any of the murky business at the bottom of the seizure. 'The Louverture account, Rollo? I take it that you were discrete enough to maintain it for me? Tell me otherwise, or you will not want to see the consequences.'

His eyes narrow, and he glances out into the street as if to check for interlopers. 'Are you sure you want to discuss that, ma'am? In front of *her?*'

'All other assets and funds are gone. Requisitioned by the United States Government, I gather?'

'If that is the information you have, ma'am.' That is banker code for 'yes'.

Sarah has gone white as a sheet. 'What are we going to do? You and your baby will be destitute. I cannot have that on my conscience, not after what you did for us, Mrs Dunwoody.'

'Please calm yourself, Sarah. There is a way.' She looks Rollo in the eye. 'I am correct in saying that there is a way, am I not, Rollo? Because you *were* discrete with the special account?'

Rollo looks like he is not inclined to do anything for Harriet, but he nods. 'Yes, ma'am. There is a way.'

'Good.' Harriet glances at her pocket watch. 'There is a dawn steamer leaving for New York. If Rollo here is quick about his business, you and your children can be on it. First Class, of course.'

'What's First Class?'

'You'll find out. It's nice.'

'What about Pat?'

'He has made this about himself.' A few tears from Sarah. Harriet doesn't want to break her, too. 'Sarah, I will do my best with him, I promise you. But you can't save him and your children at the same time.'

'Yes, Mrs Dunwoody.'

'So then, there is always a way. Rollo?'

'Yes, ma'am?'

'I would like to make an immediate withdrawal. Toute de suite, if you will.'

'Yes, ma'am. Certainly, ma'am.'

Spending cash quickly is very easy in this town. Harriet recruits a small charabanc of Hansom Cabs to go to the stables of 101 Canning Street and collect the whole family. They rendezvous upon George's Landing Stage, escorted directly into the First Class lounge of the RMS Belle Wood, a commercial liner sloop bound to disembark. Amid final calls, there isn't much time for a long goodbye.

'How can I ever thank you?'

Harriet shrugs. 'In this life or the next. You have enough money?'

Sarah nods vigorously. Pat controlled the money through his window cleaning business, so she hasn't ever possessed a fraction of the sterling currency that Harriet has just given her. Harriet knows enough about New York to gather that life will get tough for them on the other side. 'Mrs Dunwoody, I can never pay you back. Pat can never pay you back.'

'The type of debt I have with your husband can never be repaid. Pains me as it does to admit it presently.'

Fellow passengers sneer and leer at the gaggle of scruffy children and their mother huddled together in the fine smoking lounge. None of them have had a change of clothes or a bath in weeks. 'There will be a wash room and an outfitter on board. Have yourselves a good feed and a good scrub and then get yourselves some nice, warm clothes. That Atlantic air can get perishing cold at this time of year, as can New York after the fall.'

Sarah nearly swoons. 'Oh, Mrs Dunwoody.'

'All aboard! Visitors alight!'

'That's me, Sarah. Call me Harry, please.'

Sarah looks like she would like to hug her friend, but Harriet volte-faces and heads back out to the gangway, aware that her own business cannot wait a moment longer. Whoever took her daughter may have just revealed their hand by seizing the two houses.

'May God Bless you and your baby child, good lady,' she hears Sarah say just as the doors to the lounges are shut and she heads back across the deck. If Harriet is to be honest with herself, she paid for their passage not out of altruism, but so that she wouldn't have to deal with their problems as well as her own, because seas are about to get even choppier in this here Liverpool than out in the Atlantic swell.

'Neither good nor a lady am I,' she mutters, checking for her pistols, knives and beavertail sap about her undergarments. They will be put into action soon.

Next stop is back to that bank for another withdrawal.

Commander Banastre Xavier Dunwoody, the aforesaid deceased husband of Harriet who received a bullet to his bits before gonorrhoea could take them, bequeathed everything to his wife in the event of his untimely death, because he thought that she was carrying his son and heir at the time of writing his will. Further, he was quite convinced that he would never die. The fact that his wife was on the trigger of the Derringer that ended him is neither here nor there, because there is no official record of his death or even his existence in the Borough of Liverpool during the hot summer of 1863. This is because the British Government was humbled and embarrassed by the events of the day he died, events that shall never even enter classified vaults for their sensitive nature. Events that could determine the future of nations should their true nature ever be made public. Events that seem to be repeating themselves, if her senses are correct.

Which is why Harriet can determine that whoever has engineered her current difficulties must have been privy to those events and to her existence, which can only lead to a handful of characters (men) anywhere on this planet. Or God, although God is certainly not responsible for what she is doing to Mr Rollo, live-in manager of Martin's Bank of Water Street. She curses herself that she should have thought about paying this old chap a visit sooner.

Among the items large and small she inherited is Banastre's collection of thumb screws, dear items to him since he first used them as a river pirate in order to extract information and punish seditious crewmen. Used again during his stint as the commandant of the military prison at Fort Sumter and only two years ago upon the person of her friend Pat McCartney. He suffered to the extent that he has probably never recovered full use of his digits, which elicits another pang of guilt for her actions in sending his family across to America earlier this evening. How Banastre enjoyed extolling his own inventiveness with this technique, always embellished with liquor, cigars and British company. How dead he deserves to be. She accessed the screws via the deposit box at his former 'Consulate' at Fraser, Trenholm & Co Cotton Brokers on Rumford Place prior to revisiting Mr Rollo. Unbeknownst to the company, she retains Banastre's keys to the office. It was well worth the short hop for the sake of a flash of inspiration. Seeing poor Sarah leave has confirmed Harriet's suspicions about herself; that she was being far too gentle in her approach to her investigations. Maybe the banks have finally burst.

'Aaaaargh, you Yankee virago! Release me immediately, I say!'

Rollo has not quite got to the stage of begging, but he isn't far off. The quiet man is suddenly quite loquacious. Funny, that. His nose pisses blood from the wound inflicted upon him by Harriet, using Conté's beavertail sap after he was roused by the interloper in his chamber, snoring like a hog prior to the invasion. She didn't knock this time.

No matter about his defiance, for Harriet has long since learned how to deal with bank managers. She remains, because of previous embarrassment to the Prime Minister of the United Kingdom of Great Britain and Ireland and his First Lord of the Admiralty, very much a non-entity: a ghost. So this ghost is currently inflicting heinous pain upon this man who has no personal connexions of family and makes himself available to clients day or night, all as part of his professional discretion and unique service. This little tête à tête may as well not be happening because neither party should exist. It makes for infinite possibilities.

'Please, Miss Farrell...' And there it is, the whimpering doth commence. 'I implore you to have a reasonable conversation. Your approach really is not necessary, if you will permit me to inform you why.'

'Would you tell me what I need to know over a cup of tea or tot of complimentary single malt, Mr Rollo? I cannot be sure.'

'You savage harridan. Where did you learn such tricks?'

'From the best and the worst, old chum.'

'Pah. Release me immediately. I have clients in the highest office of this town. You shall not get away with this affront.'

'At best, you'll be a laughing stock, Rollo. Turned over by a silly, solitary female like this? With all your security? I'd keep this quiet, if I were you. There are enough banks around here that will gladly take all your clients.'

'Think you are clever, harridan?'

And there it is again. More defiance, just when he had started to wise up. She tightens the screws and he yelps. His staff will begin arriving in an hour, and Rollo is a stickler for punctuality.

No time to hang around. 'You will tell me what you know presently, sir.'

'Aaargh, yes. Yes, yes. Alright.'

'I believe you know the men I refer to?'

'Yes, yes. Of course.'

Rollo pants. He looks like his heart could give out, but the clock keeps ticking. 'Really, Rollo? Even now, you treat me as the dumb female?'

He spits blood. Down here in this soundproofed vault, deep into the bowels of this bank, there are untold riches and secrets.

Not a soul can see or hear this place. Harriet could make away with someone's ill-gotten fortune in diamonds just on her person, but she only wants to leave here with information. Someone has her child and even though Rollo will not be able to tell her, he will be able to divulge about who requisitioned the houses and why. She tightens the screws further, and he screams louder.

'John Surratt! Bloody Surratt, for chrissakes. He's your man. I was going to bloody well tell you presently, as per my instructions from your commanding officer, using civilised communication. There is simply no need for this.'

Butler. Of course, Butler. She just needed to hear that name from another's lips, to confirm that she isn't going stark raving mad. 'Who is this Surratt?'

She loosens the screws. Can't have him passing out just as he's getting talkative. 'Do you not read the papers? Not much of an agent you,' he splutters.

'Rollo, just who is this John Surratt?'

#13 – COUP DES ÉTATS-UNIS

New York State, October 9th, 1865

Porterhouse steak, seared rare, with a mound of fried onions, broiled mushrooms, mashed potatoes, Brussels sprouts and peppercorn sauce, replete with a generous side order of Belgian waffles with maple syrup and washed down with a quart of strong ale. Mmm, hog heaven in this finest of Yonkers eateries.

Butler spears a Portobello mushroom and gobbles it, complementing the meat juices and hoppy ale. He emits a throaty belch to the outright disgust of other customers, a habit in which he perennially delights, before stopping to observe William toying with his food.

'Eat. None of this nibbling nonsense. You're a grown man.'

'Sorry, Ben. All this business of ours has me in a spin. What of the consequences? Are you sure that we're doing the right thing?'

Butler pulls his short blade and picks steak out from between his teeth. William considers how many men he's killed with that same blade. The Major General enjoys repeating those stories. He continues to pick at his food but Butler loses patience and grabs William's setting, spearing the steak and shovelling it onto his own plate. 'You know that I cannot abide waste. Have your veggies then, at least. And no business at the table, goddamn it. Do I need to tell you about the secret to good digestion again?'

'Surely not, Ben.'

Butler cocks his leg and lets rip. Other patrons watch on in disbelief at his odious table manners. 'Surely not. Don't know why I bring you to such places.'

William knows why. He enjoys the faces of restauranteurs and customers when he brings a negro along to eat with him, daring them to challenge him. It is all about power; every decent steakhouse in every major city has come to expect this from Maj. Gen. Butler. It has nothing to do with emancipation, just one of the legion cheap thrills about the boss man's countenance, to include laughing hysterically at one's own jokes, scratching and sniffing, and spectacular flatulence. But anyone who measures him solely by such antics is always in for a short, sharp shock.

William does well to remind himself of that, and grazes his sprouts. His dining partner always has room for dessert and invariably eats his, too. It looks very much like it will be another long evening for Benjamin Butler's shadow.

Seneca Village, now known as Central Park. It used to be a settlement area for free Africans; now, it is a newly-created, manicured public garden. The holly bush quivers, and William can hear a snort, fart and grunt as the Major General finishes his business. He emerges, pulling up his breeches as some Molly Malone follows him, adjusting her skirts.

Butler observes the other Molly, whom he procured for William, leaning against a tree. 'You are not partaking, Willy?'

'Not tonight, Ben.'

'Well, I do not know why I bother, really.' He turns to William's Molly. 'Say sugar, go over there and wait for a short while with your friend, would you?' She tuts, but obeys. 'And less of the attitude; I paid good money for you two. Don't go absconding. I'm just going to have a chat with Wee Willy Winkie here.'

He turns to William, his round face expanding. 'Sorry, Ben.'

'Just what in Jiminy has gotten into you tonight?'

'May I speak frankly?'

'You never need to ask.'

'It is this England business. We are playing with fire. They may simply overrun us. I've seen the Royal Navy close at hand. They are mighty fearsome.'

'Exactly. Congress and the Senate will shit brownstones bigger than anything you'll see in Manhattan, as will the American voting public. In times of crisis, you need a good, strong leader. Then we step up.'

Is that the royal *we*? Butler sticks his chest out. 'But we risk annihilation, Ben.'

Butler chuckles at the idea as if he's just been told a lewd joke. 'The British won't invade. They just want their cotton trade back is all. That and enough corn to feed the rabble in their own cities, the manpower for their pits, looms and furnaces. It has only ever been, and ever will be, about commerce to them. Simple.'

'How can you know that? How can you trust them? I have read about India and Africa, Ireland…'

'So you think that we are some backwater asswipe of a colony to be exploited and overrun?'

'No, but…'

'The British do not invade civilised nations. So, as long as we show ourselves thus, we shall remain sovereign. They don't want to pick another fight with us, either. Leave the politics to me and just settle those collywobbles of yours, Willy. I need my best boy on form. That is what this evening is about. A bit of fun before we get back to doing the hard yards, eh? Dip your wick, eh?'

William prefers the hard yards, if anything. The 'fun' part is all Ben's. Does he believe that line about the British not invading? Butler *likes* war – it's the space in which he thrives – so therein lies the real answer. This could get altogether dreadful. 'Yes, Ben.'

'Trust me with the tactical aspects. Watch and learn, I'll get you into the Senate yet, Willy. Imagine their faces. Change is coming.'

Is this more of his sport? Just an extension of the restaurant antics? The *Senate*? Really? 'Right. Sure, Ben. I'm sorry. Just collywobbles, is all.'

'Good man. Now…' Butler observes the two Mollys and waves them back over. 'Are you having oats this evening or not?'

'Very kind, but no thank you. You know that I've got a wife back home.'

'So have I. What difference does that make?'

'Ben, please but no thank you…'

Butler holds up a hand to silence him. 'Very well, I suppose.' Much like the steak, nothing goes to waste. 'Think I've reloaded sufficiently. Now then, Miss Molly, get in that bush. Chop chop, haven't got all night. Your friend can watch, and you can have another quarter if you coo like a dove.'

William turns away, sits on the grass and looks up at the stars. He spots the Major General's personal valise next to the bush. It could easily go missing on a night like this, so he picks it up.

'Put that down, Willy. You know better than that,' comes Butler's voice from behind the foliage, then the ugly noises begin again.

Machinations with a hangover, back on the campaign trail. 'You know to trust me when I say, John Paul, that this threat is clear and present. My years of service and intelligence network are unmatched across North and South. This is not some drill to arouse political support. Several large regiments have assembled on the Canuck border. Not some brigade of moosefuckers either, rather crack British Redcoats in hordes of frigates, crossing over to Nova Scotia as I speak. Big numbers. Scots Guards, The Kings, Royal Irish, Sappers, Artillery, Dragoons, Infantry, veterans of the Khyber and Crimea. They intend to invade, and I have documentary proof that, to the South, the Palmetto forces and their allies are in cahoots on a vast scale, armed to the teeth with French guns and remobilising at this very second. Did I mention that the Frogs want a piece, too? Oh Lordy, yes sir indeed, this is the end of days for us unless we act. A pincer movement on a continental scale, no less.'

'Oh my, Benny.'

'Oh my indeed, John Paul. Send gunboats up the Mersey, Clyde and Thames, I say. Bomb Toulon, I say. Put it right back up their sneaky limey and Frenchie jacksies, I say. Old world bastards, meddling and subverting! Now it pains me to be so coarse, but this is not a moment for lollygagging, sir. Now, do I have your support in raising my motion? Do I, sir?'

John Paul Morgan, Governor of New York, smokes his pipe in the study of his uptown home. He eyes Butler up and down for the umpteenth time this morning, observing the stack of classified papers brought to his desk as evidence, then back at Butler. He accepts the handshake offered.

William waits upon the porch, hat in hand. Butler bursts out the front door and barrels down the sidewalk, fat cat with the cream, clutching his valise.

'Another in the bag. Where next?'

William consults his notes. 'Martha's Vineyard. A Supreme Court judge.'

'Ooh, you shall like it there. Amazing shrimp.' *He* shall like it there.

'I cannot wait, Ben.'

'Neither can I. So onwards to the ferry, my stout man. Quick march. One-two, one-two. Last one to the jetty is a rat's ass.'

#14 – A BLISSFUL PISS
Liverpool, October 9th 1865

The Hansom Carriage parks in the same spot that it always occupies at this time in the morning and then at dusk or whenever Messrs Prioleau and Bulloch choose to finish their day's business at 19 Abercromby Square, an exquisite Georgian square taken straight out of Bloomsbury and transplanted here in Liverpool, although many a Liverpolitan gentleman would argue that it is the opposite way around. Only serious money lives this far up the hill, the same money that dictates what goes on down by the Mersey shore.

The back of the carriage is occupied by the United States Consul and this is a ritual part of his morning commute down the hill to Paradise Street, as it will be on his run home later. Thomas Haines Dudley is a lonely, displaced American, full of physical and spiritual pain, eager to return to New Jersey but knowing that his work is far from done on this side of the Atlantic. President Johnson hasn't got to him yet in his cull of Abe's apparat, but D.C. hasn't responded favourably to any of his messages since the events of April. Dudley craves support – of family, of friends, of his own state and government – but he knows that it will not be forthcoming. They will not heed anything he tells them about the greater need being more vital now than ever before.

Thomas Haines Dudley sits in his carriage, observing those preening cocks entering their resplendent headquarters as if Lee never surrendered, as if Jefferson Davis' own gun metal grey ass rests in the Oval Office right now. They know what he knows, senses, smells, but he can't prove a damn thing. So close, just over there in that yonder garret of number 19, the Confederate White House in Europe, the nonsensical term coined by Prioleau, Bulloch, and the band of merry Rebs within. If Dudley ever sets one foot in that building, an avalanche of injunctions and lawsuits will be visited upon him in the British courts. The ruin will finish him, yet his only salvation exists beyond those walls.

The centrepiece injunction against Dudley is unequivocal. Prioleau is British by marriage, and his new premises are protected by law. Dudley's use of private snoops has been curtailed by a magistrate and then an old soak in the High Court when he challenged it. He tried to take his case to the House of Lords, but D.C. wouldn't pay for it. Why, indeed, after he had to publicly admit that he was conducting espionage on their sovereign soil? It should be those stateless criminals who are worried, not him. They circumvented the law and ran blockade-runners out of Liverpool, Glasgow and Bristol. They should be persona non grata, yet he finds himself a recluse and an outcast, as if it is the United States who are without a mandate here in the mother country rather than the insidious project of the Confederacy that somehow lingers and thrives in this strange Northern clime. Everything is bent out of shape, corrupted, and his mission has been made flaccid and anodyne.

This place does not represent even a fraction of the clever racket Prioleau has created, a banker and broker with his very own Navy Commander in tow. They should be packing up and leaving, but they are doing quite the opposite. Why so?

Dudley balls a fist, angry tears flowing. He is so close and that information is just beyond the door of number 19. He can smash this cabal and flush out the man he knows is behind all of it, but without proof (and to the world), Thomas Haines Dudley is just an old crank whose days are numbered. He is alone and devoid of courage. He is yesterday; he is history.

He sobs into his hands. As per prior instructions, the carriage moves on and down the hill, back towards another day at the office.

Rollo wasn't lying. He never lies; he just tells you when he is bound to withhold information. By some strange miracle, he remains faithful to his clients even now, after his ordeal at the hands of Harriet the Harridan.

Only the timing is moved forward. The letter was going to be released to Harriet in a week, to allow for certain events stateside to settle, or as it happens for Butler to get his goddamn ducks in a row. She sits in Princess Grace's austere but spotless parlour, replete with the fragrances of wildflowers picked from the gardens of Lord Derby's estate at the heart of the West Derby Hundred. This is where Monolulu father and daughter have settled their home and business far from that madding crowd in town. This is Harriet's sanctuary, without abode or child. A green idyll merely four miles from the heaving, dirty town and set within grounds that could be a country pile in Yorkshire were it not so close to where it all happens, exquisitely hidden. Rented from old man Derby in exchange for stabling his horses with a little cash on top, it is the best kept secret and the last place a couple of Edo immigrants might settle, but Harriet knows how hard it is for Grace to keep paying the rent, even with the discounted favour.

Not that Harriet is enjoying her surroundings right now. Her impotent fury reaches out an ocean away, seeking out the source of all her woes two years ago and once again. Butler's missive lingers long and painfully true after multiple scans. At least she knows now.

BURN AFTER READING.

My Dearest Darling Harriet,

How long has it been? I guess that you still mourn that man you called your sister, or was it that woman you called your husband? A hermaphrodite, no less! These times we live in! You two did a sterling job of keeping that perfect little scandal away from my attention. What a lark. Well done and no matter, as it has flowed under the bridge. I am now ready to forgive your trespasses and welcome you back into the fold. How thrilling that prospect must be for you after your long hiatus.

I suppose your grandest concern right now and for the past few months has been the whereabouts and welfare of your child. To be direct, I decided back in April to re-activate you as an operative in the best interests of the United States. Naturally, I understood that you would need to be persuaded and I remain not without influence in the town. I commissioned the withholding of your child and, later, the requisitioning of your properties in order to ensure your compliance as I do not need to detail your belligerent and reckless action of yesteryear in this missive. As an act of goodwill, I will arrange for said minor to be released back into your care upon completion of my project, and I assure you that she is currently well looked after. You will recall that I do not do things by halves.

This proved to be a prescient move as the stew has thickened since April. A man named John Surratt has flown the country to Liverpool. Look him up in the news archives, for he is a prominent fugitive stateside. This fellow is my prize trophy and one that requires the ultimate amount of discretion on your part. Find him, procure a telegram transmission that he will be keeping on or close to his person and return this transmission to me forthwith via our mutual friend Mr Rollo. Then, I expect our mark to be detained and dispatched in reasonably healthy fettle upon the first available steamer bound for the Eastern Seaboard. The usual level of discretion shall be applied.

Upon the arrival of said document and Surratt into my custody, I shall have great pleasure in restoring your child and your personal wealth, perhaps with a little bonus if you do it in good time and with the minimum of fuss. Until then, you shall move slicker without a minor in tow. Who knows, you may continue in my employ as an adept officer, should I choose. Yes, the thrills keep on coming, dear Harriet.

My plate is full over here. I intend to run for office, and a campaign of this magnitude requires money and time, so I would advise you not to bring me cause to revisit those shores again and that you complete the aforementioned brief promptly and to my full satisfaction.

Welcome back!

BFB

Ps You can expect a visit from the Pinkertons. Ignore them. They are toothless and desperate.

Pps Further, I would avoid beating a path to Haines Dudley this time. He is an insufferable, pompous relic of a man whose credit has vanished on both sides of the Atlantic. This was the worst of your mistakes last time out. Do not waste your, or my, time on him.

'And so it goes.'

She screws up the letter and tosses it onto the hot coals on Grace's hearth. Her friend sits and knits, uncomfortable with having a visitor, which makes it all the more special that she has admitted Harriet into her inner sanctum. Where else has she to go, though? Back to Louisiana? The workhouse? St James' Cemetery?

Well, she knows just who she'd like to put there.

'See this old pub in Donegal, up on Muckish Mountain so, is run by this mangy old fella with a limp and a glass eye called O'Mahony. Now, on me travels, I goes to O'Mahony's for a pint. Drops by, so I do, and most welcoming it is. I gets to chatting with O'Mahony and he is ever the most chatty man, so. He says, "Did ye notice that fence out there, Pat? Did you see how straight and perfect it is so?" "Yes, I did so. A fine fence," I reply. "But they don't call me O'Mahony the fence-builder. Oh they do not." Then O'Mahony says, "Do ye see this bar? What do ye make of it?" "Fine bar so," says I. 'Fine bar?" says he, "I crafted it myself out of a tree I chopped down out there in the wood. Joined it together, fixed it up here and varnished it, so." "Fine bar," says I. "Yes Pat, but they don't call me O'Mahony the bar fixer, do they? See that pint, then?" "Yes, says I, fine pint of plain. Pulled to perfection so." "Yes it is. But they don't say that O'Mahony is the best pint-puller, do they?" "They do not?" says I. "They do not," says O'Mahony and then he slaps the bar with his palm and with a tear in his eye he says, "But you fuck one goat..."'

One fella on his own who is about as drunk as Pat, wheezes in a fit of laughter. Diarmuid leers at him, polishing pots. 'Tell us one we've never heard.'

Pat leans across the bar. 'Ah, that must be worth one on the house? Just a dram for the entertainment, like. To take the rattle away. I'm awful sick, so. Poitín, or cheap, dark rum. I'm not fussy. Furniture polish even. You've got some there.'

'Ye've had two gallons of grog already on tick, Pat. Are ye going to cough up for that first?'

'You know I'm good for it, Diarmuid.'

'Ye must think I'm soft, McCarthy.'

'It's McCartney. Says so in the census. Our Finn told me.'

'Ye not in the right place to have a smart gob, so. How about I get the lads to shake you down for your coins, then?'

'My Fenian brothers? Aye, you go and do that, Diarmuid. Go on then. For all I've done for the cause.'

'All *ye've* done. Listen to him, fellas. Still dining out on two years ago, isn't it? It's all getting a bit fuckin' old, Padraig. This pub nearly burned down because of ye antics, need I remind ye?

Ye need to get home to your wife and clean yourself up, little bollocks ye.'

'What kind of business do you run if you won't give a man his drink? We should be in this together. Fuckin' traitor you are, Diarmuid.'

'Out. And don't come back until ye've got the brass. This is the last time I'll ask ye nicely.'

'There's nothing you can't do that the British haven't already done. Or the peelers. Or that American fucker who killed poor Royston. Me poor thumbs still ache.'

'Stop bleating on about ye thumbs and go home.'

'No, I won't. You'll give me my drink.'

'Right, that's it. Don't say I didn't warn yers. A boot in the arse ye will have to get.'

'Can I not have a piss first before they beat me up?'

'Boys?'

'Ah, Diarmuid. You bastard, you.'

'Boys? Take him out back. He will be putting off paying customers, so.'

'Right so, Diarmuid. Come on, Pat.'

'Get your scabby fuckin' hands off me. Diarmuid! Come on!'

'Cause a scene and ye'll get twice the walloping, old son. Wise up.'

'Diarmuid! Youse were a fuckin' pot collector before I got you this job! Diarmuid!'

Thud. A solid undercut, right in the guts. Ale and bile spew out of Pat's mouth and nose. That feels like it dislodged something inside him. Diarmuid is ready with the mop and bucket. Pat is dragged out back by the barman's regulars. Fenians, drinkers, collective owners of this fine establishment on Lime Street. Men with thick forearms. Fine Fenian men. This place has gone up in the world since the riot of '63, but don't mention that time in here, especially not in front of Diarmuid. He doesn't care to be reminded of all the damage, during and after. They're better off without the likes of Royston Chubb, God rest his soul. Better off further again without this drunken little culchie.

Crunch. That could well have been a couple of ribs breaking, but the pain is numbed by there being more booze than blood in

Pat's works. He was right about the rattle, though. It's getting worse and only the strongest Poitín will fend it off, or a good, hard beating.

Thud. Pat has been launched into the jigger behind the pub. Shadows of big, Irish man mountains loom over him. He knows every one of them, some of them even put on a blue uniform back when they marched up Water Street two years ago on that momentous day. A glorious time that was never recorded by any of the waiting press, nor remembered by Diarmuid or any of these here knuckles who are presently about to give him a good pasting for his floppy gob and his trouble. Traitors, eejits and gobshites, the lot of them.

Pat remains on the cobbles. He splutters and starts singing in their faces. '*God save Ireland! said the heroes; "God save Ireland" said they all. Whether on the scaffold high or the battlefield we die, oh, what matter when for Erin dear we fall!*'

'He's fair fuckin' lost it, so he has, Michael.'

'Aye, Donal. Don't know if we can beat any sense into him.'

'Ye know what Diarmuid said.'

'Aye, right so.'

They step up to him. Here it comes. 'Don't punch me in the bladder boys, else I might piss me pants. Square go.'

'Right so, Pat.'

A meaty fist flies his way, the first of many.

The temptation is there to go right back into The Crown and demand booze, but even in his addled state, Pat can figure that it would lead to a second beating, and this time they might break or burst something that puts him away permanently. That might not be such a bad thing given the general bleakness, but there are quicker, less painful and less humiliating ways to do these things.

He spits out a tooth, one of the few he has left in his mouth, before climbing up from the cobbles. Pat has scaled huge buildings, cliff faces, steeples, you name it, but getting to his feet just then was harder than any climb. He resolves to go home and beg to Sarah again. This time, he means it. He'll clean himself up, get his business back together and never touch another drop.

Then Diarmuid can go stick his poncey pub right up his scrawny fuckin' ginger crease. Pat doesn't need no pub, Pat doesn't need no booze. Yes, Pat needs home, Pat needs Sarah. If he can remember the way. But first, that piss.

'Oi!'

A peeler stands at the end of the alley, probably attracted by the commotion a few moments ago.

'Y'alright, Constable? Can one help one?'

'Put it back in your trousers, Pat. I won't tell ye twice.'

He knows Pat but the peeler is just another blur to him. 'Ah come on. Can't a man have a piss? There's shit and everything down here. Dead bodies, probably. Just want a wee wee.' The peeler brandishes his club and starts walking towards him. 'Alright, alright, I'm going, so I am. No need for that, so there isn't.'

That peeler followed him most of the way home. Don't they have better things to do? He has less status than a stray dog right now. At least a common mutt is allowed to take a piss in an alley, so he can.

This is all that bloody Harriet Farrell Dunwoody whatsherface's fault. Pat wishes that he had never met her. This is just what you get for helping people, so it is.

'Good night, cuntstable. Have a special evening so on your way, hic. Fuck you and goodnight.'

He slips into the closed courtyard off Scotland Road that they call home and the peeler slopes away into the dirty night. The next stop from here is the workhouse, but Pat has determined that enough is enough. He feels a little more sober now and knows that the full rattle will be coming, sure as eggs are eggs. But he will get through it, reclaim his business, work hard and his Sarah will start to love him again. His babies will start to see a proper father, a real man. Padraig McCartney is a chappy of means and invention; he just needs to set his mind to it.

He drags the rotten wooden door open and it comes off its hinges, collapsing back into the slurry of the courtyard. 'Aw, bollocks. I'll fix that. Tomorrow, so.'

The toilet is shared by the entire block. It overflows with sewage, as the landlord hasn't sent a plumber around like he said he would. Rats scurry away as Pat trudges inside. Tomorrow, he *will* fix this toilet and the whole block will thank Pat McCartney. Good man, so, that Pat is. Skilful man of means so.

But first, a piss. It gushes out of him, and it is blissful. Then it feels like someone has stabbed him in the side. He looks down to see that his water has turned dark. Difficult to know in this light, but he suspects that it is blood.

'Aaargh, bastard.'

The agony subsides, and he finishes. That's it. He is definitely stopping the drink. For good. Forever.

He buttons up his fly and wipes his hands on the filthy shack, footsteps squelching as he backs out into the court. They're living in a basement room. No candlelight from below, so Sarah will be huddled up in bed with them all by now. Maybe he should clean himself up a little rather than treading shit into their home? Maybe, but first, he needs to speak to his dear wife as a matter of priority. He needs to tell her exactly what he is going to do to make everything right. He needs to promise her, then he can go clean himself up and sleep tonight. They will all sleep tonight, and he will speak with the rent man tomorrow. Put that greedy bollocks straight on a few things, too, so. A man's man, is Pat.

'Sarah? I'm home, love.' The door is locked from the outside. There is a sign on it, but he can't read it. Should have learned how to read while he had the chance. Maybe Finn could read it for him, but Finn is not here. Nor are any of the other seven children. Nor is Sarah. Where are they? When did he last come home?

"God save Ireland! said the heroes; "God save Ireland" said they all!' The door is yanked open, and a craggy-faced man who looks twice his age answers.

He gurns at Pat. 'Who are you? What do ye want?'

Pat squints, leans back and looks up at the brickwork. It's the right place, alright, but it dawns upon him that they haven't lived here for over two years now.

'Sorry about that,' he grunts before waddling off. Pat starts laughing, from a chuckle to a hysterical belly laugh that torments his cracked ribs. Perhaps he may never stop.

It's not funny any more.

A red dawn sun lopes up over the borough, creating an Eastern glow across the grand edifices that straddle the Strand, the warehouses of Goree Piazza, and up, up, up Water Street, a thoroughfare dripping with money, getting ready for another day of commerce and collusion.

The tangle of sloop masts separates George's Dock from the waking Liverpool, towards the same Landing Stage where Pat first arrived here during the Great Hunger with his Mammy and siblings, 18 years past. They were starving and bereft of hope; they were dark days he never wanted to repeat, yet he finds himself doing so, at his own instigation. Pat saw business opportunities here with his new friend, Mr Royston Chubb. Pat was going to grow up to be a wealthy man, a Fenian brother respected by all, a man's man.

Now, his shoes hang off his feet, which dangle over the water's edge. He stinks of shit, his own or someone else's. Dried blood and stale piss complete the mess he now represents. Cholera would be welcome to take him but it just isn't quick enough for his liking. A few hundred feet away, ferrymen and customs officers prepare for the first arrivals and departures of the day, but they don't see or choose to see the poor soul whose scabby toes are about to slip into the drink along with the rest of him.

101 Canning Street was empty as the grave. People at Holy Cross said that she's gone to New York and there is no way of following her. They said so, probably because that was the only way of getting rid of him as he cried out for Sarah and his babies, wailing at the top of his lungs until some bastard said something or that gobshite French fella of a priest kicked him out of mass. Along with a damaged sobriety and the fast-coming rattle, reason returned to his mind. Of course she's gone, they've gone. He

can't go through this pain in his body, mind and soul. Better to do this instead, better all round.

On the way down here, Pat resolved to find a way to pay for his own passage and reunite with them. Maybe it would be a good opportunity, a fresh start. New York needs window cleaners. Failing that, New York's gangs always need housebreakers. Pat has the skills, but there is a problem. Although he can travel across the Atlantic Ocean, he'll never get away from himself. He's so tired of bouncing back and forth, trying and failing to find the good man inside himself. Now everyone else has given up on him, why should he go on? There is but one, simple answer, then.

A waft of salty brine comes up from the swell as if inviting him in for a dip. It is so much simpler to end it here. No one will bother. Maybe he'll wash up in Birkenhead, at Eastham or on Otterspool Beach. They will chuck him in a pauper's grave and that will be that, or the current might take him out to sea, towards the horizon, back towards Ireland, feeding fish along the way. Everyone is determined to forget about him, so why fight it? Sarah can build her new life and there will be no more palaver altogether. And the bonus is that he'll not have to go through the bastard rattle.

So here it is so. Time to go.

Splash.

Pat's backside remains pressed against the iron railing, filthy feet planted upon the damp, mossy stone of the dock wall. The tide ebbs against the side, and he can see a figure washing down just under the surface, difficult to see under the algae, the shit brown, spraying river and the morning gloom. Then the person bobs up momentarily, and Pat can't quite believe his own eyes.

'Mr... Dudley?'

#15 – THE LAIRD RAMS

Liverpool, October 11th 1865

'£220,000 total for the HMS Scorpion and the HMS Wivern. Paid for by Her Majesty's Government to the Laird Shipyard. Where's our money? We should sue.'

'Audacious. I like it. I'll instruct the lawyers.'

'Just how is Dudley after his brush with death, Jim? Tell me more.'

'You mean his brush with melancholy and mediocrity, Chuck?'

'Ha, more like. Well then?'

'Well then, some passing Mick fished him out of the river. My watchers say he dropped in the drink like a stone, and the fellow jumped in and saved him. If I had his lot in life, I'd fancy topping myself too.'

'Best idea he's ever had. High time he gave it up.'

'Likely his nerves are fritzed, and we've gotten him plain licked.'

'Pity about all the other damn Yankees.'

'Pah ha ha. True enough, Chuck.'

'Such a shame. Now that we can't do anything about it, eh?'

'Yup. Stuck in the mud are we two poor Southern fellas.'

They don't look like two fellas who are stuck in the mud. They look like two fellas who are cock-a-hoop and full of brandy bonhomie, talking out loud as if they want to be heard. Fellow members of The Athenaeum have noticed just how well they are taking their 'defeat'. At Gettysburg, in the War itself, in the British courts, kit and caboodle, they should be sunk. But no.

'More cognac, Jim?' asks Charles Prioleau, 'I'm buying.'

'That's why I like you, Chuck,' replies James D. Bulloch, 'You're always buying.'

They sip hot tea. It is all too quiet and polite, given what has just happened. In a very odd way, though, Pat feels liberated from his burden. Perhaps it was the dip in the chilly river that

121

cured him of his rattle, or it was just the sense that he is not alone, nor has he been alone at all in recent months, at least in his misery. He sips more tea. Earl Grey, tastes like soap but he'll drink it to be polite in the politest of company.

Dudley smiles. What became of such an astute and gentle fellow that he would throw himself to become eel food? Anyone might take a look at Pat and say it might be expected, but this man? With his status, his wealth, it doesn't figure right. 'Pat, you know what I was doing there, but what were you doing?'

'Catching flies, sir.'

'Very good, Pat. But I suspect not.'

'Aye, sir. Not.'

'Look at us. A fine pair. Feeling sorry for ourselves.'

'Aye.'

Dudley reaches into his desk drawer and rummages in a humidor. He pulls out two fine, thick cigars, offering one to Pat. 'Havana made. One of the rare perks of this job.'

'Don't smoke, sir.'

'And yet you like a drink?'

'Aye, too much.'

'Take one, for God's sake. They're good for the nerves and the constitution.'

Pat could do with something for his nerves, alright. He takes one, and Dudley strikes a phosphorus match. They are made up the road, not Cuba. Sarah tried to get a job in the factory, but the management found out she was married and kiboshed it. Another door shut in their faces. Still, many of the girls working in there are falling sick now, so maybe it was a good thing.

'Now Pat. Suck it in but don't take the smoke down past your throat. That's considered vulgar.'

'Right you are, sir.' Chuff, chuff.

'Nice?' Chuff, chuff.

'Very nice.' Chuff, chuff.

Chuff, chuff. They smoke in silence. Maybe there just isn't an answer about what happened a few hours ago. Maybe they shouldn't even discuss it. 'It's a welcome change to have some convivial company, Pat. Life has been… lonely.'

'What about the wife? Kids?'

'Emaline wanted to go back to New Jersey. She couldn't bear the lack of space; she hates it here thus she hates me. Still does, I will vouch.'

'Any word from over there?'

'Our new President Andrew Johnson is an awful prick. God knows why Abe chose him. He's dead behind the eyes, that kind of politician.'

'You mean every kind of politician?'

The portrait of Lincoln looks down, almost admonishing Pat. Dudley nods, taking the meaning. 'He'll be sharpening his axe as we speak. Probably post me to Alaska next, a governorship after Seward has bought it from the Russians. It is cold up there.'

'Wow. I've no idea where that is, but I shall take your say-so.' Dudley chuffs, allowing a moment for Pat to see the intolerable burden on his shoulders. 'This is the thing, isn't it, sir? What really made you want to jump in the river?'

The Consul shakes his head and his eyes darken. Whatever has been bothering him, this is at the heart of the matter. 'Palmerston ails fast. Heaven knows how he hasn't kicked the bucket already. Seymour is out of the picture, but Britain will have a new Prime Minister soon. Well, an old Prime Minister returned to the helm at least. Lord John Russell.'

'That was the same awful bollocks who told us to eat rotten potatoes? He killed half of Ireland, him and his lackeys.' Russell was Prime Minister in the late 1840s. 'He's the very reason I'm sitting here.'

'Yes, Pat. The exact same and why New York is more Irish than anywhere now. And, unfortunately, he's as clean as a whistle. No connection to the plot between Banastre Dunwoody, Palmerston and Seymour. No record of skullduggery in the lobbies. But I will tell you this: Russell wants the United States destroyed. Not cut in half, not weakened, but obliterated. He's worse than any of them. I would argue that he is actually insane. The dubious privilege of my position is that I get to meet such men in person.'

'But the war is over? Your man General Whatisface, the minty-looking fella with the white beard I saw in the paper…'

'General Lee.'

'Aye, Lee, that's him. He surrendered back in April. Didn't he? Our Finn read the article out to us. Just before someone popped your friend.'

Dudley shakes his head deathly slow, grim-faced. 'No. No. It isn't over, Pat. And those two bastards in Abercromby Square know it. I don't think that I can take much more of this. Pissy memos from President Johnson's Secretary of War criticising my spending, threatening to dissolve my estate, ruin me. And a wife that would happily have seen me drown...'

'You don't know that.'

'I am sorry but I do, Pat. So what exactly have I got left? How can I save everyone's bacon again when they're too stupid to realise what might happen next? I just can't do it. At least in Abraham we had a leader with courage, backbone. At least I had his ear. Thank you for saving me, sincerely, but I struggle to find the point.'

Pat reaches across and grips Dudley's hand. His damaged thumbs ache from hauling the sodden Consul up the iron ladder and back onto the jetty earlier. 'You're not on your own, sir. I'm sorry for being such an arse, and I am sure that you are too.'

'Thank you, Padraig. I think.'

'Good man yourself. That's where we start, then.'

They smoke and ponder. Dudley leans across to Pat. 'We let them take her baby, Pat. Well, I did, not you. I took my eye off the most precious thing in the world to her, just to try to recruit her again, just to get her to stay in Liverpool and screw Prioleau and Bulloch before it was too late. No one would listen then; no one will listen now... she was my last hope.'

'I'll fuckin' well listen.' Pat gulps. He'll never get used to being in the familiar company of rich, educated men like Dudley. The ground could swallow him up, but there has to be some fight left, like there has to be a reason that he was in the exact same spot as him earlier. Was it a sign from God? Stop being such a nincompoop. 'So what are we going to do about it? Not you. We.'

Dudley stands up and goes to his decanter. 'Port?' Pat shakes his head. Dudley thinks twice, replaces the stopper and goes back to his seat. 'What we are going to do is find that child and return her to her mother. Whether she wants our help or not.

Then, damn it, we are getting that evidence by fair means or foul.'

Pat, for the first time in an age, grins from ear to ear. It is the kind of grin that emanates from a man who has nothing on Earth left to lose. 'That's more like it, sir. I like your moxie, so I do, Mr Thomas Haines Dudley, United States of America Consul, like.'

Harriet doesn't know how much longer she can keep taking advantage of Grace's kindness, yet her horsewoman spends all her time by her erstwhile client's side, away from her business, which surely must be suffering as a consequence. They ride down Paradise Street, past the U.S. Consulate on a well-beaten path. Perhaps she should knock on Dudley's door, see if he can help? But it is not her responsibility to remove the Consul's head from the sand, thus it is simply not worth the time or effort. After what happened back in April, she'll resent him and she won't shake it off, to the extent that it will remind her to resent herself.

The wind has changed and autumn, it seems, is receding towards winter. A chilly, relentless Nor'wester pushes up the Mersey, right into their faces. No longer does Harriet pine for Louisiana, though. She only pines for Baba.

They dismount by the Customs House, its magnificent dome overseeing everything that comes in and out of the docks on the other side of the building. Union Jacks flutter in the cold breeze atop the British bastion and it is the first sight all incoming passengers have when arriving at George's Landing Stage. The American Lady and her African companion glean the usual derisive, admonishing glances from the merchants and officials, but Harriet has long learned how to disregard English fools and their ingrained obsession with rank, file and social status. They have a right to be here, and this is where their search starts. Find Surratt, find Baba. Everything else is just pomp and hogwash.

Their footsteps clack upon the wooden floor and they climb the stairs up to the top floor of the east wing, where the steerage class records for entry into the borough are kept. Grace is fastidious in record-keeping with her stables and her business. She is ready with her notebook and her deft fingers. A row of cabinets stretch across the length of the floor, but they focus upon the set of several at the far window that overlooks back across town, where Surratt and Baba will be, somewhere in the ether.

'I'll start at the bottom and you start at the top.'

'Yes.'

'Grace, are you sure you want to do this with me? You have a business to run. The wrong people might start to take notice.'

'Papa is looking after everything for me. Please do not ask me this again, ma'am. It is my obligation to you, not my courtesy.'

'That is not how I see it, but I'll accept.' Their chatter attracts the attention of a beady clerk. Only recently have these records been opened up to the general public, due to the host of private investigators about town that are doing the Constabulary's work for them. No doubt this snooty little bean counter would need any excuse to kick them out, though. 'Grace, look out for any man with the initials J.S. Let's not credit him with too much of an imagination.'

'Right, ma'am.'

The clerk snaps his head up again and holds a finger to his lips. Harriet smiles back at him and he returns to his ledger.

Grace's fast fingers and eyes sift through the cabinet, scanning every detail. It takes seconds. 'Miss Harriet, how about this?'

#16 – PRETTY KITTY

Liverpool, October 11th 1865

Two sad balladeers lilting, echoing and competing in the music room of The Washington Hotel on St George's Place, the sumptuously appointed temporary residence of any well-to-do visitor with business to conduct in the Borough of Liverpool.

The Washington Hotel is set within a terrace facing Lime Street Station, less grand at first sight than the opulent and huge terminus, but with a host of amenities that other local hostelries, grand or modest, do not offer. The proprietors of this establishment offer every discernible luxury imaginable to paying guests, with the indemnified promise upon check-in that *sir* does not need to venture out and spend his money in other, more rambunctious and dangerous local venues when anything can be procured for *sir* to enjoy in the safety and comfort of these rooms, or indeed in the safety and comfort of *sir's* suite upstairs. No questions asked, utmost discretion guaranteed and indemnified by reputation. Just ask the Concierge. For anything.

The balladeers this evening and every evening are Madame de Pomfrette, a world-famous alto channelling Madame de Pompadour, imported to The Washington directly from the select basement clubs of the Pigalle in Paris. Her stage partner is the pristine, *slightly* younger white blonde soprano, Mademoiselle FouFou, harmonising within the duo. They perform twice daily and thrice nightly in these rooms for visitors who pay by the night or by the hour. For some inexplicable reason, the gallic chanteuses, who are adorned in silk gowns and frilly boas, croon out popular English and Irish ditties and, for every performance, flash their gartered thighs at the gentlemen guests who smoke and drink and ogle. The same fellows care little for the veracity of their backstories and readily accept their cheap costume fantasy act, preferring their sentimental music hall renditions to some Frenchy or Italianate dirge. Out of all the young women on display in this human menagerie, these two have risen to the top of the pile with their witty repartee and delightful performances, which would grace any variety performance across the land, at least in Mme Pomfrette's opinion. The added benefit to any of the paying guests is that, with a rather higher stipend to their bill – paid upon checking out – a night with either or both of these Parisian courtesans can be booked, savoured and extolled by reputation to gentlemen friends and future visitors looking to enjoy their stay. That old theatrical tradition of the leading ladies being 'available' to paying customers after the show holds firm here. This hotel is the biggest Maison de Plaisir in town and the veneer of good repute is about as thin as their Parisian act.

'You can be replaced, you impudent little bitch. How do you fancy the workhouse? Or selling yourself in the docks? I took you away from all that, but you can go back,' grunts Audrey Hampson, erstwhile Mme de Pomfrette, as she slaps a warm flannel around her face to remove the ghoulish greasepaint. She leers via a mirror at little Kitty Flynn, the erstwhile Mamselle, who is getting changed from her stage into her bedroom attire, ready to deliver herself to the upstairs rooms of Sir William Francis Delahunty, MP for Stobs and Wells, her sixth appointment of the day. Sir Bill likes them young and the hotel abides.

'If you say so,' mews Kitty, pulling on a stocking. Yes, Sir Bill likes them young but acting older, to retain the veneer of respectability and slalom scandal, masking the obscene and grotesque as is his wont. Another randy, horrid old bore with sewage breath and brewer's droop, reeking of port and jism. And right now, Kitty has had about enough of him and his like. It is the first time since she arrived here that she has allowed herself to contemplate anything else other than servicing these fat ogres.

'I do say so, girl. How dare you insult my singing.'

'Miss Audrey,' Kitty begins, wondering whether or not to pacify her for the millionth time as she does have her own business to attend to, or just to let her have it, 'What can I say? You're a diva, so. I was jealous of your prodigious talent, so I am.'

'Well, I am a diva. I was in Welsh Opera at Rhyl, you know.' Christ, the woman is starting to believe her own lies, missing the obvious sarcasm. Perhaps she should be just allowed to get on with it, to swim in her own piss. Perhaps Kitty should just simply persist with the line of not making trouble, as much as she could not resist in likening Miss Audrey's singing to a cat getting fingered the wrong way to the other girls earlier, which brought much hilarity but became news that travelled back to the aforesaid senior feline expressly. Filthy mouths on them, the lot of them. Of course, Kitty knew that would happen before she opened hers.

Miss Audrey Hampson dabs slightly less furiously after Kitty's soft soak. She is in her mid-twenties but on closer inspection, stripped of all her paraphernalia and pomp, looks twice her age, older even. How long has she been singing? As long as she has been working on her back. Sharing this cramped changing room with her in the two years since Kitty arrived in Liverpool as a barefoot orphan has become a stale, sickly experience. One that, until recent weeks, it appeared there would be no salvation from.

Kitty considers her place in the world for the umpteenth time today, every moment in between shows and upstairs assignations. She recalls how, as a stowaway waif of eleven, she dodged the predators of Clarence Dock fresh off the boat and ran up the hill of Parliament Street towards them big, posh houses, not knowing where to go or what to do about the gnawing hunger in her belly, her knees trembling with weakness. Others would have succumbed to a ditch, but she kept going and going, eating berries, worms and slugs for sustenance, survival tricks she had learned in dear old Ireland. She entered a church, and the narky-arsed priest directed her to the workhouse on Brownlow Hill, the giant citadel of misery that she knew she would never leave if she entered. She kept going and going down the hill, asking in the Adelphi Hotel for work – cleaning, anything – before being chased out of the door, ear full of fleas. Following her nose down Lime Street, past gin palaces and ale houses to espy this gleaming, Portland stone edifice of The Washington Hotel, she stumbled in and again asked for work. Then she was taken downstairs to meet the aforesaid Miss Audrey, star of the scene. How it was like a dreamland at the time! How Miss Audrey was so kind to her! Miss Audrey fed her, bathed her, clothed her. Miss Audrey taught her. To read, to sing songs and to do other things. Miss Audrey set her to work.

And now, Kitty Flynn has decided that she has outgrown Audrey Hampson's fake kindness, boozy wrath and superior airs. Hampson takes her false teeth out. There's not so much as one peg left in her syphilitic gob. 'No, you're a fine singer, so, Miss Audrey. I spoke out of turn, so I did.'

Hampson waves a paw at her. Has she cottoned on that something is up? Probably not. 'I know that I am. Don't harp on. You've work to do, girl. Time to get up them stairs.'

'Pity about them crabs all about your nethers, like. They must itch and stink madly so, like the offal trough in a fish market.'

Hampson's face emits sudden puce and vitriol. Kitty can tell that she is about to explode, but this time she is ready for her. She adjusts the thick signet ring on her knuckle and punches Hampson square on the temple, drawing blood. 'Wh- wha-.'

Kitty loops a leather switch, one used for the upstairs antics, over Hampson's neck and yanks it back, choking her. 'While you're letting me do all the work, while ye sit on ye fat arse eating cakes, know that I have some important news for you, Miss Audrey. Little Kitty here's days on her back are well and truly over. I don't have to go nowhere now. You do.'

Hampson splutters. Kitty loosens the belt. 'Wh-wh…' She tightens it again.

'It's you who needs to get up them stairs. See, I've been given other business to attend to. Special business. Go ask Aston if you don't believe me. I dare you.'

'Wh-wh-wh…'

Kitty releases the cord and Hampson slumps flat on her dressing table, bleeding, sobbing and gasping. Kitty is only thirteen years old, but she grew up a long time ago. Picking up a bodice from a hanger, she tosses it over Hampson's prostrate form. 'Get up them stairs. Now.'

'He will be disappointed. He likes them y-'

'You better do a good job, then.'

A pinch of defiance remains in her former madam. 'Who put you in charge?'

'Who do you think?'

'He… He would never. I do not believe you. I will not believe you. He would…'

'All you need to know is that I am.' Kitty whips her back with the switch, devilishly hard, slashing against Hampson's skin. She yelps. 'So get up them stairs, get them drawers down for Sir Bill and be quick about it.'

Kitty has a little bit of trouble dissolving the pang of remorse about how she just treated Miss Audrey. For better or worse, the woman did save her life, even mothered her for a long time, taught her how to survive. But the idea that any of it was for anyone's good but Audrey Hampson's should never be countenanced. This is the way of Audrey's world and the way of Kitty's, too. No, she did it the cruel way, the right way, learned from the very mistress of pain herself.

See, not long ago, Kitty Flynn was given an opportunity, and you don't turn one like this down. Not ever. For it is Kitty's turn to play Mother Goose and how she will do it so much better than that toothless, crab-infested old slag ever could.

The upper suites of The Washington Hotel are a labyrinth that can only be navigated by an experienced member of staff, for there are doors and chambers that no one passes through up here without knowledge or authority. This job is far more preferable to having to listen to Miss Audrey's god-awful singing day after day, night after night, or to the regular servicing of pathetic, dirty men. She hopes that the boss will give her blessed relief from all that, too, in order to focus on the little one up here, but then appearances do need to be maintained and the hotel must continue to run. Pushing Audrey up to Sir Bill was naughty, and the Boss Man might punish her, but equally, he knows the value of her discretion, and she knows what that buys her.

Thirteen eh? She knows that she is older in guile, if not so much in looks.

The infant yelps in her cot, snot and tears stream down her face. Poor little tot. Up until the child was brought to her, someone had been wet-nursing the kid and there is no doubt she was well-fed and treated by her gait and healthy pallor. No rickets or scurvy skin, bright eyes, strong milk teeth, but she wouldn't stop crying. So, she must have come from a good home and someone will be missing her surely, with her beautiful, jet-black corkscrew hair and dark eyes. Just what is so important about some mulatto child? Well, she doesn't know and will not ask, understanding the need for discretion. No flies on Kitty.

She picks up the little one, who she has named Sally, after no one in particular. She never had a doggy or a dolly as a child and now she does. Turns out Sally has messed the sheets again without a nappy but housekeeping will take care of that. Time to bathe her, then.

'Sorry I was so long, little Sal. Mammy had something to take care of.' If Kitty had gone to see Sir Bill, she'd have been even longer. She just can't abandon her girl like that again. She's glad that she gave Hampson what for. If the child had an accident down here, there would be murder, her murder. Truth be known, Kitty would never forgive herself either. She's starting to take a strong liking to little Sally, so she is. 'I shall make things better for you, I promise. Let's get you washed and fed. Then I will read you a story, lovely baby.'

'Mammy where?'

'Right here, lovely.'

Yes, she will have a word with the bosses. Make a case. Maybe Sally is destined for similar work, or greater things, or something terrible and awful so that Kitty won't bring herself to consider, but she's here now and Kitty to Sally is her Mammy and Sally to Kitty is her baby. And that's that, for Kitty loves Sally.

She glances around the place and curls a lip. 'You know what, Sally? Mammy's going to get us some better lodgings. A place fit for a Princess like you. Just you watch, aye.'

Sally has no idea what she is saying, but she smiles and hugs her, getting a little bit of poo on Kitty's legs. What a lovely baby.

#17 – LORD JOHNNY AND
HIS REDCOATS

Whitehall, London, October 11th 1865

A tincture of laudanum before work. *GC Cruickshank's Opium Tonic*, as it says on the label, *a remedy for all maladies!*

'Ah. Ooh. Ah.'

Several half pint bottles of the magic glug sit in the cabinet of his ensuite at 300 Whitehall. A constant supply is maintained at Chequers, the townhouse in Bloomsbury, Pembroke Lodge in Richmond, and various estates about England and Ireland. Wherever he goes, it is ready and waiting. Vital fuel for a man with ceaseless business. Pity that his wife, family, and fellow peers will not see it that way, which is why he must be discreet.

It is a potent concoction of opium and alcohol. Proven as much in medical circles and debated upon in the Commons as to whether or not it should be declared legally verboten, such is the degenerate behaviour of the common man when allowed it.

He adjusts his collar and strides across towards the briefing rooms. Civil Servant mandarins and housekeeping staff gape and ogle at his magnificent figure. Who can blame them? How those nouveau riche twits, in-bred parasites in the Commons, and the guttersnipe press mock him for his stature, but not for much longer. They shall rue the fucking day that they called him 'half-pint'. A private secretary shuffles over to him, pale of face. 'Sir, I must tell you…'

'Away, lad. I have business.' Lord Johnny shoves the awkward fellow out of his path and he nearly careers off the balcony to a certain death on the tiles below. It would have served him right for getting in the way. No one gets in Lord Johnny Russell's way.

No. One.

'He shouldn't be allowed out of his quarters in that state.'

'It has taken all of my wits to stop the snoopers.'

'He's as stoned as a monkey. This is not befitting office.'

'Befitting office, befitting office not. Nay, no, nyet, non, nein.'

'What? Stop talking about me. I can hear everything, you know. Bloody mandarins. I'll have you fired. I'll have you shot, I will.'

'Beg pardon, sir? Are you quite well?'

'He's a fucking disgrace. Foreign minister! Prime Minister! Pah!'

Voices, voices, whispers, voices. Rasping, accusing, judging. J'accuse, j'accuse.

'We are replacing one sick man with another. This really won't do.'

'Prime Minister Palmerston, Palmerston, Palmerston.'

'This really is the limit.'

'Seymour, Seymour, Seymour. Pretends Pammy isn't at death's door. And now this weasel returns for more.'

'*What* really is the limit?' screeches Lord Johnny, arriving at his chosen room. Eyes move to the carpet, collective winces and sharp inhalations. 'Be still your tongues now, eh? Um? Speak when you're spoken to, I say. I'll have all of you shot. Nay, beheaded.'

Lord Johnny opens the door and marches inside the windowless, gaslit room, slamming the door behind him. A scale map of the Eastern Seaboard is set upon a huge table. He straightens up to his full height and ramrod posture, striding measuredly around the model. Die-cast Redcoat Troops assemble on the edge of New York State. Arrows depict the path of steamer carriers across the Atlantic towards Nova Scotia and New Brunswick. To the south, Palmetto regiments are dotted from the panhandle to Texas and up through the Carolinas, ready to activate, brothers-in-arms with the Fighting Tigers of Louisiana and other militia that have held tight since Lee surrendered, waiting for orders, waiting for leaders.

Flotillas of Royal Navy ships presage a beachhead off the Gulf of Mexico, ready to surge up the Mississippi and sack New Orleans. An unprecedented, glorious mobilisation is about to get underway in the name of Her Majesty Queen Victoria. Weakened by four years of war, the United States of America is ripe for a drubbing. They shall not threaten the Empire, upon which the sun will never set. This is Lord Johnny's favourite project, his masterpiece, his legacy, his Great War. Won't be long now. Rule Britannia.

'Oh bravo, old boy,' he announces to an empty room.

He runs a finger along the dome of the Capitol Building in Washington, then flicks the balsa wood model over. He does likewise to the adjacent White House. Soon, it will burn and – this time – it shall not stop burning.

'The British are Coming, the British are Coming, and this time they are fucking well staying. Ha. La Victoire et La Gloire.' He does a little impersonation of Bony. Well, Bony has nothing on Lord Johnny. Everyone will see soon. Her Majesty, too.

A slight gnawing rolls up in his guts. Perhaps it is time for more of the sweet mixture. Lord Johnny heads out and back onto the landing. The same cowed figures await him. Must they ruin his ooh, his ah, his buzz? Insipid rodents.

'Oh my.'

'Oh my what, son?' Are they laughing at him? Is this pesky chatterbox oaf of a boy laughing at him? Perhaps he *should* push him off the balcony. And what of it? Who will challenge him for it? 'What is your name, lad?'

'Humphrey Smith, sir.'

'And what do you do, young Humphrey Smith?'

'I am your PPS, and I have been in post with you for 18 years, sir. I am 52, sir.'

He eyes Smith up and down. Perhaps not so young. Perhaps he recognises Smith. Perhaps he is who he says he is. Perhaps he *has* been in post as his Private Secretary for years now. Pish though, he shall have better staff when he reaches number ten. Staff worth remembering after he's been at the special sauce.

'Very well, Smith. Carry on.'

'Yes sir, but...'

'What is it, Smith? Spit it out.'

'You are not wearing any bottoms, sir.'

Lord Johnny glances down, and it does appear that he is naked from the waist down. He nods and ruffles Smith's grey hair. 'Ah. Very good, young Smith. Carry on, fellow-me-lad.'

Smith holds a sealed envelope out to him. 'From our operative in Liverpool. For your eyes only.'

He snatches it and waves Smith away. Now, back for some sweet mixture. If only he can remember the correct door back to his chambers.

#18 – MISTER SPITZ

Liverpool, October 15th, 1865. Sunday

JS. Jacob Spitz. Canadian National. Age 23. Heir to a timber company out of New Brunswick. Visiting Liverpool on trade business. An adequate enough cover for their likely lad, but for three, small details: his date of birth matches Surratt's, his initials likewise, and his religion is logged as Roman Catholic. Fewer lies, fewer Hail Marys to say as penance.

More grist to the mill. How many Canadian Catholics of his age travelled as single male passengers during that period? One.

What Harriet knows about the Holy See is one thing that you can never deny; if you're in that club, you'll never mark yourself out as an apostate heretic, even for the sake of an adequate cover. Those in thrall to the faith must always practise it wherever they are in the world. God comes first; just ask all those poor souls who contribute their pennies to the collection basket and scrub up smart for Mass on Sunday, then starve for the rest of the week. So, is *this* their man? Or is it wishful fancy?

Grace accompanies her up on the driver's seat of the box car, pulled by a pair of sturdy fillies, scouring the churches of the borough, tempting the priests in with that familiar rich young widow cover. How they lap it up, especially if they're smelling money. She plays the generous benefactor who wants to bestow a gift towards the construction of a new cathedral at Everton, in this instance. He could be a bank manager in New Orleans, or a Bishop in Liverpool, but the same play works just fine. If only they could help her find a dear and long-lost cousin, an American man going by the name of Spitz, real name Surratt, then it would make her *even more* generous. The rest is a condensed version of the truth that Surratt is on the run from the United States, unjustly accused of being part of the Lincoln plot. Bishop Alexander Goss, a man of sizeable appetite, wrings his sweaty palms at the prospect of a donation, less so at the description of Surratt. He orders his housekeeper to bring out his best sherry, pulls the ledger and finds the church of the Holy Cross on Tithebarn Street to be the likeliest haven for such a fellow because Father Jovliet has connections with the one true

Catholic and apostolic Church in Quebec and with the Southern States. In exchange, Harriet promises a huge donation to his future cathedral fund forthwith. They leave the Bishop gay and flushed with the promise of swollen coffers. At this rate, they might get their Big House faster than the Anglicans and the town of Liverpool will finally be called a city.

So, of course, it had to be Jovliet. Best day to catch the rat Surratt? Sunday, of course. Eight am is the first Mass of the day, to be said by none other than Harriet's dear recent acquaintance. Even the Bishop thought he was a prick, without using that exact word. Father J keeps some strange alliances, but he has powerful connections all the way to Rome.

A grand swathe of parishioners, mainly poor and Irish, mill into the large church, guaranteeing yet another full house. Jovliet stands up on the altar with his back to the congregation, muttering in Latin before the proceedings start, already entranced in his own aura. Harriet and Grace file in with the rest of his flock. She grips the Daguerreotype image of Surratt, taken from his days as a farm boy in a Maryland militia to commemorate the victory that never came.

They stand at the back, scanning every likely-looking lad who files in. Most of them have families and none match the daguerreotype image or height description provided by Rollo within Butler's brief. Poverty doesn't normally raise these boys too big. Flat caps are clutched in reverent, penitent hands, and children and babies bade quiet. As if commanded by the Holy Spirit directly, the whole congregation stands.

Jovliet pipes up, keeping his back to everyone. '*Fratres, agnoscamus peccáta nostra, ut apti simus ad sacra mystéria celebránda.*'

Grace watches on in awe. Harriet elbows her. 'You tempted, Princess?'

'I beg your pardon, Miss Harriet? I do not follow.'

'You know. To join the flock? His flock even?'

'I have enough to deal with, Miss Harriet. Please do not tease me.'

That is unusually barbed a response for Grace. It is unfair to put her under this much pressure. 'I'm sorry, Grace.'

'*Confiteor Deo omnipotenti et vobis, fratres, quia peccávi nimis cogitatióne, verbo, ópere et omissióne.*'

The adults strike their breast three times and they say, '*Mea culpa, mea culpa, mea máxima culpa. Ideo precor beátam Máriam semper Virginem, omnes Ángelos et Sanctos, et vos, fratres, oráre pro me ad Dóminum Deum nostrum.*'

'Mea culpa, mea fucking culpa. Keep letting them blame themselves for their shitty lives, like it's their fault they are poor.' Harriet can hear herself mutter while scanning every head and body in this packed church. There must be four, five, six hundred souls in here, and not one of them appears to be Surratt. 'Damn man. Where are you?'

She considers slipping out of the back, continuing the search elsewhere. But where?

'*Et incarnatus est de Spiritu Sancto ex Maria Virgine, et homo factus est. Crucifixus étiam pro nobis sub Póntio Piláto: passus, et sepultus est et resurréxit tértia die, secundem Scripturas, et ascendit in cælum, sedet ad dexteram Patris.*'

'Suppose any of these people speak Latin, Miss Harriet?'

'You could translate for them.'

'I am not sure Father up there would appreciate it. He looks stern.'

'Stern is not the half of it, Grace.'

'*Et iterum ventúrus est cum gloria, iudicáre vivos et mortuos, cuius regni non erit finis. Et in Spiritum Sanctum, Dóminum et vivificantem: qui ex Patre Filióque procédit. Qui cum Patre et Filio simul adorátur et conglorificátur: qui locutus est per prophétas.*'

'This is looking like a damp squib. I think a hole might open up and I might fall down to hell if I have to stay here much longer.'

'*Et unam, sanctam, catholicam et apostólicam Ecclésiam. Confiteor unum baptisma in remissiónem peccatorum. Et exspécto resurrectiónem mortuórum.*'

'Are you sure that he is not here?'

'*Et vitam ventúri sæculi . . .*'

Harriet continues to scan. She's tempted to walk the aisles, but that would get the attention of Jovliet and, however appealing such devilment would be, causing a ruckus would not be too bright an idea right now. The priest and his altar servers continue with their backs to the throng, as if turning away from the direction of Jerusalem is turning away from God and hence a sin. It seems plain that Surratt is not here in the congregation, though. Will they have to do this in every Catholic church in the borough? They might be a while, but that Bishop said Mr Spitz *was* here.

'Amen.'

'Sweet baby Jesus, Grace. Would you look at that.'

There he is, up on the altar, swinging a thurible of incense around like he's David trying to slay Goliath, dressed in a white cassock. Jovliet's Head Boy in plain sight. Of course he'd be up there, taking part in the show like a good Catholic boy.

'Is that him? Hardly what I expected.'

Harriet nods at the altar and folds her arms, attracting a few more sideways glances from members of the congregation. 'Let's wait this one out.'

'Ssssshush!'

She smiles at her irritated fellow Catholics. It has been a while since she last went to Mass. Perhaps she has forgotten the decorum; perhaps she couldn't give a rat's ass.

'*Virginum omnes Angelne et Sanctos et vos fratre.*'

Mass takes an age, an epoch. Baba Conté might have grown up herself in the time it took Jovliet to get through the liturgy, but the congregation leaves having had their money's worth and their sins wiped clean.

If Surratt was bold enough to join a heinous conspiracy, he might fancy he could handle himself with two mere women. Guns, of course, have their special way of persuading people, but Harriet sees that this detail might require more direct and immediate action to subdue the mark and Butler wants him alive for his show trial. They stash themselves in the choir loft until the church empties, which gives the perfect view of Surratt's movements in and out of the sacristy. He snuffs candles, folds cloth, polishes communion silverware, kneels and crosses himself every time he passes the altar. Jovliet has retired to his presbytery, perhaps to count this morning's take from the baskets, or to consider his next visit from a poor female parishioner.

Grace watches on with her. She seems on edge herself, as if the surroundings or something else is spooking her. The closer they've got to Surratt, the more nervous she has grown. The Princess is a faithful friend, but she is no Conté, who would have been down there, bagging and tagging Surratt before you can say the Lord's Prayer. This is just not her line of work and Harriet knows that she must let her about her own business after they have taken care of this fellow. Let the horsewoman be a horsewoman.

He looks almost innocent down there, but his momma swung low because he fled, which is a dirty deed in anyone's book, if not Father Jovliet's. Does that make this right? Are Butler's intentions righteous? Inevitably no, they will not be. Does that matter now? It's him or her child and she might not get a better opportunity.

At last, Surratt finishes his chores about the altar and he kneels down on the hard marble for one last prayer, perhaps. Harriet reaches into her shawl and pulls out the beavertail sap. 'Watch my back, Grace.'

'Surely ma'am,' whispers her tense friend.

Harriet whips off her shoes and she is right back in the glade, hunting for bushwhacker trespassers on Choctaw land, fleet of foot but quiet as an avenging angel. Just as she gets within a few feet, he stands, crosses himself, and turns on his heel. Harriet cracks him across the jaw with the sap, sending him reeling to the floor. He groans, but the blow is powerful enough to almost knock him out cold. Saps have been known to kill men before, but they make excellent bludgeons for close work and are in plentiful supply around the Mississippi, which is why they are so favoured.

'What in hell?' he groans, 'Who are you?'

'I work for the United States Government, Mr Surratt. You will need to come with me.'

She pulls her Colt .45 and points it at him. A supercilious smile invades his face. 'This is a house of God. How dare you.'

She cocks the hammer. 'I won't ask again.'

'I think you will. You won't shoot me on an altar. I can see that you won't.'

Dazed as he is, Surratt is clearly feeling righteous and he has a decent enough instinct about people. Harriet, on the other hand, is feeling like she needs to haul ass before Father comes back into the church to see about all the kerfuffle. Shooting him would be a very bad idea, too, as then he might not make it to the Infirmary, never mind Boston Harbour.

'Very well, Mr Surratt. We'll take this elsewhere.'

'Wh-'

She saps him again, this time with a hard, backhand swipe. He collapses to the floor, blood and teeth spattering the stone riser. His God willing, he'll live.

Harriet frisks Surratt, hoping against hope that he keeps Butler's precious memorandum upon his person.

'Miss Harriet, we really do need to go.'

'I know, Grace.' Finally, she finds it in the ass pocket of his breeches. She breathes relief.

'You feeling strong, Grace?'

The word spread across the borough faster than any telegraph. The cabal of snitches in local government, about the dock estates, and among the plentiful numbers of scallywags and upscaled criminals forming Dudley's network of information gathering against the illegal Confederate shipbuilding has been activated again. As anticipated, it has yielded a very rapid response. He'll have to justify the spend to D.C. – but hang it, that will keep for a while.

'What have we got that a determined and whip-smart operative who happens to be the mother of the missing child hasn't?'

'That is a difficult question to answer, Mr Dudley,' says Pat, enjoying the comfort of the Chesterfield armchair in the Consul's bureau after a long day of footslogging and interviewing the collective chatterboxes and ragamuffins of old Liverpool town. Many familiar faces who were altogether surprised to see him in the company of a gentleman like Mr Dudley.

The old Yank fella has been given a second wind. He skips around on the spot like he's just discovered the elixir of life.

'Money, all the money of the United States government, or all the tea in China. And a net of snitches across town willing to take our cash for information. Timely, our renewed intervention was too, Pat.'

'That's grand so, Mr Dudley. What have you got, then?'

Dudley beams, gets up, opens the door and guides a woman into the office. Pat is pretty sure that she's a brass of some sort by her look and manner, but he pins his gob shut. 'I present the noted stage actress, singer and impresaria, Miss Audrey Hampson. I got that introduction right, didn't I, dear?'

'Quite so, sir.'

Pat observes her and remembers. *Actress* eh? Yes, she's a brass alright. 'Charmed, Miss.'

'Miss Hampson has the residency at The Washington Hotel. Remember, Pat?'

'Aye. Sure, very good you were too, ma'am. Delightful, like a bird singing, so. Or a crow cawing.'

As is her wont, Miss Hampson easily spots his sarcastic barb and matches it with an acidic sneer packaged as a smile. They both come from the same side of the tracks, but there's no point in playing any common ugliness out in front of Mr Dudley. It makes Pat wary of any word spilling out of her trap, though. He knows that the gentleman Consul is smart enough not to be taken for a mug by some ha'penny trollop, but Pat is right on his guard.

'So, Miss Hampson. Please tell my friend here what you have just told me.'

'Him? *Your* friend?' Miss Hampson looks at Pat like he's just crawled out from under a stone.

'Surely, Miss.'

'Righto. Well, I know where your baby is. Well, whoever's baby it is. Well, I'm pretty sure that's the right one.'

'And how do you know?' asks Pat.

'Mulatto, right? Birthmark on the back of her neck, right?' Miss Hampson makes the shape of a U with a finger. She looks highly satisfied with herself.

Pat nods. That's Harriet's nipper, alright. 'Great work, Mr Dudley.'

'Only putting it right, Pat.'

'Surely.'

'Do I get my money then?' says Hampson, not caring for all the interlocutions.

Pat leans into her. She stinks of cheap wine and rotting fish. His sense of smell has returned since he laid off the booze, but that isn't necessarily a blessing in this town. 'Where, exactly, is the baby then?'

'Money first.'

Mr Dudley smiles and waves his hands about in amelioration, as if he's charming a jury in a civil case. 'Of course, remuneration. Do give me a moment, please, Miss Hampson.'

'Certainly,' she mews, unable to wipe off the contemptuous smirk directed at Pat. Mr Dudley heads out back towards the basement, where Pat knows he keeps his coffers.

Pat eyes Hampson. Hampson eyes Pat. She lights up a cheroot and blows purple smoke. 'Whassamatter with you, Paddywhack? You looking for business? I'm a little tied up right now and you can't afford me.'

'Even if I could, I don't want it dropping off, love.'

'Don't 'love' me, you ugly little ginger rat.'

'Know this while the big fella's gone. You trick us, you shall rue the day.'

'Ha. Is that your promise? You going to punish me?'

'Looks like life has already punished you and then some.' She hisses at Pat just as Mr Dudley returns with a lump of cash that could solve all of his problems in one fell swoop, including passage to New York and a fresh start with Sarah. Or a really good swill in the Crown. As the Consul hands the money to the brass, Pat feels a bit giddy at how base temptation has just visited him.

Hampson couldn't care less. 'So, there's this nasty little Irish slut called Kitty Flynn working at The Washington. The Rabbits got her this special number from some American. Take care of a child; tell no one. Thick as mince she is, for all of her smart mouth. She forgot that nothing happens in my hotel without my knowing about it. God knows why Aston didn't ask me.'

Pat lets her rant settle in the air for a moment. 'It's hardly *your* hotel now, is it love?'

'Please refrain from goading her,' says Mr Dudley.

Hampson tucks the dense roll of cash into her cleavage. 'Yes, listen to the gentleman.'

'So?' grunts Pat.

'So slutty Kitty's got the baby in the top floor suite. Best rooms in the house. Set up all cosy. She thinks she's got it made.'

Dudley turns to Pat. 'Mr Tierney was lying to us, it seems.'

Pat's eyes light up in indignation. 'Whoa. Hang on a second. How was I supposed to know that he was yer man, eh?'

'You didn't, Pat. I know.'

Hampson swaps sly eyes for Pat with doe eyes for Dudley. 'Aston is a personal friend of mine. I am putting everything on the line here, sir.'

'Not that good a friend, it would seem,' says Pat, although it is scanning as true. The woman has got some big balls in coming here, bounty or not. This must be quite a gripe.

She ignores Pat and continues with the Consul. 'My name does not need to be mentioned in any of this, does it?'

'Of course not, Miss Hampson,' replies Dudley.

Pat breathes through his teeth. This is tough. Aston could crack the dock wall in half with his forehead. They'd best be careful here, especially if Tierney's sponsoring the babysitting. 'You think you can get us in, then?'

Hampson throws her head back and laughs. 'Even this gentleman here doesn't have enough money to pay me for that service, Paddy. You have your information, and that's your lot.'

She heads out of the door. Mr Dudley holds it open for her. 'Thank you, Miss Hampson.'

Hampson flicks a feather boa in his face. She's a living, breathing caricature of a bawdy Hogarth tableau. '*You* are welcome any time, sir. Feel free to drop by and see me. Ask for Audrey. I promise to attend to you, as you Americans say, PDQ.'

Mr Dudley tips a salute to Hampson and she sashays out. Pat gurns derision. 'Not if you don't want a dose, Mr Dudley. Dear fuckin' Jaysus.'

'I can see that.' Mr Dudley clearly doesn't appreciate coarse references when he isn't drunk himself.

'Surely, sir.'

He reaches down to his humidor for a pair of cigars. They're going through them at a considerable rate. He passes one to Pat. 'Tell me everything you know about these Dead Rabbits, Pat.'

'Everything?'

'Yes.'

'Christ, I'll be a while. We go way back.'

He put up quite the struggle when he came to, even when bound and gagged. Harriet was forced to sap him again, but that will have to be the last time. He will be damaged goods if she's not careful, and that breaks one of Butler's foremost edicts when it comes to the apprehension and transit of enemy assets.

She applies some ether to a cotton handkerchief and pushes it against his airways as the box rattles along the road. It is difficult to see, with only light squeezing in via the cracks of the double doors at the back, but she can feel the tension draining out of him. He will doubtless wake up with one hell of a headache, but by then, he will be in the hold of the timber sloop MV Leopold, bound for Boston Harbour. And then, just maybe, she might begin to countenance catching a break from Butler.

The cabin is separated from the driver by thick wooden slats, and she can barely make out the seagulls from the rumble of the wheels and the horses' hooves clacking. The smell of the docks is unmistakable, though: a fugue of faeces and brine.

'Grace, how are we getting on?'

'Nearly there, Miss Harriet.'

'Good.'

This was the only carriage that Grace could procure at short notice, borrowed from Lord Derby's estate. It is used to transport fertiliser manure, which doesn't make the journey any more pleasant. Still, they are nearing George's Dock, where Surratt will be removed to a strongbox and Grace will be able to ride off back to her own business, at last. Then Harriet will write to Butler via his snivelling lackey Rollo, and he will tell her where to find her Baba, in spite of the gnawing feeling that he will do nothing of the sort.

'Whoa!' She can feel Grace pulling the carriage to a stop. Harriet will have to alight, and the dockers that Rollo commissioned will enter the car and box Surratt up. It is nearly always in the transfer that something goes awry.

A knock on the doors and Harriet opens up. She is faced with grim, burly, grey-eyed peelers and moustachioed, suited chappies in black derby hats, leering in at her. It takes no time at all to figure out what has transpired and another piece of her heart breaks off and falls away into the bottomless chasm.

'Grace, why?'

A little voice emanates from behind the hat brigade. 'I am so sorry, Miss Harriet. My business was going down. We were for the poorhouse. They gave me no choice.'

'I could have helped you.'

'No, Miss. Not even you had it in your power. They said they would deport us. To Brazil, to Demerara. My Daddy would not survive the crossing.'

Harriet's guts knot themselves, and she pulls on all of her reserves of strength not to lash out at the hats or at Princess Grace, as either would mean a messy, violent death. 'I understand, Grace. I forgive you.'

'Miss Harriet, I...'

Gruff tones break their exchange. 'We can be dignified about this or not, ma'am.' A peeler offers Harriet a hand and she accepts. Another carriage, this one with bars on the windows, awaits her. Where is it taking her? To gaol or hell, same difference.

Behind her, she can hear Surratt stir and grunt. He's a strong boy, that one, for sure. Harriet passes Grace on the way to the Black Maria. The Princess is ashen and the cat has got her tongue in some death grip. 'Who are you? Which mob?' she asks the hats.

'That is classified, ma'am,' says one of them, which is enough to confirm to her that they are British Government agents, as is her dear friend Princess Grace Monolulu. Intelligence Branch, doubtless. It makes sense now. They have been watching her ever since the debacle at the Town Hall with Banastre and the Prime Minister. Liverpool has been crawling with London spooks ever since. Once bitten, twice shy.

'I hope you look after the horsewoman properly for her trouble, lads. She's done a fine job. Do not dismiss her, for she is your equal and probably your better.'

A few sardonic sniffs meet her statement, but anything else would be a surprise. She climbs up into the back of the cab, and the door is deadbolted and padlocked after her. The Derby Hat Boys can't be all that good because not one of them checked her for her sap or pistol. Mighty sloppy, that.

#19 – PAT THE CAT IS BACK IN BLACK

Liverpool, 16th October, 1865

Aston Tierney appears nearly as wide as he is tall, without a square inch of fat on his entire body. That's the way it has been with the men and the women of his family for generations back in the old country. They were the toughest knuckles in Roscommon, but they were smart enough to get out of Ireland long before the blight. It was opportunity that brought the Tierneys to England rather than hunger, which goes to prove how not every Irish family saw the disaster of the 1840s as the end of the world.

Richer pickings were and are to be had in England, and the clan didn't need to go any further than Liverpool. He was a bare-knuckle champion from the age of 16, flooring men twice his age, but opponents kept dying in the ring and this had a way of putting off the tipsters and gamblers, cutting off the revenue. Perhaps young Aston was a victim of his own success, but it was a lesson he learned early: go where the money goes and let no bastard get in your way.

So his firm, the Dead Rabbits, is loosely associated with the gang of the same name established in New York, Boston and Chicago, with mutually beneficial trading links in terms of contraband and stolen goods travelling between the four cities, but that's really where the affiliation ends. 'Dead Rabbits' is a suitably vile and macabre name for a gang, or at least a franchise name, a gang that he inherited from the poor prick who preceded him who ended up with old Davy Jones after a tragic accident in Liverpool Bay during a fishing trip. So tragic it was.

The best earner in the entire borough comes from the percentage of profits from the hotels that are on the books of the Rabbits, the places that offer those extra services and comforts which form the main source of Aston Tierney's revenue, even more than the 'trading' activities on the docks. Aston can get you, your business, or your clients anything, provided you pay the man his worth. It's tidy and there are no competitors. For very good reasons.

Any eejit in the entire borough with half an idea about what really goes on could tell you this information, which makes Pat's current assignment all the more beset with jangling nerves, heebie-jeebies and a swarm of mad, stinging wasps about his guts.

It is around 1am on a Monday morning, as quiet a time as any to be picking your way up the back whitewashed wall of The Washington Hotel without attracting attention. A new phalanx of business types will arrive later, whereas many of the other guests would have checked out to catch a train or a steamer, so there is a minimal number of eyes and ears around. Having said that, haystack Tierney will be somewhere on site, as The Washington Hotel is Dead Rabbit central, the biggest and best earner of all their portfolio of interests, close to many of the other 'sponsored' establishments. As Pat climbs, wedging his fingers into cracks between bricks, bare feet gripping window ledges and finding impossible toe holds, he half expects Aston's giant fucking head to pop out and that beady, black-eyed glare to be upon him, his long-bearded mouth frothing like an ogre with a hard-on. Even the thought of Tierney terrifies the shit out of him more than any other man he's met, and Pat has met some extremely terrifying men up close and personal in his time. Pat has a long and colourful history with the Tierney clan, one which would cause him to avoid them in normal circumstances. The problem is, normal circumstances haven't existed for many months now. Why does he keep getting himself into these pickles? Why did it have to be Aston Tierney on the other end of this?

The layout of the hotel is such that he can only access the upper corridor rather than the suite directly from the rear of the building. He'd thought to go right up the front or sneak in via the lobby, but he'd have been a sitting duck right from the get-go. The blessing is that he is able to jemmy the sash window with ease and without making any noise. He goes in feet first, making a soft landing upon the plush pile carpet. The corridor is dimly lit and quiet as a cave, red like a bruised womb. This place is a glorified knocking shop, the biggest in town, and it stands out prouder than a honeymooner's dick, plumb opposite Lime Street

Station. God knows how many poor girls have ended up in here, but he can only save one of them tonight.

He glides along the soft carpet, grateful that it isn't bare boards, towards the middle room of the passage. At the far end, he can make out a very Irish-sounding fiddle, guffaws and grunting, which indicates that the Rabbits are having themselves a nice little seisiún tonight. It reassures him, as a place can be too quiet sometimes. Closer and closer, but then the far door opens.

'Ye arse stinks, Collins!'

'Go and have a shit willya!'

Collins stumbles out, farting and laughing. Another bruiser of a man. He has his back to Pat, who must move quickly. The middle door is locked as expected, so he pulls his wire and slides it into the mortice, finding the catch and slipping inside just as Collins turns, nearly tripping over his own feet.

Pat guides the door shut and waits for Collins to traipse past, heart thumping, his own arse going but for very different reasons to the malodourous Rabbit. He could swear that this type of work used to be much easier. Cleaning windows has made him soft, but then while Pat has stolen all kinds in his life, he has never stolen a baby.

The smell of lavender is everywhere in the suite and the carpets are even softer and deeper. It is pitch black, so he negotiates the short passageway carefully, mindful of vases and furniture. One trip or clumsy knock, and he's deader than a dead rabbit. He gets to the far room, which – according to that Hampson trollop – is where baba Conté will be, and mercifully it is flooded with moonlight. The kid sleeps in a cot, but there's another in here, beneath a blanket on a chaise longue, no older than a child herself, given the shape's size. Miss Hampson went to great lengths to describe this one, but a half-crazed idea pops into his head to wake her up and save her into the bargain. Christ, it's that other one from the ballroom, the one who can sing. How close were they on the day that Harriet finally lost faith in them? This older kid might not know it, but she needs redemption just as much as the two-year-old snoozing in the cot. His eldest boy, Finn, must be the same age, or thereabouts.

Silly, silly ideas, Pat. Yes, far too soft these days. The problem with not drinking is that it allows a conscience to fester and nag him. He edges towards the cot and peeps over the rail. That's the little pig alright, same button nose, same rosy little angel face, just a bit longer but no less cute. Now it is time to right a wrong. No child should ever see a place like this, and this one will mercifully not be able to remember it.

Baba Conté's eyes flicker open, and Pat presses a finger to his lips. She smiles and copies him. 'Ah, little angel y'are,' he whispers, 'I'll get ye back to ye Mammy.'

'Mammy!'

'Who the fuckin' hell are you?' grunts a voice behind him, way too old and coarse to ever come from a thirteen-year-old's mouth.

'Ah, right then,' says Pat.

They don't normally throw women in this bridewell, but they made an exception for Harriet. They're clearly unsure what to do with her, else she'd be packed and trussed and on a train to London and some godforsaken HQ. Still, she's expecting some sort of interrogation, followed by the neatest possible way of getting rid of her. The only hope is they don't fully understand her role in all of this, or the connection back to Butler.

She is in this particular gaol by accident or by invention, but it does not matter as the resulting distress is equal. This is the very same bridewell once run by Payton Ake, that man whose very name Harriet can barely countenance, that man who ended her world. Certain things run around the issue, like the orphans he left, which Harriet placed into a good home, or the killing of his dear friend Captain Frank that led to his actions, but the question remains of how such a devoted father could do such terrible things? Terrible times make for people doing terrible things, of course, but even so, she will never fathom it. Perhaps some of the monster escaped from him into her when he did that deed, an insatiable thirst for revenge bubbling under at every waking moment. She struggles to contain it, not least in this red brick dungeon.

Rats assemble in the dark corners, with the gaol free from Ake's famous hygiene regime these days. That smell of sandalwood is what she'll never forget, lingering about Conté's room at 101 Canning, on his person just before she tugged the string on her booby trap and ended his world too. It has long gone but is immediately present at the same time.

Keys jangle, and the cell door opens. Here we are, the Derby Hat Brigade. Finally, they've worked something out for this American troublemaker, have they?

'Hello, Harriet.'

Except it's not. Not a bowler hat in sight. Just a woman in plain dress, but replete with a certain poncho made up of human scalps and that signature thin smile. Kate Warne offers her a handshake, but Harriet is straight to business. 'How did they let you in here? Have you done a deal with the Limeys?'

'Not likely, young lady. Never likely.'

'Then how?'

'There are two types of police officer in Liverpool. Straight-up British ex-servicemen and Irish knuckles. One type you can bribe, the other will let you rot in here until told otherwise by their superiors in London. Fortunately for you, the Irish are in the majority here. Rather like Chicago, if you recall.'

How long has it been? And still she tries to instruct Harriet like a schoolmistress. Warne's presence indicates that the Derby Hats have bigger fish to fry than her. What is at play here? What does she want after all this time? 'So, go on, Kathy. Prey tell.'

Warne leans against the door frame and takes Harriet in. There's always been this weird flirtation about her body language, at once sexual and motherly. This is not about currying favour or extracting information, this woman has a genuine shine for her, albeit in a corrupted mind. Where reciprocation or even acceptance is ever possible, that would be fine, but right now, Warne just makes her skin crawl. 'I'd like to say I've missed you, Kathy. But, well, this is kinda all your fault, I'm afraid.'

'*My* fault?'

'Well yes, if you go back far enough. You and Allan sold us to Butler.'

'Oh, my giddy Aunt. Bitter are we?'

The poncho looks bigger than last time, like quite a few more additions have been made since they last crossed paths. 'You handed us over to Butler, so this is all on you and the

Pinkertons. This whole, sorry mess. Be careful with the monster you created, Kathy.'

'Ha,' she chuckles, reaching into her pocket for a pack of cheroots. She offers one to Harriet, who declines. Then she lights up. 'Can't get decent baccy anywhere in this country. Too stale.'

'So you don't deny it?'

'You're entitled to your opinion.' Warne glances around the cell. 'Which is just about the only thing you have in the world right now. And if you are looking for someone to blame, you have done an excellent job of contributing to your own mess.'

Harriet pulls her Colt .45 and points it at Warne's nose. 'You're right, Kathy. I shouldn't take it personally.'

'Now, how far is that going to get you? Silly girl, I thought you'd learned a thing or two over the years.'

'You said it, *old* girl. I've got nothing left. So tell me why I shouldn't let you have it and take the satisfaction to the gallows? Or end it for both of us right here and now? You rather deserve to get popped, things you've done.'

'Because you'll never give up on your baby girl, and then you want Butler's ass on a platter.' Harriet can't help but curl a lip. 'Which is exactly what we want, too. Thus, we have come full circle. Oh happy day.'

'I don't believe a word that comes out of your mouth.'

'Well, I am leagues below Benjamin when it comes to lying and manipulation, dear. But consider the case for my defence. He's forced you into apprehending Surratt. He played you and Conté two years ago, all to gain traction in his campaign for power. The man is a singular disaster for the United States, for me, for you, for your baby, for the entire civilised world. He will never stop until he *is* stopped.'

Harriet keeps the pistol trained on her. The proposition of disconnecting Warne's brains from her skull is no less tempting, but she feels mercifully cold. 'You've changed your tune.'

'Let's just say, things came to a head between him and Allan.'

'Tell me something I don't know. I don't care.'

Warne glances down the corridor. 'Oh, I think you do.'

'Oh, I think you're full of shit.'

This is all getting a little Mexican for Warne. Harriet is enjoying the moment. 'Want me to call the warder, then? Yell that I am being held hostage?'

'Do what you like, and I will do what I like.'

'Seriously, smart-assed repartee forgiven, we are together in one hell of a bind, Harriet. Butler has spies, even within The Agency. That's how he got to Lincoln. Three bodyguards that should have been at Ford's Theatre that night didn't show. They vanished. He's played all of us and he's still playing you. I can get you out of here. Get your baby back.'

'And what will you want from me?'

'You return to the fold. You work for Allan Pinkerton again. Equilibrium restored.'

'Him? You? Not fucking likely. I don't work for anyone now, nor will I ever again.'

'You work for Butler. You will *always* work for Butler unless you do something about him.' Warne holds up her hands in surrender. 'Shoot me if I'm wrong.'

'You came halfway across the world to tell me that, Kathy? You *gave* me, us, to Butler. We didn't choose him.'

Warne offers that thin smile again, a pathetic attempt to appear human. 'Allan authorised it because we had designs upon New Orleans and Butler was best placed at the time. I argued against it but to no avail.'

'I'm sure you argued real hard, Kathy.'

'Harriet, I came halfway across the world to tell you that we are trying to save it. I know the plans the British have. Do you?'

'Not interested.'

'Oh, you will be.'

'Cocksure, ain't you, Kathy? You forget what happened in this town two years ago.'

'You want a Congressional Medal of Honour, honey? National hero, heroine?'

'That would be a good start, yes. I'll have all of those if you can arrange them for me.'

'Stop playing hard to get, you naughty girl,' mews Warne. There she goes again. 'Name your price for that note. Anything you desire.'

'Except for a medal?' she says, unable to progress from her sour tones.

Suddenly, Butler's precious memorandum burns a hole in Harriet's pocket. She could knock Warne out with her sap and exchange outfits before escaping, but she will put up a fight and that will alert the peeler station, which will mean endgame. Ditto for a gunshot. That clothes swap thing never works, either. 'So you want to destroy Butler, bully for you. But how are you going to defeat the British Empire? Where is it going to stop?'

'Not defeat. Subvert. Protect them from themselves. We want an ally, a trading partner, not an enemy. Common language, common principals and laws.'

'Like burning natives out of their homes. Or starving them, enslaving them. Yes, plenty in common.'

'Great Britain and America should never be at loggerheads again and that is the policy of President Johnson himself. All that other business is not for the likes of us to change, dear. You, of all people, should know that this game is messy.'

'Why always me, Kathy? Goddamn, just tell me. I'm just one woman and her daughter. Can you people not just leave me alone?'

'Are you coming, or are you going to stay here and scratch that nice ass of yours, gal?'

If she goes with Warne, she'll have to put up with her weird ways. But there's no sign of any other way out, bar shooting a peeler and ending up dead, real fast. Then where does that leave Baba? The opportunity that she wanted has come, unexpected as it was. Warne smokes and smiles at her, comfortable that Harriet is doing all the figuring now.

The Pinkertons must have paid good money for this bust as questions might well be asked, but Harriet is able to stride straight out of the Campbell Square Bridewell with Warne at her side as if she is a ghost. Warne even has a sturdy horse waiting for her in the yard. 'Follow me. And for God's sake, don't go waving that shooting iron at anyone.'

They mount and canter out of the yard before turning onto the wider drag of Duke Street and forming a gallop.

Letting the dirt settle, Princess Grace watches from the shadows, just as adept at staying out of the eyeline as any other agent, including the two women who have just ridden away in quite the brazen bust.

'Oh, Miss.'

It got a bit rough, but not as rough as it is about to get. Pat sits cross-legged on the floor in the adjacent suite, arse planted into the plush pile carpet. Aston is daubed across an armchair like it's the throne of England. He eats a meat pie, enjoying the crust and jelly. Pat expected tarts and booze everywhere, but as far as Aston is concerned, he is a family man with no compunction to drink or fornicate, although he lets his entourage indulge to their hearts' content. Provided his boys and girls do a good job, they're grand, which they will always do for Aston because they love him. Or so he would lead them to believe. Not a person in this room isn't shit-scared of Aston Tierney, and that fear – masquerading as love and respect – runs long and deep across the Borough of Liverpool. Pat knows Tierney of old and his clan. Pat knows the truth about them and him.

Aston chomps the pie and picks up another, scoffing it down. The man enjoys his food alright. He must be one of the richest hoodlums in town, yet he looks like he has just come off a stevedoring job on the docks, working nights. Huge, pile-driving fists, forearms like ham-hocks, neck as thick as a Doric pillar. Pat can only wait here and hope, aware that Aston's boys and girls have indeed done a good job for him again tonight.

'Savoury, mmm.'

'Aye, Aston.'

He belches and wipes his mouth on his sleeve. 'Was starving, Pat.'

'Aye, Aston.'

'Aye. This job keeps weird hours, so. That was me dinner, would ye believe it? Gone two o'clock in the morning. I barely see daylight or me ankle-biters. But there's no one else to run the business, not until my own boys grow up.'

'Aye, Aston.'

He interlocks his fingers and regards Pat. 'I'm a bit curious as to the nature of your visit this evening, Pat. You're after stealing nippers now? Jewels not enough for yer?'

'I stopped all that years ago, Aston. On account of Royston dying and so. And it isn't theft. All I want to do is return a child to her mother.'

'Ah, right so. Royston Chubb. Can't say I ever liked that fella too much. Caused the riot on Lime Street, so he did. Cost us thousands, so he did. Damage to businesses. All a bit shitty. Someone did us a favour in slotting him, I'd say.'

'He was my friend, Aston.'

'You keep telling yourself that, son. Royston feathered his own nest.'

Pat feels a well of anger forming in his stomach, bubbling up with the toxic, mortal fear. It is a poisonous stew that ferments with the knowledge that Aston Tierney usually gives people who cross him short shrift.

'Aye.'

'Aye. This looks like an inside job, though. I'm awfully suspicious of it. You mind telling me who put yers up to it? Was it that very important Consul fella? The American?'

'That baby is the daughter of a very important person, Aston. There are bigger things happening. Bigger than even you. You should have said something when we came to see you.'

A collective gasp in the room. Aston picks his teeth. 'Bigger than The Rabbits? That so? Wow.'

He gets to his feet and stands on Pat's balls with the heel of his hobnail boot. Pat yelps. Here it comes. At least Sarah and the children are far away enough to start a new life without him. 'You fuckin' know it, you big, nasty, greedy fuck. Get off me. Let me fight you at least.'

Aston chuckles and lifts his boot, rewarding Pat for his open insolence. 'Aye, that's me, Padraig. Greedy, and it's the only way to be in this town. And what are you, son? The second coming? A martyr? Dirty, ratty Cavan culchie, so. Scurrying up walls and pretending it's normal.'

Pain wracks Pat's nethers, but he forces himself up onto his knees and to his feet. 'What of it, big man? You can do your worst.'

'He makes it sound like he's giving me permission. What a silly bollocks you are.' Aston pulls out a long blade. 'A bollocks soon to have no bollocks. What will we call you then? Paddy no bollocks? Ye've had the last of ye ten kids, so.'

Laughs. Aston likes to perform his discipline personally and with an audience present, to maintain his repute and create folklore, but he's just another fucking bully when it comes down to it. Pat adopts a fighting stance to Aston's further amusement. 'Come on then, Tierney. I'll die with me boots on so, not like all ye simpering pricks.'

Everyone is laughing now, including the young girl who raised the alarm. A party of 20 people all in thrall to Lord Aston, savouring the impromptu entertainment that is about to be served up to them involving the removal of Pat's knackers. He considers making a dart for the window, but then he'll never get to the sash on time. This is it, to the death. He knows that it won't last long, probably quicker than drowning in the Mersey with a bit of honour thrown in.

There's a kerfuffle in the corridor, and then a couple of peelers, O'Driscoll and Rafferty, barge into the room. Aston tucks away his knife and sweeps back his greasy fringe, mopping out pie crumbs from his beard. 'Howyer, Martin. Bit sudden this, isn't it?'

'Howyer, Aston,' replies O'Driscoll, taking in the range of scumbags in the room, all of whom he will know on a first-name basis. This isn't the first time this fella has saved Pat's bacon. At least, that is what he is hoping the peeler is here for.

'Did ye not enjoy that bottle of Powers I sent ye for ye 40th?'

'Aye. S'alright, like. Thanks a million, Aston.'

'Just alright?'

'Prefer Bushmills, like. To be honest.'

'That northern piss? Alright, I can organise a case of that for ye if ye like. Now, what are you doing here then, apart from interfering with me business?'

'Come on now, Aston. You were about to slot poor little Padraig here now, were you not? Plain as day. I've good enough eyes, so.'

Pat pipes up, probably unwisely, but the only way is attack. 'This giant, knuckle-dragging fuck kidnapped a child, so he did. He's in the business of buying and selling them. Fuckin' wholesale, like.'

Aston is wide-eyed and incredulous. 'What? Mad culchie, so! He's been at the poitín again, Martin. Look at the daft, squidgy face on him.'

'He has got a daft face, but you just let it go, Aston. Then we'll have heard the last of it. You've no need, have you? Really?'

'Like I say, Martin. You're interfering with my business. This isn't the arrangement. And I made that arrangement with your boss, not you.'

'File a complaint, then.'

Aston holds up his huge hands and grins, but Pat knows that Aston Tierney never lets something go. Whatever Mr Dudley did to persuade the two peelers to intervene, it is only a temporary reprieve. Pat has to take this opportunity to talk sense into Aston, as impossible as that is.

'Aston, look,' he says, 'You're my countryman, a Fenian Brother, yes?'

'Not sure I'm that arsed. What of it?'

'So there are things afoot that threaten our cause, our country, perhaps even damn it. I assure you and the United States Consul.'

Aston nods, as if he's listening. 'Martin, this little knacker's definitely been at the sauce, so he has. I mean, look at him; he'd drink piss out of a leper's boot, so, the dirty ticket. Can ye not just leave it to me? I really want to scrap him now. He's as useful as tits on a nun and altogether more troublesome.'

'No Aston, you heard me first time,' says O'Driscoll, deciding that enough is enough, 'Pat on your way and no more burglarising, like.'

'I so wasn't burglarising! I don't rob no more!'

'Out, Padraig. And Aston, don't you be worrying about the small fry, eh?'

Aston winks at Pat as he files out with the other peeler. It is not worth arguing with O'Driscoll, but Pat knows that this isn't over. 'Square go. He's only a sprat, aye. Don't you be robbing from me again, Pat McCartney. Let that be a lesson to you, ye scamp.'

Pat leers back at Aston, whose deep, brown eyes look jet black in this dim, smoky suite. 'Pat, out, now!' grunts O'Driscoll, keen himself not to spend any more time here than he has to. Pat obliges, but he knows that his card is marked, and there is nowhere he can run. Reputation is everything. His blessed balls are on borrowed time.

He slopes out, accompanied by the two peelers who just saved his life. Will the baby be moved now? Or is Aston arrogant enough to believe that no one will challenge him in Liverpool? Probably no and probably yes, but Pat must remember that none of this is about him any more, lest he will shit his pants in terror. He has to stare the demon in the eye, whether that demon is Tierney or it is the demon drink, until the devil finally calls time on him.

Now to find Mr Dudley and work out what on God's good Earth they are going to do next.

#20 – THE DEAD RABBITS

Liverpool, 17th October 1865

'Forgive me, Father, for I have sinned.'

'You'll have to leave the Borough, John. It is not safe for you here.'

'As we have just seen, Father. Who in hell was that woman? Forgive the cursing.'

'An extra Hail Mary for that. My sources say it was Harriet Farrell, a former United States operative. Quite a piece of work for a female. She was, ahem, the cause of some mischief in this parish not long ago. She has Butler's note, no thanks to those protestant idiots who arrested her and then let her slip away.'

'What, she's gone?'

'Yes, John. Who knows what damage she can inflict? Troublesome.'

'But as long as the British don't extradite me, surely I can stay?'

'Look, John, this is a busy parish. It seems patent that you are a soft target who knows rather too much to be falling into the wrong hands.'

'Cannot the British protect us?'

'Do you have any idea about the scorn they have for Catholics, John? Your release is part of the deal we have with certain powers, but they will not play nanny to you. I am quite sure that they will not bestow the favour again to us.'

'I should stay. I will stay. I have nowhere else to go.'

'You were part of a conspiracy to murder a head of state, John.'

'It was a noble cause. You absolved me, Father.'

'Giving you further sanctuary will see this church exposed.'

'My momma said that you would protect me.'

'You are a good boy, but you need to go and leave me to the affairs of God's bidding. I have connections in Rome. No American or even British agent can penetrate the Vatican. Rest assured.'

'But they don't speak English there.'

'They speak Latin. You speak Latin.'

'Sure enough. I suppose. Oh Father…'

'What is it, John?'

'I have sinned. I let my own mother go to the gallows to save my skin.'

'That is a sacrifice any good mother would make for her son, John.'

'And then I escaped with my tail between my legs. What is to be done?'

'We have a Holy Order waiting for you in Rome. You will be set for life.'

'But will I be free? No. I want to go home, Father.'

'Then you will join your mother under the sod.'

'Yes. I want that.'

'Pull yourself together. You are going to Rome.'

'This is all on that piece of shit, Butler.'

'Say another decade of the rosary for the language.'

'I'm going back to Virginia. Hang it.'

'You will hang.'

'So be it. Amen.'

'Don't try to be a hero, son. You saw where that got you last time.'

'It was a just cause to kill Lincoln. Many in the church agreed to it, including you. Including the…'

'You need to be very careful about what you say in public, John. This is exactly why you need to be in the Vatican.'

'The Vatican will be just another prison. You just want me to keep my mouth shut, and so will they. I am plain tired of secrets, Father.'

'You *will* keep your mouth shut, John.'

'Two Hail Marys, right? Or was it three?'

'Now you listen, boy.' The curved blade forged half a millennium ago in Constantinople thrusts through the curtain and is a hair's breadth from Surratt's eye. Jovliet has clearly done this before. 'Who do you put your faith in, then?'

'Almighty God. Only Him.'

'Good. That means you will do the bidding of His representative upon Earth, will you not?'

Surratt dry gulps. Father is saving his body, if not his soul, by holding this blade to him, even if that is a bitter truth. 'Yes, Father.'

'So you may assemble your meagre possessions and follow the Holy Order to the Vatican, where you will receive sanctuary. Breathe a word of our involvement in this affair, and you will pay the full cost of death and damnation before you even reach American soil. Am I clear?'

'Yes, Father.'

'Now get out of my sight and remember your penance, my son. Add two decades of the rosary.'

'Dear Lord, young Grace.'

'Yes, Mr Dudley.'

Grace shrinks into the sumptuous, burgundy leather upholstery of the chair opposite Consul Dudley, who scratches his bald eagle pate. Her business, her Papa's life, and her life are all at risk just by being here, as the Ministry has warned her about consorting with any Americans, especially one like this man. Dudley gets up and paces, massaging the bridge of his nose. President Lincoln stares down at Grace. She never wanted any of this, but her association with Miss Harriet and the events of two years ago brought some evil men to her door. Experience tells her to trust Mr Dudley, even if the burden of guilt is making her want to grab Papa, their best horses, and flee Liverpool to start again. Ireland perhaps? Or New York?

There is one problem with that. 'The British have not paid me, sir,' she says, ashamed to let money corrupt the conversation.

Dudley goes to move, then checks himself. 'Just answer me a few questions, if you will, Miss Grace.'

'Surely, sir. If I can.'

'Why are the British protecting the conspirator Surratt?'

'I am not privy, sir.'

'No. Of course.'

'Sorry, sir.'

'Did the Foreign Office have a hand in Abraham's death?'

'You mean Lord Russell?'

'Yes. John Russell, or others.'

'Not to my knowledge. But my knowledge is thin, sir. They tell me what I need to know and no more.'

Questions he knows she cannot answer, but Grace can see that he is thinking aloud, trying to see the whole canvas in order to spot the flaws. Dudley nods and walks out of the room. She is left to herself, her own inadequacy and powerlessness; her mind beset with the turmoil of Harriet's arrest, of the betrayal of a friend. What about the child Conté? Did Russell's men really leave her with no choice? Penury is a choice; death is a choice. She could have opted for either over this wanton act. God have mercy on her.

The Consul returns with a manila envelope. He hands it to her. 'This should tide you over, Miss Grace.'

Grace doesn't need to look inside. 'That is most generous, sir.'

'It isn't my money, dear. It is the United States Government's, and the United States is buying something from you. We are buying your loyalty, if that is still in your gift.'

So, it comes to this. Britain or America? How about Africa? How about the Edo or all the other peoples? More than you can ever imagine, across vast lands. Do they ever get a choice? 'The Englishmen in round hats will hunt me down if they find out, sir.'

'We all have to take risks, I am afraid to say. Our world is not a safe place.'

A knock. O'Driscoll and Pat pour into the room. 'Thank Christ for you, Mr Dudley,' splutters Pat. Then he notices Grace. 'Oh, hello, love. Howyer?'

'Hello, Pat. I have been better.'

Dudley nods at O'Driscoll, who leaves. His man in the Constabulary never sticks around. There's someone who knows how to pick his side. Dudley hopes that it is the right side, for the sake of everyone in the room. For the sake of everyone in America.

'Are you injured?'

'No, Mr Dudley. Thanks to that peeler. How much did you slip him? Surely I cannot afford to pay you back.'

'Do not think on it, Pat. And it isn't all about the money, you know. America still has allies in this town.'

'Aye, but…'

'Your return is good timing, Pat. Miss Grace, tell him what you've just told me about Miss Harriet.'

'Darjeeling. Now the baccy here is dry and insipid. The coffee ain't much better, but these here limeys do know how to move, preserve and serve tea, for sure. Dee-lish-ous.'

'It tastes like boiled gnat's piss, Kathy.'

'Having never tasted gnat's piss, I'll just have to take your word for that.'

Harriet doesn't acknowledge Warne's retort. Gentlemen and ladies in the tea rooms glance over and mutter about them, as if two loud American women is an aberration in this town. Harriet has seen enough real aberrations in Liverpool not to care a jot about their opinions or conversations.

'So where next?'

'Show it to me, Harriet.'

'What, here?'

'Show me the note, and we'll get about the business.'

Butler's memorandum is stashed neatly within her petticoat. The chattering classes recoil as she goes for a rummage.

BURN AFTER READING.

Confirmation of plan. Mr Surratt to handle Lincoln alone. Mr Booth and Mr Atzerodt to handle Johnson, Mr Powell to handle Seward. Security will be lax tomorrow, as per my instructions. You will not see me again.

Godspeed,

BFB.

'Of course, that's not how it happened. The Surratt boy's mother was trying to protect him, so she switched the job with Booth. She ended up swinging for it, saw that myself.'

'Did you enjoy it?' says Harriet, nodding at Warne's poncho, 'Did you slip the undertaker a dollar and add to your collection?'

Warne adorns pince-nez and squints at the note. She reaches out to hold it, but Harriet snatches it back. 'You're being preposterous again, girl. You will make a scene.'

'Won't be the first or last.'

The senior woman leans in further. Warne's scent is a Parisian fragrance that fails to mask her sweating onions body odour. She could do with a good scrub around the nethers, but Harriet won't be the one to tell her. 'The stamp is genuine. Harriet, we are so, so close. I know where your child is. I can get us in.'

Yet again, Harriet considers sapping the bitch right here and now to extract the information, then going in gung ho. But the likelihood is that whoever holds Baba will have some form of protection, the extent of which is an unknown quantity. Crossfire is not good, especially as far as infants are concerned. Far better to serve that dish cold, despite the feeling that none of this will end well.

'I see.'

'You see? The thing that you want more than anything in this world is given to you, and you look like butter wouldn't melt?'

'All I have is your word, Kathy.'

'Yes, and it is a bond.'

Harriet slips Butler's memo across the desk, and Warne pockets it. The Darjeeling drinkers of the Lime Street tea rooms have returned to their pomp and gossip. They shall never know the violence that nearly occurred.

'Can we go now, Kathy?'

Warne slurps tea. 'Can I not finish my pot?' Harriet is on her feet. 'Clearly not.'

Harriet motions for Warne to lead the way. She wipes her mouth and gets up, leaving a handsome tip for the staff.

They make their way out of the rooms and through the magnificent lobby. A grand staircase of wrought iron and mahogany fittings snakes up to the top of the building. The rhythmic chuffing of steam trains and a faint smell of burning coal from the adjacent Lime Street station augments the bakery.

'I could do with the restroom,' says Warne, just as they get to the grand, revolving door.

'Not before I see my baby.'

'I will not be a minute or so.'

'You can piss your bloomers for all I care, Kathy. Do not vex me.'

'Such a touchy one, are you not?'

'I can still blow it all up and take you with me, so no tricks. Allez.'

'Right, right. Such a headstrong girl.'

They head out onto Lime Street, the townscape spreading out in front of them. St Georges' Hall is the most imposing vision, with its Doric neo-classicism, and endless length. Then, there is a succession of hotels of varying repute and quality on either side of the thoroughfare. They jaywalk the carts, traps and carriages, slaloming cattle and sheep being driven towards the docks and the horse slurry which can readily stick to ankle-length dresses. Many come a cropper in merely trying to cross these roads, but it ain't the traffic that worries her today. Harriet has a firm hand on her pistol inside her petticoat, alert to Warne herself and any other dangers that may accost her.

They cross St George's Plateau towards a grand terrace of semi-palatial establishments, 'semi' being the operative disclaimer as Harriet knows all about their reputation, particularly the most notorious of them, The Washington Hotel. As Warne leads her towards the entrance, she curses herself for missing such an obvious lead. Who would you go to in Liverpool for any service or goods if you really wanted the very best with no questions asked? Why, the Dead Rabbits, of course. She circled the den for months, even entering it at one point. How close was she?

'Shit. Fuck.'

'You see, Butler may have his spies in our camp, dear. But we have our spies in *his*.' Warne couldn't look more pleased with herself in making this statement. The great scramble for power continues, and Harriet is all too aware that she has found herself in the middle of something altogether awful again. So has her sweet baby girl.

They enter the lobby, which will never be the Ritz of Paris, but harbours even more wealth than its salubrious cousin, albeit from nefarious sources. A garish billboard depicts *"Madame de Pomfrette avec La Mademoiselle Foufou" – Matinees and Evenings at The Washington Hotel Ballroom*, with de Pomfrette's name scrubbed from the bill. The reception committee is dressed up to the nines, just Aston Tierney himself in a three-piece suit, clutching a dragon-headed cane with a gold handle. Tierney has made an effort for Warne.

'Hello, Mrs Warne. Welcome to The Washington.'

'Ms.'

'Right you are. And this must be *Miss* Farrell again?'

'Do not fucking talk to me,' mutters Harriet. She last sampled this cocktail of fear and loathing with her deceased husband Banastre, but at least this time she doesn't have to hide the contempt across her face.

'Feisty. I get it. You're the mammy.'

Warne is keen to interject. 'Darjeeling, please. I thought you'd never ask.'

'Beg pardon, Miss Warne?'

'Do you have Darjeeling tea?'

'We have anything you desire, Miss Warne. Come this way.'

'You know, Major General Butler's office and our business go back a ways. It is a real shame to banjax all that so.'

They're in the penthouse; a splendid view across the curved roof of Lime Street Station is available from the large window. Tierney perches on an armchair, legs spread rather too wide, spouting self-aggrandising small talk, although everything he says has some kind of barb hidden inside the dense, Irish country vernacular. Warne savours her tea, Harriet leers through him, hoping that she can will his head to explode. Of course, she could make that happen, but the room is full of Dead Rabbits and there is still no Baba. Her trigger finger itches.

'You are two peas in a pod,' says Warne, 'at either side of the pond.'

'Surely, ma'am. He put the tender out to every firm in town for that little Cammell Laird job your little agent here ballsed up. Remember that? He gave it to that Donegal donkey-arsed eejit Chubb. That was an error of judgement. Should have come to the Rabbits, so he should. Always come to the Rabbits, in any town or city.'

If Butler had chosen the Rabbits, Harriet probably wouldn't be sitting here right now. She thanks God for small mercies, but she didn't force herself in here to listen to this bluster. 'Where is my child, Tierney?'

'Safe, dearie. Safer than anywhere in this town or even the world.'

Harriet's heart thuds. It is so difficult to retain composure, for all of her training and the bitter, hard taskmaster of experience. 'So bring her out to me.'

'Kitty,' says Tierney, his teeth canine, like the mouth of some feral, mythical beast, 'Come and meet Miss Farrell.'

A young slip of a girl dressed to appear rather older appears from behind the throng of knuckle-dragging men. She approaches the floor, standing between the Americans and Tierney as if she is about to begin a recital. The kid is a little too familiar to Harriet, even though she knows that they have never met in this lifetime.

'You must be La Mademoiselle Foufou.'

'Right you are, Miss Farrell,' says Tierney, enjoying the sport of it. 'Such a Foufou she is.'

Eyes sear into Kitty. She has dressed – or has been dressed – for the occasion in a tight black dress that exudes respectability where there is none. Even the Rabbits understand the importance of appearances. The kid looks hard beyond her years, which is probably what Harriet sees in her that reminds her of herself. Either way, she has a dreadful feeling about this. 'Miss…'

Tierney's brow folds as she stutters. 'Spit it out, Kitty. I can't fathom what has gotten into her today. She's never this nervous, usually such a brash little thing. Come on, girl. You've nothing to worry about, so.'

Kitty bursts into tears. Harriet wants to grab her and talk to her, console her even. She knows grief when she sees it.

'Speak,' interjects Warne, a little too forcefully.

'Sally…'

'Who?' grunts Warne.

'Your baby… Miss Farrell. She was well taken care of. I looked after her myself. Loved her. She was lovely.'

'*Was?*'

'Ah, would you look at that,' says Tierney. 'That's what my customers pay for. Madamwhatsit Foufou. Top billing now, so she is.'

'*Was?*' Harriet seethes, seeing this play starting to unravel. She should have kept that note, but then she never would have made it through the door of The Washington.

'I never meant for Miss Audrey to get hurt. Too bad, like. Even though she was a bitch.'

'Not now, Kitty.'

Kitty glances over at Tierney, and her tears are immediately cancelled. Harriet sees even more now. This is a hand of poker and this big, greedy, dirty bastard knows he holds all the cards. He signals Kitty to stand down. The kid shuffles out of the room, head bowed. Crossing paths with her is an instantly recognisable man in a tweed suit.

'Your child is safe, Miss Farrell,' says Allan Pinkerton.

'You must be mighty desperate, Pinkerton. Coming all this way,' grunts Harriet, pinning herself to the chair. The room is full of demons, and the head demon has just checked in.

'How dare you address your superior in that tone,' says Warne, in that indecipherable, half-joking, half-serious manner of hers. Of course, Allan is where her bread is buttered, always and forever.

'Shut up, cunt,' says Harriet, fair ready to make an example of her, to show these terrible bastards what she is made of. Is she worse than Pinkerton just because she is a woman? Is this her own bias at play? Yes, no, maybe. So what?

Pinkerton steps up to Tierney and puts a hand on his shoulder. 'Thanks to Mr Tierney's impressive logistics, we have moved young Conté to a secure location, a safe house if you will.' His Scottish burr barely fits a man of such influence in American political life.

So just what is at play here? Why does Pinkerton want this? Why is he here, outbidding Butler for the sake of a small child? Why not just ask him? 'What do you want, then?' asks Harriet.

'I couldn't possibly tell you in present company,' says Pinkerton. He turns to Tierney, 'Need to know, you'll understand. But I will say that you are perfect for the role, Harriet. A veritable model of the skills required.'

'So, it's a job? Butler had the same mind and there is no difference between you.'

'Ah, but there is. You see, he is a traitor of the worst order, and I am a patriot of the first order.'

'You are a Scottish turd. Why can't you leave me alone?'

Warne steps up. 'How dare you.'

She turns back to Warne, inches from her insipid breath. 'And you, are just a cunt.'

Harriet goes for the only angle she can see. 'You best be careful, Aston. You've just double-crossed one of the most powerful men on the planet. He will come after you.'

'You mean that fat knacker?' retorts Tierney, the wilful ass amused at his own reply, 'Let's see him try. Nah. And he's friggin' miles away, so.' He blows a raspberry. Guffaws.

'You really have no idea, have you?' replies Harriet.

Pinkerton turns to her. 'Look at you, all grown up. With a child of your own now. What will you teach her? What promise you still have.' Harriet spots Warne flinching at Pinkerton's flattery, as if that matters more than anything to her. 'You can go amazing places, dear. You just need a helping hand.'

'I don't want or need anything from you.'

'I think that you're missing the obvious. Come with Kate and I. We will brief you.' Pinkerton motions for Warne to stand, and she obeys like the poodle she has always been. A channel opens up through Tierney's thugs to the door. 'Mr Tierney, we will be in touch.'

'Good man yourself,' says Tierney.

Harriet gets to her feet and follows The Pinkerton Detective Agency out of the room, ignoring the grinning Tierney and his slavering gang of Dead Rabbits.

For the second time in as many days, John Surratt arrives at the Landing Stage at George's Dock, but this time he knows exactly where he is going. This here Liverpool was far from being the sanctuary he sought, rather it is identical to the pit of snakes that he fled in D.C. Stick around for longer and it might get worse, even.

The boat awaits, and he traverses the jetty with Father Jovliet at his side, him not taking his beady, narrow eyes away until his charge is safely on board the Naples-bound barque. Upon arrival there, young Surratt will be collected by members of the Swiss Guard and transferred to Rome and the Holy See, to be bound over in Vatican City until the threat has diminished to the church's reputation in the United States. This is the price of faith and of his flight to freedom, which has just become another form of bondage.

He boards the gangway and Jovliet watches him walk up before leaving without further ceremony or so much as a goodbye. Surratt clutches his small, tatty case and waits for the priest to turn his back before popping it open and pulling out a $20 bill and an envelope addressed to *Mr C. Prioleau, Fraser, Trenholm & Co, 19 Abercromby Square.*

'For you, momma. And for my sins.'

A passing Customs Officer takes the bill and the envelope in a single deft move and heads back up the gangway and back onto the jetty just as the ship's horn blows. Surratt spits a morsel of his bitterness into the Mersey swell and enters the passenger lounge.

#21 – THE EUSTON EXPRESS

Liverpool, Hampshire and London, October 18th, 1865

Foxhills at the Romsey estate in the idyllic meadows of Hampshire, mid-morning. Surrounding Lord Palmerston The Prime Minister's bed are his wife Emily, the stepson William Cowper-Temple, the family physician, Edward Seymour, the 12th Duke of Somerset and First Lord of the Admiralty, and Inspector Blake of Scotland Yard. The Prime Minister had caught a chill a few days previously, which is the story that the press will get in due course.

'Any traces?' mutters Seymour. Palmerston is getting colder by the second.

'If he was poisoned, they knew what they were doing,' replies Blake, checking Palmerston's temperature and scribbling notes.

'So, he was poisoned?'

Emily cries. Cowper-Temple leers at Seymour. 'Must you? Now? He was an old man, for God's sake.'

'Shut up, son. I repeat, Mr Blake. Was the Prime Minister poisoned?'

'I have no evidence, sir.'

'Oh, Henry,' wails the old wife, and Palmerston starts to gasp, his breath shortening.

The Prime Minister sits bolt upright and stares directly at Seymour, who flinches with surprise. 'That's Article 98; now go on to the next, Eddie.'

'Yes, Pammy.' How many years has he nursed Pammy? Waiting for this moment, waiting for the succession. Not once did he consider slipping his old friend some sort of concoction to speed up the process, even though Pammy hung on and hung on. Then, that short-legged bastard Russell steams in at the opportune moment. He can't say that to many people in private, let alone public, but Eddie knows alright. Pammy holds his hand in an iron grip.

Lord Palmerston smiles and relaxes, drawing his last. His physician checks his vitals. Emily wails, Cowper-Temple comforts her. Seymour shakes his head and leaves the room.

'We're done for. Done for. That opium-crazed maniac will get the reigns now. Bah, fuck it.'

The door slams. All those at Palmerston's bedside glance at each other. Emily resumes her wailing.

The steam train powers through Hertfordshire, green scenery slowly giving way to canals, warehouses and pea-soup fog. London looms like the mouth of a giant, blackened, sandstone monster, the centre of the civilised world receiving more visitors from its upstart satellite in the North. It does not care if those visitors are American; it is never outraged by the novelty or culture that it imports. This metropolis announces to any visitor that it is bigger and better than anywhere on the planet, and its inhabitants know that any other place – even within the British Isles – is forever going to be inferior and copyist in comparison.

Harriet steps off from the carriage onto the platform at Euston Station, flanked by Warne and Pinkerton, those two tweed shadows hidden in plain sight again. If British agents were watching, they would be picked up in moments, which indicates that they are not. A whiff of rotting meat and choking, smokestack grime invades her nostrils, similar to Liverpool but without the cleansing brine to mitigate it. They enter a spectacular entrance hall that could well be the Roman Senate, such is it an ode to Classicism, to impel the visitor again to be immediately aware that London is indeed bigger, better and richer than anywhere else. Perhaps, but it still stinks of shit, piss, smoke and death.

'We can proceed on foot from here,' says Warne as she parades through the arch, pointing in the direction of Bloomsbury on the other side of Euston Road, a slightly greener environment, which is their destination on what Harriet hopes is a flying visit to the capital.

'I am not an apothecary. Need I repeat?'

'Harriet, my sweet,' there she goes again, flirting. 'You only need to know what we have briefed you.'

'Why can't you do it? Or one of your local snoops? Why all this?'

Pinkerton bristles. 'If you have any more dumb questions, you can ask them on the train back. Let us get on.'

He pushes her forwards, and they cross Euston Road into an unfamiliar place with hidden dangers. Yes, it was a dumb question. They need a patsy, lest all of this goes wrong, which it is very prone to doing. American intelligence got them this information, but if the British are to find a smoking gun, the perfect rogue agent is Harriet Farrell: disaffected, unhinged and even a bit Irish, all of which has a convincing ring to it. Pinkerton knows that she will keep her mouth shut and stick to the story she has been given for the sake of her daughter. Both him and Warne are indeed just as bad as BF Butler in every way, whatever their agenda.

She still has her sap and pistol on her body, but they are not of any use in this situation. Harriet scans around her, looking for a conduit or alley to dash to – make an escape and reform – but her heart pumps too hard as she drags the anvil of grief and sorrow behind her. Something has got to give today.

'What kind of a world are we living in when a young woman is slain like that, and the man who did it is not brought to account? It is evil, so. Plain evil.'

Pat's outburst is partly due to the nagging worry that a similar fate to Miss Hampson awaits his own person, once Aston Tierney catches up with him. She was found in a pit behind the under-construction Prince of Wales Theatre in not much of an encore performance. Her throat was slit with her tongue pulled down and out of the wound like some grotesque Oxford knot, a signature Dead Rabbit murder and a message from Aston to all and sundry. He leaves them regularly.

'I tried to task Mr O'Driscoll to investigate it, but there isn't enough tea in China to pay him for that one,' says Dudley.

'Jaysus, Mary and Joseph.'

'Do not curse so,' mutters Grace, so subdued they'd almost forgotten that she was in the carriage, save for the fact that her horses draw it along.

'Sorry, Grace.'

'Accepted. I understand your fear, but I tire of so many oaths.' Who knows if the British men in hats aren't watching Grace? They could come calling at her stables at any moment. Along with her Papa, they are defenceless.

They all know these things, but they have to carry on. Harriet's child has been moved from The Washington Hotel; that much is clear from Dudley's remaining snitches, or those who dared to snitch. No one knows to where, but the story went that their friend was seen parlaying with Aston and a couple of tweed-wearing Americans: a middle-aged male and a male-acting female. Harriet left with them, and that is where the trail runs dry.

Dudley offered Pat a ticket to New York on the next steamer, plus some recompense in order to set up with his lady wife upon their reunification. It conflicted the Consul, but he wanted to offer Pat safety after what had happened to Miss Hampson. Tempting as it was for Pat and dangerous as it is to his person right here, Pat resolved that this is not the right time to cut and run. There are three left in Harriet's corner, whether she knows it or not. She never abandoned him, so he shall not abandon Harriet. Mr Dudley was grateful beyond words, perhaps more than anything not to have to proceed without him.

Thus, they sit outside the erstwhile unofficial headquarters of the Confederacy at 19 Abercromby Square, now the second, bigger garret in town of Fraser, Trenholm & Co, a South Carolinian company. It has made some $9 million from blockade-running vessels during the war, according to Mr Dudley's assiduous figures presented time and again to British courts, during the Consul's relentless campaign to challenge this illegal activity and get the assets seized.

As seems plain by the opulence on show here and inside the building, this campaign stalled and failed for the better part, prolonging the war by months, perhaps even years. All they can do now is watch and wait for Messrs Bulloch and Prioleau to leave for the night, so they might enter the building and search for any evidence they can find that can subvert their new supporters in Westminster. It's a long shot, but apart from saving Harriet and her baby directly, this is all they can do right now.

A carriage draws past and stops outside. As the front door opens, Dudley spots the painting of a Palmetto tree just inside the entrance, fully aware of the regiment it represents. The banker who fronts it all, that French Huguenot Carolinian swine Prioleau, struts out of the Georgian façade and enters the carriage, followed by Bulloch.

'Why didn't ye do this before, Mr Dudley?'

'Because I was acting in accordance with British law and maritime law. What we call breaking and entering, they call trespassing. An imprisonable offence.'

'So, what's changed?' Dudley glances at Pat, tilting his chin. 'Oh, sorry. Yes, I savvy. Had too many punches in the face over the years, so I have. Gone a bit thick, so I have.'

'Grace, can you get this carriage around the rear entry?'

'Surely, Mr Dudley.'

Grace climbs up into the driver's seat and manoeuvres her two ponies across the cobbles. 'It's a good job I don't care much for the rule of law now, Pat. Not with what we're about to do.'

'I've never cared for it either. Or the people what make them.'

'Good then. So my lesson to you two fine people today is that if you want to discover anything at all about the rich and powerful, you follow the money. Your lesson to me is about how to conduct an illegal entry to a building.'

'Grand, so watch and learn, and vice versa like, Mr Dudley.'

'Let me look at you.'

Warne examines Harriet from head to toe like she is a child entering her first day at Sunday School. The brown coat fits rather too snugly over her frame, being tailored for a smaller woman, but Harriet will pass for a shop assistant at *GC Cruickshank's Apothecary and Modern Dispensary* on Marchmont Street, right in the heart of an estate of London almost exclusively owned by the 1st Earl Russell. A regular shopping visit with the utmost discretion guaranteed. No need for Derby Hats, she would hope. It is late afternoon and already dark, not far off closing time. Russell is as regular as clockwork in his daily visits here, as if stocking up too much on his favourite elixir might rouse his enemies and sully his reputation.

Even after the overtures in Parliament to outlaw the concoction, laudanum remains widely available, but Russell is a man who requires such discretion, given his status in the public eye. *GC Cruickshank* rents the property from the Russell estate, upon one special condition that it supplies the former and possibly future Prime Minister with what he wants, when he wants it. Undoubtedly, too, Cruickshank makes the best laudanum concoction in all of London.

Warne licks her thumb and brushes a few stray hairs back beneath the surgical bonnet adorned by Harriet. Pinkerton consults his pocket watch. 'He's due.'

'Out you go, Harriet,' says Warne, still in schoolmistress mode. Fuck her to death.

Harriet walks out from the storeroom into the shop. She is the only assistant on duty today, as Mr Cruickshank and his staff have been unavoidably detained by a series of planned mishaps. Due diligence complete. Copies of the keys to the shop were procured and the rest is as straightforward as such a plot should get.

Harriet glances at the wall clock, then at the jars and phials of just about every surgical substance, elixir and tincture available to the public. Under the counter is everything that is unavailable to the public. To the sound of a bell, her one and only client strides through the door and approaches the counter.

'Good afternoon, sir.'

Russell squints at her and glances over her shoulder to the back. 'Where's Cruickshank today?'

'Unavoidably detained.'

'Oh? Ah?'

'Staff illness in his other shop.'

'Ah, you are new.'

'I was drafted in from the other shop in Southwark as cover, sir. Mr Cruickshank left very specific instructions regarding your requirements.'

'Other shop, other shop, other shop. Mr Cruickshank should have informed me directly of the change. I deal with him exclusively.'

'He sent a despatch to your office. Did you not receive it, sir?'

Russell twitches. Why do the Pinkertons want this? She curses herself for being so out of touch these past two years, but nothing sickens her more than political machinations and the men behind them.

Harriet produces the pint bottle, neatly wrapped in a brown paper bag, complete with a complementary dose of concentrated strychnine infused into the tincture. One decent swig ought to do the trick.

He eyes the bottle, then Harriet. He chews his top lip, then taps the table. 'This is most irregular. I take it that you know who I am?'

'I have been briefed, sir.'

Russell chews his lower lip, then contemplates the bottle. 'If he didn't make the best stuff, I might take my business elsewhere.'

'Our sincere apologies, sir. But I can assure you that your medicine was formulated according to Mr Cruickshank's exact concoction. And at your discretion.'

'Discretion, is it? Well, of late I have been indiscrete and it is well to remember it, I would vouch.' Russell taps the side of his nose. 'Enemies, you see. In every nook and cranny.' He glances at his watch, then takes the bottle and about turns without ceremony before striding out of the shop. As per instructions, she waits behind the counter, as she was, in case the Foreign Minister decides to return. He slams the door shut and the bell rattles. Through the window, she watches as Russell climbs up into the waiting carriage outside. The driver giddies the horses.

Bang.

Crash.

Smash.

Thud.

She is blinded by the white-hot flash. Shattered glass sprays across the shop, jars and phials explode in the shockwave of a devastating explosion. Harriet is prone behind the counter, which protected her from the full force of the detonation. She finds herself on the sawdust floor, her ears ring like a continuously sounding peeler's whistle. Smoke and the aroma of burning flesh and cordite fill the space. Are Pinkerton and

Warne still in the back? Is this their doing? Is not poison enough?

Moaning comes from the outside. She gets to her feet. Glass crunches under her boots as she picks her way to the door, which is hanging off its hinges. The carriage is almost completely destroyed save the back compartment. Horse flesh and the remains of the poor driver are scattered across the road in a scene from the abattoir. Then Harriet gasps as a blackened figure emerges from the cab and hops back onto the sidewalk. He still holds the bottle she gave him moments ago, but the bottom is shattered and the contents have been expelled. Russell looks at the bottle, then at the carriage and back at Harriet. 'Fucking Fenians,' he mutters, then he starts ambling down Marchmont Street like some addled vagrant. 'Stiff upper lip.'

Harriet feels for her pistol, intent upon finishing the job, but the ringing in her ears suddenly abates and it is replaced with the real whistling of peelers as they run to the scene of the attempted killing.

It is probably time to make a sharp exit.

Dudley sifts through the filing cabinets of Charles Prioleau's personal bureau. Pat works on the safe, stashed at the far end of the room, beneath the garish red Confederate Saltire that adorns the wall above the fireplace. They've done their damnedest to make this look like an official consulate, perhaps even an Embassy, in the choice of indoor plants and sumptuous furnishings, all imported from former Confederate lands. Look hard and something can be found representing all 11 of the secessionist states. The audacity is stunning.

Pat turns the dial on the safe, listening hard for giveaway clicks and feeling for the tiniest variations in the cogs that will offer clues to the mechanism. They might have the best cat burglar and safecracker in town on their side, but it may still take time.

Dogs bark outside and there is a short kerfuffle. Probably, hopefully, strays. Dudley snuffs the candle and all three of them stop dead for a moment. It passes and they get back to work.

Click. Pat says a little prayer and pulls the lever on the safe. The door eases open.

She checks herself as she sprints down Marchmont Street, suddenly aware that a woman alone running would glean the wrong type of attention. She settles into a quick march, disposing of her brown coat and branded Cruickshank Ltd accessories as she powers along.

Getting out of London quickly is no mean feat in regular circumstances. The news of an attempt on Russell's life may or may not spread in order to presage a manhunt, or womanhunt, but making it to Euston and on the first available train out of town is her best bet. Where are The Agency? Not far, probably on her tail, but catching her is their problem. They will happily let Harriet take all of the consequences, even if the blame is attached to some freak occurrence of Irish Rebels trying to kill Russell at exactly the same time as them.

Euston Road, with an endless array of passing wagons, omnibuses, carriages and horse trams, is even more of a free-for-all than it was earlier. She focuses on the giant arch of Euston Station and steels herself.

'Now then, Harriet,' says Warne, stepping out in front of her, holding a pistol. Pinkerton takes the rear.

'What a work of genius that plan was, Kathy,' she replies. They're close to the kerb. Horse silage is everywhere.

Warne giggles and twitches at once. 'Silly little girl.'

'Our business is done, Allan. I tried, but as you can see, someone else got there first. Find someone else to do your dirty work.'

'None too patriotic, are you, my dear?' says the Scotsman to the Irish Choctaw foundling. True Americans both.

'What is it about you and patriotism, Allan?'

Warne is straight to the point. 'You take one step further and I'll shoot you where you stand, Harriet. We have a whole cabinet of excuses ready to draw upon. You know how we work.'

Doubtless, Warne would pull the trigger, for all of her fake concern and weird flirtation. That macabre poncho of hers might get another extension soon. Harriet takes a slow step towards her. 'Make it a telling one, then.'

'Why didn't you finish him?' grunts Pinkerton, as if to snatch control of the situation back from Warne.

'Because I'm done with taking orders from meddling bastards with agendas like you and Butler. Now, both of you, get out of my way.'

Warne pulls back the hammer, ready to administer discipline. 'I will kill you, Harriet. Get back in line and there's a satisfactory way out of this.'

Peeler whistles in the distance. It won't be long before the whole area is swarming with them. Russell will have his work cut out keeping this quiet from the press mob. 'Say, Kathy?'

'What?'

'You're standing in shit.'

'What?' She glances down, which is all that is needed. Harriet swings the sap hard and it connects flush with Warne's jaw, taking out a couple of teeth in the process. Pinkerton pulls his revolver, but Harriet grabs the bar on the back of an omnibus and his bullet thuds into an advertisement hoarding for Pear's Soap as she is pulled along in the momentum. He tries again, but she hops off the bus and sprints across the road, dodging traffic like gators on the Mississippi. She makes it to the other side and glances back as peelers appear. Warne and Pinkerton have conveniently vanished.

She runs into the station concourse, discretion be damned. Darting onto the platform, a mail van finishes loading on the Birmingham train, and the engine is fully stoked, so it is bound to depart at any moment. She slips into the back of the van, just about evading the attention of the guard. The doors to the van are pulled shut, and she is left in near darkness, the only stream of light coming from a small, opaque window. Pinkerton and Warne arrive upon the platform gasping as the train moves away, but thankfully, the Liverpool departure is on the other side, and they gravitate in its direction, boarding at First Class.

Harriet massages the sap in her hand and lowers herself to the wooden floor. She might try to catch a nap, but who is she fooling? There is a list in her head, and she knows exactly where to start. It took an explosion to bring this out of her, but now she is not going to stop until her baby is back in her arms.

Dudley holds a jeweller's glass up to his dominant eye and peruses the range of documents spread out in front of them on Prioleau's enormous oak desk. Pat stares out of the window, now on lookout detail.

'My God,' mutters Dudley.

'I reckon we should be going, Mr Dudley.'

'Yes. Just a moment.' The man is transfixed, like all of his birthdays have come at once, but Pat is altogether more alert to who might be in the vicinity.

'Mr Dudley?'

'I said just a moment, Padraig. This is incredible and terrifying at once.'

'Mr Dudley?'

'Please, Pat. Just…'

'Mr Dudley, five Dead Rabbits are heading down the alley. This place must be on their rounds. They're a frigging scourge.'

Dudley still doesn't look up. 'Ridiculous. Why would they work for Prioleau when they are in the pay of Butler?' He continues with the glass.

'Sir, I know a fucking Dead Rabbit bastard when I see one. No offence. They don't much care for whose side they're on.'

Dudley pulls himself away and sees for himself. 'Oh my.'

'Aye. All very good. We need to go now.'

'Yes.' Dudley sweeps up all the papers and stuffs them into an attaché case. 'Yes, I think we do.'

'Good man yourself. Jaysus.'

They scramble towards the door and out into the ornate landing, moonlight streaming through a stained-glass skylight depicting the South Carolinian flag. 'Pat, they are working for Prioleau. All of them.'

'No? Really?'

Pat's sarcasm doesn't even touch Dudley, whose nervous excitement belies the peril they are suddenly in. 'Because Prioleau

185

works for Butler.' He jabs his valise, papers jamming out of the clasp.

They get to the front door. Pat tries the handle. 'Fuck off.'

'No really.' Dudley slaps the side of the case. 'It's all in here.'

'No, I mean… ah bollocks…' Muttering, gruff voices. Very familiar to Pat. They're Aston's boys, alright. Pat grabs a fistful of Dudley's sleeve and pulls him into the boardroom, which faces West towards Dixie. He goes for the bay window and shoves it up. 'You first, Mr Dudley.'

Dudley climbs out of the window and drops to the pavement below. Pat gets one leg out and then a Rabbit appears in the boardroom doorway clutching a lantern.

'Howyer, Pat.'

'Howyer, Gerry.'

'Aston wants your balls on a stick, Pat.'

'That's too bad, Gerry. They're my balls, not his.'

'Aye, Pat.'

Pat slips out of the window and finds himself on the pavement next to Dudley. On the corner of Abercromby Square, several more Rabbits hang around smoking. They must protect all the posh houses and commercial premises around here, keeping thieving rabble like Pat McCartney out. Another string to Aston's golden bow.

'Rabbits, street to street, wall to wall. Shit.'

'Where's Grace?'

No carriage. She must have cleared off when the gang turned up. The front door flies open, and Gerry piles out and down the steps, accompanied by his pals. All have blades drawn. Gerry whistles, and the men across the square are alerted. Some of them have shotguns. Mr Dudley and himself seem to be the game tonight.

'We'd better run, Mr Dudley.'

'Where?'

'That way. Go!'

Pat hasn't lost any of his pace, and might even have been able to lose them had he been alone, but Dudley gasps along with a full briefcase pulled to his chest and a few more decades' worth of timber on him. Gerry has pulled a shillelagh, and it's likely he'll take a chunk of Dudley's head off in a few yards, but Grace appears and pulls the carriage over the kerb, just enough for Pat to get a grip. Dudley throws the case at him and dives inside the cab. Buckshot slaps into the wooden frame, and it takes all of Grace's horsewomanship to steady the carriage and key her two colts back onto Grove Street and away.

Pat sweats and gasps, peeking out the window to see a line of Dead Rabbits watching them go.

'Ah, that's me dead twice then.'

'Ignore them. They're just hoodlums.'

'Now you'll have a price on your head too, Mr Dudley.'

'With respect, that is poppycock. I am the United States' Consul.'

'That don't mean diddley shite to Aston. With respect.'

The carriage galumphs along the cobbles. Grace isn't sparing her horses yet. Dudley grabs the case and clutches it to his chest again. 'They might cause problems.'

'Yes sir. They *might.*'

'So, how much?'

'Beg pardon?'

'How much of a price?'

'Ah, come on, now.'

'This Tierney fellow likes money. We'll give it to him.'

'His reputation as an evil bastard counts higher. Not long ago, you were scrubbing their shit off your windows; now you want to start paying them?'

'Every man has his price. This is how we find Harriet's child. Outbid our competitors.'

'Just how much cash have you got in that basement of yours, Mr Dudley? I'd be careful who you tell about such things.'

'Pat, how much?'

Pat rubs his stubbly jaw as Grace giddies up the horses again. He slowly nods, reluctant to admit that he's heard worse ideas over the last few weeks, although there is the possibility that this whole business has sent them both away with the mixer and towards a slow and painful death.

The United States Consulate on Paradise Street is no longer the safe haven of officialdom that it should be. Dudley sent out messages to O'Driscoll and the loyal peelers in his confidence to come and protect the building, but most of them will not be on night shift, and Aston likes to do his business swiftly and decisively.

Oriel Chambers on Water Street is one of the newest marvels in the borough as far as architecture goes, featuring a metal-framed glass-curtained wall. Dudley has instructed city halls and businesses in New York and Chicago to visit and take note, going to the extent of investing his own money into the building, which has only just finished completion. Tenants are waiting to move in, but it was just about the only place in Liverpool they could go this evening.

By gas lamp, he peruses the papers spread in date order across the bare floor of the office. It is empty and unfurnished, but all he needs right now is some time and space.

'See?' He holds a paper up to Pat, as if expecting that he could understand a word printed upon it. 'The CSS Shenandoah. A floating fortress and a match for anything in our fleet. Built in Glasgow and registered as the British merchant vessel, the SS Sea King.'

'That old trick, aye.'

'Yes Pat.'

'Still active in the Pacific. Last seen in the port of Melbourne, Australia. Where they got a civic reception, no less.'

'I don't get the appeal, I really don't.'

'Cotton money. Southern heirs and graces. Mint julips, nice uniforms.'

'Whipping people to death. Claiming ownership over them. Working them until they drop. Oh yes, I get it.'

'Yes, Pat. But the last point is the thing some people find the most attractive of all.'

'Sick, sick, sick. So this boat, maybe no one told them the war was over.'

Dudley shakes his head and grabs another paper. 'Because the war isn't over, Pat. Or another one is about to begin. Same difference.'

'Sir, that's some claim.'

Grace takes her cue, herself combing the papers. She holds another up. 'From the Emperor of the Deuxième République.'

'The French are in on it, too. Bonaparte's nephew has designs on parts of Louisiana and New France. This is a carve-up with the British, another land grab.' He waves the paper in his hand again. 'And one man is at the centre of it all.'

'Butler,' grunts Pat. His name will just not go away.

'Yes. Benjamin Franklin Butler.' Dudley picks up John Surratt's note to Prioleau, which simply states *Destroy Butler, JS* in an almost illegible scrawl. As usable evidence, it is inconsequential, but it speaks volumes about Butler's involvement with Abe's killing: recruiting, training and manipulating a small troop of young fanatics before clipping each one of them. Small wonder that Surratt fled as far as he could, repulsive as his actions were. What a heinous man Butler is and will continue to be if he isn't stopped.

'So odd that he has those first names when he only wants to destroy America,' says Grace.

'Not destroy, dear. Partition. Weaken and reform. Do a deal with the European powers and old Empire. He's offered Russell corn, grain *and* cotton from North and South. Give the Rebels a tidy little Republic of their own and make D.C. bend to his will. Russell buys it hook, line and sinker because it removes a future check on British power and lines his pockets and the pockets of all of his political chums on both sides of the Atlantic. It all figures. A British puppet state, a Commonwealth arrangement.'

'What about those two others? The Prime Minister fella in the chair with wheels, and his mate with the toffee up his arse?'

'Palmerston is dying and Seymour is finished. Every report I've had from Whitehall says so.'

Pat chews his fist. Be all this as it may, but it all pales in comparison with the idea that he'll be walking across town shortly, right into the lair of Aston Tierney. But the only other option is to run, and that only serves to help all these corrupt bastards. That debt remains to Harriet, too.

Dudley prods the document with a finger, noting Prioleau's scrawled handwriting: *The South will Rise Again.*

#22 – ALL DOWN TO THE CROWN, AGAIN

Liverpool, October 19th, 1865

By the time morning came, Constable O'Driscoll had received the message and had accompanied the three back to the Consulate. Dudley had expected the place to have gone up in flames, such was Pat's skittishness about that Irish gang, but his staff were punctual as ever, working on the long list of orders of state business with Liverpool. Perhaps it was a storm in a teacup? Or, more likely, Aston Tierney was biding his time.

'Do you think you should let us speak with Aston, first? Smooth it over?' O'Driscoll stands above everyone as they sit around Dudley's desk. O'Driscoll always stands, it seems.

'We haven't much time, and this will be seen as more of a tribute. Pat assures me.'

'He's an odd fish is Aston, alright. But don't go blaming me if all three of yers end up in a ditch somewhere.'

'Then we won't be around to blame you, Martin,' grunts Pat.

O'Driscoll leers down at him, a full foot taller. 'Nice gob, you've got on you. Since I saved your skinny little arse twice, and now you're asking me to do it again.'

'We are asking you to oversee proceedings. At a neutral venue,' interjects Dudley.

O'Driscoll doesn't look too comfortable altogether with the idea. He copped a reprimand from his Sergeant after the last time he pulled Pat out of The Washington before Aston could slot him. It is all too recent. 'This plan of yours seems a bit, well, dumb, is all.'

Dudley slides over a manila envelope. O'Driscoll takes it in reflex. 'We are all taking risks here, Constable. Right, Pat?'

'Damned straight. No need for her to be involved, though, is there?'

Grace is almost as short to Pat as Pat is short to O'Driscoll, but fiercer by a country mile. 'There is *every* reason for her to be involved,' she says, 'And I have saved your backside even more times than Constable here.'

Dudley exchanged the attaché case for two carpet bags full of bundled cash, representing the last of the big bucks war chest given to him to buy favours and information when dear old honest Abe was still around. Contrary to his nickname, Abraham Lincoln knew what it took to win wars. There is not much chance of getting further funds and even less that he won't ultimately have to account for every penny to D.C., as Johnson's reputation as a bean counter precedes him. It may result in ruin, but just like with Pat, this has gone way beyond personal interests. He can only hope that the small fortune in these here bags are enough to sway the allegiance of the nasty piece of work they are about to meet. What other choice do they have? Run?

Doing business with criminals bothers him less, though, for he has met worse than Tierney, holding office on both sides of the pond. He reassures himself about this, but he is not altogether convinced, but it is time to pick one's battles.

They walk straight up Church Street, past the Athenaeum, up and across to Great Charlotte Street, where the pubs and hotels of Aston Tierney's Empire line up thick and fast on a slight incline towards the station. And there's The Crown, one of the few establishments to remain out of the hands of the aforesaid hoodlum, a last relic of Royston Chubb's fiefdom, now owned and operated by the Fenian Brotherhood. For how much longer is anyone's guess.

'I'll speak first. He'll be expecting that,' says Pat.

'To beg for your life?' replies Dudley.

'We came here of our own accord. That has to mean something. And with two fat bags full of cash as tribute. Don't tell me you're having second thoughts, Mr Dudley?'

'Of course not. Proceed, Pat.'

They enter through the double doors. Diarmuid is on the other side of the bar, serving Aston a pint of fresh milk. They've a cow out back, and it is a nice sideline from the booze.

'Howyer Diarmuid. Aston.' Diarmuid holds a finger to his lips. He's white as a sheet. Pat frowns. 'Ah, I'm not still barred am I?'

'Shut your hole, Pat. Aston is speaking to me.'

Aston has not even looked up at Pat. He sups his milk and massages his chin. 'See, Diarmuid, the cost of everything has gone up, hasn't it? I'm having to pump the boys' wages, and they've got families to feed. I've got a family to feed. See, that's why.'

'But you're asking for double, Aston. That's a bit much, you'll agree.'

'Aye. Hard going it is so.' He looks around the place. 'But you're never empty, are ye? And of a Friday and a Saturday night, ye've got a tidy crowd in here without fail. Every night, trade is brisk. Wall to wall.'

'Still. It's too much. It will close us.'

Aston massages his sandpaper face, as if he is thinking of a way to help his countryman out of a tight spot. What a darling man. 'We could chip in, Diarmuid. To manage ye business. Sure, I'd be happy to help a good brother such as yourself. How about it?'

Pat can't help but feel a pang of guilt. He brought Aston here today. Of course, Aston turned up early to do a bit of grifting on the side, prior to his main order. He can only try to distract him. 'Aston, I've brought the United States Consul here to meet you. He has a proposition for you. A very interesting one at that.'

Aston still doesn't even look at Pat as he rubs both sets of thumbs and forefingers together to denote cash. Their exit is blocked by Rabbits now. No one is going anywhere, and this could well be a fatal mistake coming here. Thank God they brought O'Driscoll. 'Did I ask you to speak, you thieving little maggot? No, I did not.'

O'Driscoll steps in. 'Now come on, Aston. Hear the lad out.'

Aston gets up off the stool, drains his milk and wipes his face. He goes eyeball to eyeball with the peeler. 'You've come as protection then, Martin? More fool you.' He shanks O'Driscoll in the guts. Pat didn't even see the blade. All three gasp. O'Driscoll daubs claret over the bar as he collapses. 'See, I had a word with your Sergeant, on account of your interference the other night. He told me that you were getting your cards for breaking the code. I told him that I'd be the first one to tell ye. So no more Billy Big Bollocks from ye. Gobshite, ex-Constable.'

Aston towers over Grace. Dudley tries to get in between them but is pushed back. 'I will bring the full force of the law to bear on you, Tierney.'

'Put a cork in it, Yank,' says Aston, not taking his eyes off Grace. He strokes her cheek. No fear is shown from her, which excites Aston even more. This is what he likes, more than cash, more than anything, and Pat curses himself for not stopping her from coming. 'See, this small one's cute so, more spunk in her than any of yers. Horsey little spade. Which one of your boys fancies a go on her first? Break her in like one of her fillies?'

'Get your dirty fucking hands off her.' Harriet's shot rings out. Aston groans and then looks down and yelps. His kneecap is shot clean through. The big man buckles, then collapses. Pat can make out the open trap door behind her in the lounge. He hits the deck and prays that the other two follow suit as a hail of bullets fizz past. Thudding, grunting and howling ensue, and he dares to look up. Harriet Farrell grips two, smoking six-shooters, one in each hand. She approaches the be-decked Rabbits, twitching and moaning. She reloads.

'Please, Miss. Lady. I've a wife and seven little uns.'

She puts a bullet in Gerry's head and follows suit with the others before the screaming and begging can start. The stricken Aston jumps each time, himself spread across the killing floor. He reaches for the blade in the prone O'Driscoll's heart. The air is full of gunsmoke and fresh death. Dudley is aghast.

Harriet approaches Aston, kicking his flailing hand away. 'Where's my baby?'

He grits his teeth and bites his lip so hard that blood runs. 'Have a shite, ye fuckin' old whore's geebag. Ye'll have to kill me.'

Harriet unloads into his forehead and his brains splatter Diarmuid's bar. All is still for a moment. Grace takes her side.

'No joy there,' says Harriet. 'Let's try The Washington.' She steps over the bodies and opens the doors. Grace follows her. 'You two coming or what?'

'Harry, fuckin' hell, love. Harriet, stop! We need to talk.'

Pat scrambles in her wake. Dudley and Grace trail behind – scared and wary of anyone following – but Liverpool seems to be business as usual. Someone, probably Diarmuid, will have to deal with that mess. Names may have to be named, especially with a dead ex-peeler and a gang boss whose brains have just been disconnected. Not just any gang boss, either.

Wagons and carriages seem to dodge Harriet rather than the other way around as she strides across the thoroughfare towards the entrance of The Washington Hotel. She pulls her sap, then bounds up the steps and into the lobby.

"But says he "My fine fellows if you will enlist
It's ten guineas in gold I will slip in your fists
And a crown in the bargain for to kick up the dust
And drink the King's health in the morning..."

The sweet, old ditty *Arthur McBride* emanates from the ballroom, calling to her from another lifetime. Harriet follows it.

'Harriet, please stop and consider!' yells Dudley, breathless and struggling to keep up.

'Miss Harriet, he's right!' Grace follows, at the top of her voice.

'Harry, stop, please! She's just a kid!'

To her, Pat isn't there, nor the others. It is a zero-sum game, and it has come to this; immediate answers are required. The girl is on a small stage, accompanied by piano and fiddle, dressed in a garish ensemble for the Mademoiselle Foufou matinee. A fog of pipe and cigar smoke greets them, the audience being middle-aged men of substance to a person, all ogling the little French Fancy on the riser. Kitty Flynn doesn't notice the woman bearing down upon her until it is too late.

If I could find a handsome boatsman, to ferry me over to my love and die...

Harriet slips a foot behind Kitty's ankle, and she drops to the floor. The audience gasps like it is some sort of Vaudevillian sketch, but – in a blink – Harriet has the hard sap underneath the girl's throat and she struggles to breathe.

'Harry, no!'

'Where is my baby? Tell me now, or I'll gut you like a pig.'

Kitty screams. Pat tries to pull Harriet away. 'Harry, she's only a child herself. Please, you'll never forgive yourself.'

Harriet keeps Kitty pinned with one hand and points her Colt .45 at Pat, fury engulfing her every sense like a tempest. 'She will tell me, Pat. And no man will stop me.'

'Miss Harriet. Please calm yourself. Miss Conté would not want this.'

'Clear off, Grace.'

'Miss Conté would tell you different. Mr McCartney is right; she is only a child.'

Harriet jams the sap harder into the girl's throat. Any firmer and it might do for her and there will be no answers.

'Breathe, Harriet,' says Dudley. Harriet is barely aware of any of them, only Kitty's frantic, frightened eyes. She takes a breath and pulls the sap away.

'Fuckers. The lot of them.'

Pat crouches by Kitty, who is distraught. He holds her. 'Aston is dead, love. You're free.'

'Wh- what?'

'It's true. Harry there plugged him in the head less than five minutes ago. You can believe it just by looking at her, can you not?'

'Dead?'

'Tell us where the child is. You know, don't you?' Kitty shakes her head, a tiny bit of defiance and a heap more of fear overtaking her. 'Tell us where Sally is. Her mammy wants her back.'

'Sally?'

'Yes, baby Sally. That's her mammy, so you'll know why she was awful angry.'

Harriet stares down at Kitty, who takes in all of her assailant, head to toe. 'The convent on Mount Pleasant.'

Pat nods. 'The Carmelites. I know it. Spitting distance from the Workhouse.'

'Aye. Give Aston's name. They won't try to stop you,' croaks Kitty.

'A small mercy.' Pat squeezes Kitty's hand like she's one of his own, but he hopes to God that none of his children go through what this poor kid has had to endure. He looks up and Harriet has already gone.

They leave Kitty and head for the doors in the wake of the tornado.

#23 – BUSTING UP THE HUSTINGS

Cambridge, Massachusetts, October 24th 1865

'Our beloved nation is at a critical juncture, gentlemen. President Johnson bleats about how the war is won and that he has a plan for the South. I would tell you, as erstwhile, de facto Governor of New Orleans and its New French environs, that your commander-in-chief is spouting bubbles of drivel again. I know the South, you see, intimately. I know the thinking, and I have the information. See for yourselves, Otis Hillard and the Palmetto Brigade have sucked up recruits from every branch of Lee's army, from cavalry to infantry and artillery, the best of the best of the Dixie vanguard. There are hearts and minds to sway, and many are looking for their next leader, towards a fresh secession. This is not scaremongering; it is based upon proficient intelligence, and I can submit it to you here and now for peer review.'

On the campaign trail among the intelligentsia of Harvard University. Convincing the academics that this future Republican candidate has the chops for power is no simple task. Butler faces a lecture theatre full of stern beards with conservative outlooks on the world, but they are not recalcitrant. Not one of them would back Johnson or even Lincoln to run this country, except into the ground, but the more documentary evidence he can offer them, the more support he can glean. Ledgers of scrupulously copied intelligence are passed down the aisles by undergraduate students under Butler's thrall. Next, it will be Yale, followed by the College of New Jersey.

'Let us not wait for the next election to act, as it will be too late to avert disaster. Unelected President Johnson must be impeached and impelled to stand down for the good of the United States of America and for our future peace and prosperity in this critical moment.' He holds a finger up to the heavens, as if to prod God directly. 'Again, read the evidence for yourselves, but we have direct information that the British have assembled a huge garrison of Redcoats near the Canadian border, inordinate with the Canuck population. Troop ships have been arriving at

Halifax for months now, and sightings have been made of a massive fleet of Royal Navy vessels in mid-Atlantic, converging at a proximity to our waters that is far too close to be explained as manoeuvres. This danger is clear and present... Willy, what in hell is it? Can it not wait?'

Butler's incandescence is tempered by the knowledge that William will know better than to interrupt him here for any other reason than an issue worthy of his immediate attention. He gets as close as he can into Butler's ear hole. 'Ben, there's been an attempt on Russell's life, and Haines Dudley is at it again.'

It's enough to take the wind out of Butler's sails. 'To the point, esteemed gentlemen. I have just heard sobering news requiring me to assume military duties again. Without delay.'

'What is it? Have the British invaded?'

'Are the Palmettos attacking?'

Learned men reduced to small boys, wrapped around his little finger, wits trembling. They can add so much coal to the furnace, but he must speak with William before concluding this event. 'I urge calm. My staff and I will attend to the issue. You can have confidence in me that your donations and trusteeships will be put to the best conceivable use.'

'Tell us, Benjamin.'

'Friends, I will in due course. In the meantime, do peruse the copies of documents that I have provided and help yourself to complimentary sherry and cheese savouries. The canapés are to die for.'

Butler barrels off the lectern and into an anteroom with William in his wake.

'Could it not have waited a few more minutes?'

'There is a steamer due to depart. We'll lose days if we don't leave now, Ben.'

'Jesus. It must be dire.'

'It is, Ben.'

'Dudley? What has that pompous old fart been up to now?'

'He got access to Fraser & Trenholm, Ben. They kept a record of everything. Well, almost everything.'

'Those fucking dolts! I told them to keep my name out of every conversation and they kept fucking records! You were there, Willy. Were you not?'

'Yes, Ben.'

Butler wipes sweat off his brow. 'And what of Surratt? And that Irish virago? Can she not take care of it?'

'Surratt absconded with the help of friends in Rome, but he made sure that he stuck the knife in before he left. Farrell is a loose cannon. The Pinkertons got to her. They have your memorandum now.'

This brings Butler near to apoplexy. 'Cannot anyone take simple directions? Do not speak to Allan, I said; do not speak to Thomas, I said. Explicit orders, dammit. Must I do everything myself? I am trying to run a goddamn campaign here.'

'Masterfully so, Ben.'

'Don't blow smoke up my ass, Willy.'

'Sorry, Ben.'

Butler straightens up, bracing himself. 'And the Lincoln business?'

'Yes, that too. They have it all. Verified in paper.'

He balls his fists like an angry toddler. 'Goddammit, Willy. They could use it as a plea bargain now a man like Dudley is privy. Baldy ass will take it straight to the courts. That alone would ruin everything. Ruin us, ruin me. Aargh, botheration!'

'Yes, Ben.' Butler takes a moment for stock. 'Sir, we need to go.'

'We need to go. We need to go, we need to fucking go. Pah!' Butler bowls around the floor like a loose cannonball on a stormy deck.

'Yes, Ben.'

'Pah. That infernal, insipid village.' Butler sits and chews his nails. He gazes up. 'Guess you had better arrange a berth for us both. Post haste, Willy.'

'Already done, Ben. Bags are packed and stowed. I'll get us a cab to the harbour.'

Butler grabs his small valise, the one that goes everywhere with him and William knows never to touch. 'You can brief me fully on the way.'

#24 – THE HISTORY OF STUPID IDEAS

Liverpool, October 24th 1865

Grace's carriage trundles down Water Street towards George's Landing Stage on this murky, still morning. Tall masts and smoke stacks peek through the gloop. Here they are, again.

'In the history of stupid ideas, that was right up there,' says Harriet. Pat wears a new, dapper, tailored suit and sports a freshly-coiffured beard and hair. It only adds to how foolish he is being made to feel right now.

Dudley holds up a fistful of papers, the last remaining to be copied and sent to President Johnson directly. 'We have evidence, at last.'

'Not that, Thomas. You and him. Sucking up to the Rabbits, to Tierney.' She turns to Pat. 'And you should certainly know better.'

It is the first time she has spoken at all about it since she shot up a pub, killing several knuckles, including the aforesaid head knuckle, yet it suddenly feels like all of it is their doing. And here's soft-arse Pat, thinking that the subject was done with.

'It wasn't sucking up, so. We were banjaxed, Harry. If you hadn't shown up, we'd have been dead either way.'

'Don't thank me yet.'

Baba sits on Harriet's knee. For all her stern talk and outrageous courage, Pat can tell that his friend is still struggling. He almost preferred her when she stuck a gun in his face.

'I'll ask you again. Is there no other option? If what we hear is right, America will be a roughhouse again soon. Best steer clear.'

'It's always been a roughhouse, Pat. Do you have somewhere else to go? Do you have a cunning idea that you can magic up? Not on current form, I will vouch.'

'Jaysus, I'm trying me best, like.' Pat shakes his head. The carpet bag full of dollars is at his feet. It burns a hole in the bottom of the carriage. Money meant for Aston, now for Sarah. He hopes it doesn't carry a curse.

'Pat. Papa.' Baba reaches for him as Grace pulls the reigns. They've arrived.

'No, Baba. Just Pat,' says Harriet. Pat should know better than to expect tears from her, even in a moment like this. She's had less than a week with her dear daughter, and now she is sending her – and him – halfway across the world.

Harriet hands Baba over to Pat, and the child chuckles. 'No goodbyes. I may send for you. If I don't...'

'Then she'll have a fine Mammy in Sarah.'

'And you really will be Papa Pat.'

'No bother there. Them's comfy shoes, but it won't come to that.'

'I was never going to shoot you, you know. You believe me, don't you?'

'No, I fuckin' don't, love.'

The carriage trundles to a stop and Grace pulls open the compartment door. 'Cussing again, Mr McCartney?'

'Alright, alright. Bleeding hell, Princess.'

Grace tilts her head. 'Children present.'

He glances back to Harriet, but she has turned her head away from the unbearable sight. Dudley nods at him. 'You make contact with those friends of mine on the Upper East Side, Padraig. They will look after you and your business. More windows to clean in New York than anywhere on Earth.'

Pat clutches the bag and Baba. 'Grand so, Mr Dudley.'

Grace kisses the baby and mounts the driver's seat. Without further ado, she giddies, and the carriage turns, heading back through George's Dock towards the bustling Strand.

The gangway towards First Class awaits: an open invitation to the New World. Pat arrived here off a cattle boat 17 years earlier, starving and desperate with his mammy and siblings, all of whom are with Jesus now. Two years ago, Harriet Farrell gifted him a way out of poverty and he blew it. Now, she is doing it again. Well, Mr Dudley is, but it was all her idea.

'Mama?' Baby Conté's face screws up as she becomes aware that her mother has gone again, just when she was getting used to having her real Mammy. This could be a longer trip than he anticipated.

'Would you like a sweetie, sweetie?'

'Yeh!'

'Aye. Come on, then. Your Uncle Pat will teach ye how to talk proper, so he will.'

They head up the gangway.

A choppy ocean, three days out of Queenstown, five out of Liverpool. The squall washes salty spray across Pat. Baba sleeps in a cot next to him, oblivious to the ill-tempered high seas and pending gale that is already agitating the hull of this steamship. She's a natural sailor, alright. He prefers the deck to the cosy comforts of the First Class lounges and cabin, forever having the feeling that he doesn't belong there, in spite of all his cash, fancy clobber, and a ticket to prove it.

The ship's horn bellows and another vessel copies it in the distance. He gazes out into the horizon, spotting another vessel heading this way, sharing a shipping lane. It could be another passenger steamer, by the order of things. Yes, White Star Line. Where is it heading? Southampton? Cherbourg? Liverpool?

He gets the strange urge to turn back, to commandeer a lifeboat and return to England in order to help his friend finish the job, little knowing that upon the deck of that passing vessel is a certain Benjamin Franklin Butler and his man William, intent upon murder and correction, in no particular order.

Butler takes in the bracing air, cocks his leg, arches his back and breaks wind in a trumpet salute lasting all of five seconds. Fellow first class passengers look on aghast.

'We shall return to the lounge now for a juicy steak with fried onions, Willy.'

'Very good, Ben.'

Across half a nautical mile of clear water, more wind and rain batter the ship bound for New York and Pat has had enough.

Baba stirs and starts to cry, missing her Mammy more and more. 'Alright then, back inside with you, small pudding.'

#25 – THE ATHENAEUM
AND THE CABINET

Liverpool and London, November 1st, 1865

White rabbit, white rabbit, white rabbit.

Her child has been ripped from her twice. Still, the fundamental difference is that Harriet knows that Baba Conté is going to a safer place, protected by the swarming masses of immigrants in a town that is becoming the capital city of the World. So, her red mist has lifted, but a dark hue remains.

Now she is left in Liverpool trying to clean up this mess, or at least make some sense of it. Dudley seems to have aged tenfold in the months they have been separated, as if the guilt and the perception of failure had taken a toll. He even revealed how Pat had saved him, in the process saving himself. Now, in spite of the wear and the tear, that resolve he had when they first met during the crisis of two years ago has returned, and it adds a rod of iron to his countenance.

It's a fresh, crisp November morning. They promenade from Paradise Street towards Church Street on the same route taken back on that awful day in April, but this time altogether wiser. They are emboldened further by a telegraph wire this morning from Charles Francis Adams Sr, Dudley's only true ally in the United Kingdom and himself appointed by Lincoln as United States Minister to Great Britain. They must both make the most of their borrowed time.

Thomas STOP Documents received with thanks STOP Confab with our contact confirmed STOP Go after P and B with everything you have STOP You have my sanction. STOP Your friend C.F.A. STOP

The Athenaeum stands as impassive as ever, welcoming to anyone with gentlemanly credentials, with its own set of inclusion criteria that is never swayed by the moral compass of the day. The names and portraits of slavers adorn the walls: Secretary of this, Treasurer of that, Chairman of the other. This club was built with their money and is maintained by their progeny's money. It may as well be in Richmond or Atlanta as Liverpool.

Dudley pulls the cord for the bell. Halls opens up.

'Ah, Halls. There's a good chap.'

Halls looks like he's just discovered something on the bottom of his shoe. 'Good morning, Mr Dudley. I am afraid that your membership has been withdrawn by order of the committee.'

'I apologise for my drunken outburst, Halls. But surely I am not the first, nor shall I be the last?'

'We expect a level of decorum, sir. Alas, sadly, I must decline entry. The same applies to *all* females.'

Harriet points her Colt at him, and Halls jolts back. 'You can make a little exception for us? We are on official Government business, you see.'

'I shall call the peelers.'

'Proceed, my good man, if you can after she puts a hole in you,' says Dudley, pushing past him, 'And while you're at it, we will parlay with a couple of real hoodlums at large.'

Harriet winks at Halls as they enter and climb the stairs. They breeze into the smoking room, which is half-full and descends into an immediate, frozen hush upon sight of the disgraced American. How dare he. And how dare he bring *that* woman in here with him. They make a B-line for Prioleau and Bulloch, seated at their favourite table over cards, scotch and a breakfast of kippers. The two Southern Gentlemen look like a pair of scalded cats as Dudley hovers over them. Furtive glances and snide asides wash across the room.

'You will gather by now that your game is well and truly up, traitors.'

'It won't wash in the courts over here, Tom. That is all that matters,' replies Prioleau, attempting nonchalance and avoiding eye contact. Not so cocksure now.

Dudley slaps down a piece of foolscap. The printed text is in Prioleau's own hand, with lines and paragraphs redacted in thick, black ink, illegible. It is dated 14th December 1864. 'In relation to the heinous assassination of my friend and the President of the United States, Abraham Lincoln, I hereby charge you with aiding and abetting, conspiracy and treason. What say you?'

'I say you can prove nothing,' says Bulloch, ever the gruff Navy type, sharp as a tack when it comes to commissioning ships but thick as two short planks when it comes to law and diplomacy. His bosom chum Prioleau, on the other hand, is rather more erudite and slippery.

'In the law of the land here, which is the only law that matters pertaining to this conversation, you will find that these documents were obtained via illegal trespass upon our business premises and as a result of grand larceny or common burglary, take your pick on the definition. So, get out of here before you are kicked out, Tom. Again.'

A few awkward chuckles ripple from the throng, who are rapt in this bit of impromptu theatre.

'You financed the assassination project, did you not? The same way you financed your blockade runners, by selling cotton bonds? It is all in your records. You helped Butler to kill the President.'

'Your President, not ours. And you cannot prove it, Tom.'

'Yes, I can. I will see both of you extradited and tried in an American court. You will swing, dammit.'

'Any such court will not be in session by the time you get there. Your beloved America will not be the same place.'

Dudley grins. Harriet pats his shoulder in support. The Consul didn't come here to arrest these two bastards; he came here to put the wind up them. He waves the document in front of Prioleau's nose just as peelers enter the Smoking Room, Halls in their wake, wittering and prodding a finger in their direction. 'I wouldn't bet upon it, old boy. Perhaps you would like to know where we are headed today? Perhaps it is to secure your extradition.'

There's a purplish countenance to both of them now. 'Get out,' grunts Bulloch.

They stride away, pushing past the peelers who are still loath to lay a hand upon the United States Consul. 'You can keep your membership, Mr Halls.'

Harriet follows him, rather glad not to be the centre of attention for once, but wary of the eyeballs searing into her back. 'Ah, the good gentlemen of Liverpool, kindly and generous as ever.'

Lime Street Station, again. Liverpool is draining her, but Harriet suspects that her business in this town isn't quite finished yet. All but two of her friends have gone now and a new dawn beckons, but business remains in this damned country yet.

'Are you quite sure about this, Thomas?' she asks Dudley as they stride down the platform. She is ever wary of watchers and snoopers.

'You have every right to be in there with me.'

'They might bar me. A female.'

'Then it will be a short conversation.' Harriet is impressed with his solidarity, even if social convention screams the contrary. Dudley maintains a stoic and chipper manner. 'Ah, this is our compartment, I believe. Let us board. I do like a trip down to the Big Smoke, as they call it.'

Early evening and a cold London by gaslight is still bustling busy. They procure a Hansom Cab from Euston to 98 Portland Place, Piccadilly, setting of the American Legation to Great Britain. The United States of America has not been deemed fit to have a full Embassy in London, due to some half-cocked excuse that they are a Republic, even though the French are fully represented here. Another legacy of colonialism, as they stand on this knife edge between lurching backwards or powering forwards. Perhaps the events of this evening will have a bearing upon that outcome and the whole shape of things.

They enter through a pristine arcade and Harriet spots her reflection, walking along next to Mr Dudley, an odd couple on a an odd assignment. They sashay past a United States flag, which denotes that they are crossing into sovereign territory, a homecoming of sorts. Then, through a vestibule where they are immediately flanked by two enormous men in blue US Army uniforms who allow their entry without a word of salutation.

They are guided along a passage of plain, shut doors towards a single door at the bottom of the row, replete with the nameplate of Envoy Extraordinary and Minister Plenipotentiary Charles Francis Adams Senior, Minister of the United States and de facto Ambassador to Great Britain.

One of the men knocks, and a voice immediately responds. 'Come.'

The group enters to find yet another grey, old man with a silver underbeard, perched behind an even bigger desk than Dudley's. Harriet swears that a factory must produce such men for these roles as they all look the goddamn same, but she'll judge him on deeds rather than his appearance. An identical portrait of Lincoln to the one in Dudley's garret hangs above them.

Another such chap sits opposite Adams clutching a cane, upright and uptight. He fits the same mould, but they recognise each other immediately. Neither he nor Adams rise to their feet, more preoccupied with Dudley's stolen documents piled upon the desk.

'*You*,' seethes Edward Seymour as he spots Harriet from the corner of his eye.

'Yes, me. What of it?'

'Your Grace,' Dudley interjects, remaining on point, 'Thank you for joining us. I can see that you remember Miss Farrell fondly.'

Seymour leans back into the chair and massages the bridge of his nose. He glances across the desk. 'Really, Mr Adams? These two?'

'This is simply how we must do it, Your Grace.'

'My enemy's enemy is my friend, perchance. But this is taking that adage rather too far, Mr Minister. She's bloody insane, I am telling you from bitter experience.'

'Just wait until *he* claps eyes on her,' says Adams, a devilment suddenly in his eye, 'He will fill his breeches. Is that not the desired effect?'

'It works for me,' says Harriet, beaming back at the mean old buzzard, First Lord of the Admiralty. All's fair in love and war.

What a beautiful morning. Crisp sun, dancing and dappling through the spindly trees that line this grand drag, belying the grey fog that has finally lifted just in time for this auspicious occasion. Lord John Russell takes a brisk ride upon a carriage as part of the Prime Ministerial retinue travelling down The Mall via Admiralty Arch in order to complete his formal induction and formally accept the premiership from Her Majesty Queen Victoria. Russell is aching to get down to business, but at the same time, rather looking forward to meeting the fine old girl again, especially in taking the tiller. She never made a secret of detesting Palmerston and still loathes his cronies, whereas for the brief time he was PM back in the fifties, they delighted in each other's company, especially his horsemanship

Rule number one with these Royal types is to always bring the conversation onto horses. Eschew the important issues of state as Her Majesty chooses to keep a dignified silence upon them and favours conversation about which of her nags is going to win at Ascot in the Summer. See if she has any hot tips. Equine platitudes win the day, every day. You *clever* boy, Lord Johnny-John-John.

Russell considers a quick sip of the special sauce to tide him over, but he needs to be clear, articulate and respectful in his gestures. He shall crack this lovely elixir open later and enjoy it, then get down to all the urgent matters of state.

Half an hour, in and out. He played fetch with her collies and buttered her up nicely about Balmoral and hunting legislation, before artfully segueing to runners and riders. The returning retinue bumps along Whitehall, hanging right into Downing Street. Russell takes another big swig of Cruickshank's tincture, realising that the bottle is now half-empty. Matters not.

The carriage stops, and a footman opens the door. Oh well, it shouldn't impair him too much. On the contrary, he finds that he can deal with the hobbledehoys in his cabinet far better after a quick swig than without. It makes everything honest.

He strides past the throng of press men scribbling their scoops. 'Sir, what have you got for us in your statement? Give us an inkling, would you?'

'Ah, you shall just have to wait, lads. I will speak with my cabinet first.' Russell barrels through the front door of number ten; the great leader finally returned with Her Majesty's mandate to where he was born to be: at the helm of the most glorious and powerful nation on earth. 'I shall see them now. A new dawn awaits.' How they want to feed from the palm of his hand.

He knows every manjack Minister, where they went to school (the houses they attended), which ones pissed the bed, who got buggered, who did the buggering, who did both. He knows his allies, and he knows which ones will put the knife in his back faster than Brutus upon Caesar. Right now, *they* will be the ones fretting about him rather than the other way around. It is a glorious day indeed, far too long in coming. Just wait until he really gets started.

The doors to the cabinet room swing open and Prime Minister Lord John Russell verily does nearly fill his breeches at the sight.

'What? What in infernal damnation? What? Ah!'

At the far end of the long, long table sits Edward Seymour, the only member of Russell's cabinet in attendance today. He is flanked by Adams, another American whom he vaguely recognises and a straight-backed young female with intense, green eyes. Now, that's a face that he will never forget. 'Ah, it was something fishy about you, young lady.'

Russell spins on his heels and makes to go straight back out of the door.

'I wouldn't do that if I were you, Johnny,' says Seymour, altogether far too chipper and menacing than he should be.

Russell whips around and puts his back to them, as if seeing his face would show his weakness. 'This is an outrage, Seymour. I'll have you thrown in gaol, I say. I shall have you strung up. Sent to the fucking guillotine, I will.'

'Oh, do shut up. Such a bore. This is Mr Adams, who you will know, and Mr Dudley. I gather that you have met Miss Farrell, too. Now…' Seymour glances at his pocket watch, '…I've furloughed the boys in the cabinet for another half an hour. Then you will address the press corps, I gather?'

Russell slowly turns around, deportment like a chastised child. 'Yes.'

'Very well. Then we shall put our case to you, and then you will put it into process.'

'If you think this stunt will change my mind, you have another thing coming.'

Dudley places his attaché case on the table surface and rummages inside. Adams reaches down to his feet and pulls up a bottle of *GC Cruickshank's Opium Tonic*. He observes the label.

'A remedy for all maladies. How about that?' says the Minister of America.

Harriet smiles at Russell. 'So, Prime Minister. Tell us the first order of business?'

Russell turns and snarls, 'How dare you speak in here, woman.'

'I speak as much as I like and you'll listen, you weird old bastard.'

Seymour nods. 'Johnny, trust me when I tell you that she means every word.'

'Ah, I must address Parliament first. My private secretary will release a full press release to you all in due course detailing forthcoming foreign and domestic policies.'

'Your Grace, your press secretary promised us a speech, sir. A gargantuan story, he said. What do you call this?'

'What are your plans regarding the American Question?'

'And the Irish Question?'

'Throw us a bone, Lord Johnny.'

'Ah, a full statement is pending. Now if it is quite acceptable with you, I have urgent matters to attend to. Good evening, gentlemen.'

The press moan and clamour, cheated of the news they craved, items stoked up by Russell's own rhetoric, fed carefully to editors and correspondents via his secretary, priming a military intervention in the United States. Now, the man himself has cut them dead. Without the official word, it is all worthless tosh.

Russell enters the sanctuary of his carriage and pulls the door closed, shutting out a tide of irate pressmen. He can feel their breath upon him, a collective, seething indignation on behalf of the Great British public that will scan directly to the broadsheets tomorrow morning. He reaches down to find the bottle he left earlier, lifts it to his mouth and drains it empty.

'American bastards dashed it,' he slurs, and he slumps into his seat. The carriage moves away, bound for Cruickshank's of Bloomsbury.

Seymour arranges for them to leave via the back exit and through the garden. What looks like a splendid terraced house from the exterior on Downing Street is a complex burrow of offices and residences, all linked together, betraying number ten as only a façade.

Bidding adieu to Adams but not Seymour, who scampers away without any airs or graces, they take a Hansom Cab directly back to Euston and now sit on the train due to depart for Liverpool. Dudley is beside himself with joy, but Harriet remains circumspect as the engine begins to shunt them away.

'We should get something to eat. Is there a trolley on this?' she says.

'Of course.'

'Good. I didn't travel back in First Class last time.'

'I gathered, Harriet.'

Footsteps along the corridor. The compartment door slides open, and Allan Pinkerton steps inside. He is followed by his obedient attack dog with the singular poncho. 'I knew this day was going far too well, Thomas.'

Pinkerton and Warne invite themselves in and sit down opposite Harriet and Dudley, who is singularly unimpressed with their little invasion. 'This is a private compartment. Please leave.'

Harriet pats her left side, where at least two deadly weapons are kept. It is always an advantage for a shootist to be a southpaw. Warne smiles back at her. No sign of them busting any moves, but that doesn't mean it won't happen.

Pinkerton leans forward with an earnest face on him, as if he is about to impart a fascinating fact to a new protégé. 'You achieved the desired result without a drop of blood being spilled, Harriet. Exquisite work and it makes our job all the simpler, does it not, Katherine?'

'Indubitably,' says Warne. Harriet wants to shoot her where the sun don't shine for her antics at The Washington Hotel, but she reminds herself that it is equally possible that Pinkerton himself came up with the scheme. Either way, they're a pair of tiresome oafs, struggling to stay relevant.

'What about a butchered horse and that poor driver?'

'That was the Irish. Don't be flippant, dear,' says Warne. 'And if they're going to plant a bomb, they should know how to do it properly.'

'Like you'd know how to do anything properly.'

Pinkerton is still beaming, like he is unable to read her body language, which is a hair's breadth away from killing the pair of them and dumping the bodies out of the window into the English countryside. 'I'd like to offer you a job with The Agency, Miss Farrell. Excellent pay and conditions. Childcare, the best education for her, you name it. Let's make it official, hey?'

The man's sheer gall is quite spectacular. 'Why don't you recruit Consul Dudley here, too, while you're at it? He orchestrated the deal.'

'You engaged a dangerous Liverpool gang single-handedly. You paved the way for the negotiations at the highest level. We want you on our team, Harriet.'

'So, you can look halfway competent and take credit, Pinkerton? Make yourself scarce. There are two doors you can see; one leads out of this compartment, the other to a steep embankment. Choose.'

Pinkerton ignores the threat, eyes still on the prize. 'Name your price.'

Harriet issues a wide grin. 'Push her off the train?'

'Wh- what?' mutters Warne.

'She's joking, Kate. That's what I like about her. Pure spunk.'

'I'm not joking,' replies Harriet, 'push her out and then we'll talk.'

Dudley has kept his own counsel for now, but this is his moment. 'You were hired to protect Abraham. You failed.'

Pinkerton looks vexed. He's not used to conversations not going how he planned them. 'We were compromised, Thomas. That is not your concern. Stay out of it.'

'As a serving officer of the United States Government, I would say this very much *is* my concern, old boy. Who are you? A gang of hired guns? Untrained thugs? Privateers? You amount to no more. I will be petitioning for an accountable Government Intelligence Agency and full diplomatic status once this mess is fully resolved. High time we had a seat at the table and a coordinated defence strategy, lest incompetent grifters like your lot will keep making a godawful mess of things.'

'Bravo, Thomas,' says Harriet.

'You will be out of a job soon, so do give it a rest, Dudley. We are the future, and to you, Harriet, I say that this is a once-in-a-lifetime opportunity. You have no idea of the plans we have. We will do great things.'

'*We*? What is this *we*, Allan? It's all about you, is it not?'

Pinkerton leans forward again, in her face now. His breath is putrid, like sewage. 'You will join us. I can take you all over the world in the service of our great nation.'

Harriet pulls back her head and cronk! She butts him hard, feeling the gristle of his nose giving way. Pinkerton yelps, blood pissing all over his tweed blazer. Warne has a short blade drawn. Harriet clutches her sap. 'Get. Out.'

Pinkerton grunts and ushers Warne out of the compartment. Harriet gets up and slams the door shut to keep out the smell.

'Very good, dear,' says Dudley.

'They're not done yet.'

'Yes, I do concur. But then I suspect that they will never be done. Now, how about that trolley? Cake?'

Grace waits for them on the platform, clutching a scrolled-up document. She looks relieved to see them. Further up the train, Pinkerton bounds off the carriage and lopes away, sopping red handkerchief still pressed to his nose. Warne takes the opportunity to leer back at Harriet over her shoulder before catching up with her boss' wake as he trails towards the Hansom Cabs.

'How was your trip, Miss Harriet?'

'Fruitful.'

'Very good.'

'How was your research, Princess?'

Grace nods. 'Also fruitful.'

'Excellent,' says Dudley. 'You could teach my staff a thing or two.'

'He arrives on Sunday, early afternoon. Got this from your contact in Boston, Mr Dudley.' Dudley takes the note and peruses it. Harriet looks over his shoulder. Unencumbered with passengers, lighter and smaller, the information arrived to them altogether faster on the RMS Strafe. It pays to have contacts in every shipping office either side of the Atlantic.

'Grace?'

'Yes, Miss Harriet?'

'You know all the comings and the goings down there? Tide times, schedules, etcetera?'

'Surely, Miss. It is my business to know.'

Dudley smiles at Harriet. 'What are you cooking up?'

Harriet starts walking towards Grace's carriage, which is parked by a siding. 'Food first. A proper meal. That cake just didn't fill the hole.'

#26 – THE SOUTH WILL RISE AGAIN

Liverpool, November 5th, 1865

Pissing rain gives way to sleet, then a snow drift, the first freeze of the Winter. Add a few sharp blobs of hard, driving hail, a river that could well freeze over if it gets any colder and George's Dock on this raw Sunday afternoon is about as far away from Dixie as it will ever get.

Prioleau rubs his gloved hands together and pulls the mohair blanket tighter into his chest. He is grateful for the body warmth of Bulloch sitting next to him in the back of the carriage. Having slipped on a patch of black ice and bruised his elbow, the Carolinian banker is even less pleased with the idea that he may never see his home again or reap the rewards of his years of service to the cause. Dreams of a ticker-tape parade in Charleston are busted, alas. Bulloch is altogether more po-faced about his predicament. The Commander looks at his pocket watch and pulls a telescope, eying the river for a particular incoming vessel, the single-screw propeller SS Avuncular.

'Here.' Bulloch passes the scope to Prioleau. He can see Major General Butler with his manservant laden with luggage, waiting at the First Class slipway for docking. He looks fair keen to get down to business. Prioleau emits a long, dry gulp.

'Just what are we gonna tell him, James?'

'The South will rise again,' grunts Bulloch.

'It's all very well you saying that, ain't it? Oh, my sweet Aunt Fanny.'

Passengers file past Butler and William as they wait on the jetty. Prioleau and Bulloch approach. Butler primes his pipe.

'Chilly, Ben,' says William, pulling his thin blazer around his frame.

'Brisk,' grunts Butler. 'Real weather. I like it.'

William looks askance at Butler, debating for the ultimate time with himself about his commander's sanity. Like most things to do with Benjamin F. Butler, it is an enigma that can never be solved or resolved. 'Gentlemen, why the long faces?'

Prioleau lets Bulloch get ahead of him, keen not to be in the direct line of Butler's wrath. 'Ah, Benjamin. Welcome to Liverpool.'

'You act like I have never been to this fine town, James. Why, it's like a second home.'

'Really?' whispers Prioleau, unable to get the word out of his throat.

'No, Charlie. It's just another shitass garret with ideas above its station. Now, are we going for a debriefing or what? Or do you prefer to freeze to death out here?'

It was pre-agreed between Prioleau and Bulloch to get the hard lines across in a public place, as neither man could fathom or predict how Butler was going to react in private quarters. His reputation preceded him.

'I trust that you have not heard our news, sir?'

'Lest there is a magic telegraph in the sea. No, Mr Prioleau. I guess you have better spit it out then, seeing as you're both set upon shivering your plums off out here.'

'Allow me to interject,' says Allan Pinkerton, barging through the oncoming traffic of disembarking passengers with his flunky Warne in tow. Butler's face crumples. He snaps his fingers, but William does not respond. He is frozen to the spot, and it has nothing to do with the temperature.

'Whassamatter with you?' Butler pushes William out of the way and grabs his personal valise. He flicks it open.

Warne points a pistol at him. The jetty has cleared now. A moment of silence runs between the players, frozen in an ice-blue winter relief. Butler looks at every one of his companions, finishing with his loyal valet. 'Willy, then. Why, boy?'

'For my country.'

Butler smirks. 'You led me all the way over here to get trapped by these two gumshoe ass hats? How much were they paying you, son?'

'Nothing, Ben. I told you once already, it was for my country.'

'Your country. *Your* country. Goddamn it, well I've just about heard it all now. Your country, damn. See, I blame all this namby pamby bullshit on Abe Lincoln and his simpering lackeys in the Senate. Emancipation Proclamation, my ass. What emancipation? Did he ever even go to the South? Never going to happen. It is this type of thinking that will damn us all. That is why he had to go.' William joins Pinkerton and Warne. He pulls his own gun and points it at Butler. 'Well, just swell now, is it not? Look at you, Willy. Shaking like a shitting dog. You better kill me with that, else you'll open a whole tin of whoop-ass, son.'

'Greedy pig.' William's hand wobbles. Warne steadies him, but his eyes are red with anger. 'You ate my beef. You use people and then throw them to the dogs. I will *not* let you take our country.'

'Hark, the true patriot. I am so disappointed in you. Wake up, son! It will never be *your* country. You're the wrong shade, boy!'

'So much for making me a senator,' says William, 'not that I ever believed such bullshit.'

'All hail the smartass negro! Lies are the currency of politics, you dolt. Anyone else want to join the little old firing squad slash reception committee I've got here? You two morons? Spit it out.'

In synchronisation, Prioleau and Bulloch shake their heads. Prioleau opens his mouth to speak, but Pinkerton gets there first. 'I think the most comfortable solution for all would be for you to get right back on that steamer, and we will accompany you on the return journey? How about it, Benjamin? I'll buy you a steak to say no hard feelings.'

'Oh, look at him, the Scottish mongrel. Delighted, are we? Think you're a hero? Got your collar, have we?' Butler's toes twitch next to the case. 'I say they'll have bigger things to worry about in D.C. when we return, and I will have you two clowns hauled up before a Federal court.'

Pinkerton grins. 'He has no idea, does he? This is delicious.'

Butler notices the splint on his nose. 'What happened to your face, Allan?'

'Sir. Major General,' Prioleau hustles over to Butler's side. 'I have to inform you that The Agency has full knowledge of your involvement with our, ah, project? Evidenced and verified.'

'What in dipsy fuck are you talking about?'

'I-I am sorry but we took a plea bargain with them. It seemed to be our only course of action, in your absence.'

Butler's many chins wobble. His entire vision is dominated by cretins and enemies, some in the same skin. 'Don't you try to throw this back on me, Bubba. What did they offer you?'

'Haven in Liverpool. Free from indictment, as long as we never return to American soil.'

Butler's laugh is as bitter as the cold. 'You'll never leave. Figures. Save your skins. That is base, common form, boys. Considering the sacrifices made by your brothers-in-arms.'

Pinkerton guffaws. 'You really have the hots for the Confederacy, don't you? Why didn't you switch sides and have done with it?'

'Because I *really* believe in my country, old Jockie.'

'What a load of old pish.'

Bulloch mutters. 'It's not so bad. My brother Irvine is arriving tomorrow with Captain Waddell to ratify it all.'

'What are you wittering on about, man?' says Butler.

'The end of the war,' says Prioleau, the blue hue of defeat across his eyes.

'Fucking cowards, the lot of you.' Butler shuffles on his feet, sap rising.

Warne primes her pistol. Pinkerton forces the attention. 'Now don't you go doing anything rash, Benjamin. You're a soak yourself, so you will have a chance to defend yourself in court. There is no need to end it here. We just want our bounty; the rest is up to the judiciary.'

'So, it is all about the commission, Allan?'

'Aye. Bottom line.'

'Honest enough.' Butler nods, and his lynx eyes dart around his head. 'Willy?'

'What do you want, Ben?'

'See this little portmanteau at my feet? Will you at least verify that this is the one item of luggage that you didn't pack?' William glances down inside the valise, and his eyes light up in horror. All he has to do is strike that match in his hand and the whole dock goes up.

'Yes, Ben.'

'Good. Then you will be able to verify that said valise is packed with enough explosive material to send all of Allan Pinkerton's hopes and dreams right back home to Glasgow?'

'Well, I don't know.'

'Details, son. It's all about the details. Say it how it is.'

William's face drops. 'Yes, Ben.'

Pinkerton's eyes squirt down to the object at Butler's feet. Behind him, a huge herd of cattle are being corralled across George's Dock, waiting to be moved into place for transport to Ireland, where there is ample land for grazing and beef production.

'Good then. At last, we're all on the same page. Try to railroad me, would you? Goddamn horses' asses, all of you. Now, here's what. Willy here is going to take that carriage and drive you all up Water Street there, all up the long drag where I can see you going, going, gone. Then I might vanish from your sight for a short while or a long while, but I can just about guarantee that all of you shall be seeing me again. Is that understood?'

Warne looks fair ready to shoot, but Pinkerton gently lowers her arm. 'Understood.' He gets in her ear, but hardly out of Butler's earshot. 'We'll catch him later, Kate. Patience.'

'Fat chance of that, you inept jock,' mews Butler. 'You all know what it means to cross me, you can't shit a shitter. Now, be gone. Go. Vamoose.'

Warne glances down to the valise. 'How do we know he's not bluffing?'

'Kate, do you know this man like I do?' replies Pinkerton.

'Yes, I rather think I do.'

'Now is not the moment for backchat, dear. We've got him pulled in with a rope, so let us fall back and regroup. Look at his eyes, like I trained you.'

Butler winks at Warne. 'But-'

'Not another word. Come on.'

Warne lowers the gun and leers at Butler, who blows her a kiss. William's eyes fill with tears of fear and rage, but he forces himself to turn and heads over to Prioleau's carriage. The others follow.

'Thaddaboy.'

Butler watches them board the carriage, and William tickles the reigns, turning it around. It bounces along the runway and past the driving cattle, slipping onto Water Street before heading towards the Goree Piazzas and up the steep climb out of town.

Butler takes a breath and closes the valise. It's amazing how a dud fuse and a hemp bag of desiccated horse shit, allied to a notorious appetite for destruction, can put the fear of God into people. He looks around himself before sniffing, striking the match, and relighting his pipe. No big bang, but a big mess to clear up. Still, comebacks are what this game is all about. He starts back up towards the gangplank, fumbling in his pocket for cash and his diplomatic documents for the formalities of the return voyage. 'Royal pain in the nuts.' He kicks one of his cases into the river and leaves the rest. Ben Butler only ever carries one bag of consequence.

A wolf whistle. He stops and turns. 'Well, Harriet Farrell? For sure, I missed your scowling face in all of this reckoning. Come on down, child.'

Harriet sits atop the slate roof of the arrivals hall wearing Warne's infamous poncho. It keeps her neck and shoulders nice and warm. She pinched it from Warne's hotel room, the guilty pleasure makes it all the better. Perhaps she'll burn the rotten thing later, or get Diarmuid to mount it in the Crown like a stag's head.

'Keeping me out of the loop as ever, sir?' she yells.

Butler can barely make her words out. He puts a hand to his ear, reaching for his pistol with his other hand. 'What did you say, dear? Come down here, and we can talk it through. You're still my girl, you know.'

'Not this time. Nor ever again.'

She pulls her Colt .45 and fires it into the air. On horseback, Grace and Dudley take this as their cue and gallop towards the herd of cattle milling across the dock, caterwauling and shooting into the sky as if they're on the Great Plains. Harriet issues a rictus grin Butler's way. Butler's eyes widen in terror as the cattle stampede towards him, driven by the rogue rustlers.

'By Jiminy fuck…'

The snow has dialled up to a blizzard now. Harriet yells. 'How do you like your steak, boss?'

'No, girls, no…'

He backs up as far as he can until he gets to the railing. With incredible alacrity for a man his size, he scales the railings and jumps over, right into the freezing drink. Cows pile into the jetty, thudding against the pen.

Harriet gets to her feet and gazes over the edge, but she can't even see bubbles.

'Juicy. He likes it real juicy.'

#27 – SURRENDER AT THE TOWN HALL

Liverpool, November 6th, 1865

'Sail ho!' yells young Mr Campbell up above in the crow's nest, espying the Liverpool pilot in the mouth of the river. The Shenandoah is a merchant ship with a military crew, since all armaments have been decommissioned and offloaded. Even the paint scheme has been changed to divert any unwanted attention. As the last Confederate vessel upon the seas, once it was commissioned and built in Govan, Glasgow, under the guise of being civilian; now, after years of wreaking havoc on the high oceans, it is returned in a similar guise.

Captain James Waddell and Master Irvine Stephens Bulloch possess the only American accents aboard this strange and timorous vessel, as if that is something that can only be bestowed upon the most senior ranks. The rest of the crew, from midshipmen to the cooks to the first mate, hail from Ireland and Scotland. Waddell will miss the nightly concertina and fiddle reveries, the nips of whisky and whiskey, and the dirty tales, but not as much as he will miss ramming and boarding Union whalers or scuppering their gunboats, wrecking that damn blockade in the Atlantic and performing brigandage in the Pacific. It was beautiful while it lasted, almost as if they were something distinct from the war itself, taking the fight right across the world. It was a triumph of military seafaring that should go down in naval lore, but instead, it ends today as a whimpering footnote.

The engines cut and they follow the pilot under sail, in no particular hurry this afternoon as their haven is guaranteed in this friendly port, although it looks very much like the Mersey is freezing over with great hunks of ice making them grateful for the guidance into harbour. Safe hands make for a settled mind. Master Bulloch's own brother commissioned the glorious CSS Alabama out of this very town, and he will personally vouch for the safety of any man aboard this ship. Still, such a shame to give up the fight when all they ever did was win.

'Raise the Stainless Banner,' mutters the captain for the last ever time. Oh, sad day.

They draw up alongside HMS Donegal, the Royal Navy barque assigned directly to the task of final surrender.

'Howyer, Conor.'

'Howyer Eamonn, been a while.'

'Aye.'

The two crews know one another for the better part. Many have even served together in previous military and merchant commissions. Waddell fostered a tight camaraderie aboard the Shen, rivalling any grey platoon at Sharpsburg. It would be a disgrace to call them privateers; better simply to label them sailors. Some might disagree through the prism of victory, but they are safe here.

A gangway is drawn between the two mighty ships. Waddell goes first, as is the protocol. Many a time, he has performed this ritual to subdued Union sloops, capturing or sinking 38 ships, taking more than a thousand captives and inflicting $1.6 million worth of chaos upon the blue menace. He will happily take that record to his grave, but this tops any humiliation dished out to Union captains, in spite of the warm welcome.

A long whistle. Royal Navy tars stand to attention. Waddell is a might touched to be afforded such pomp and ceremony by the British, but there was no way on God's green Earth that he was surrendering to the Federals, not since they'd never even once bested him in a straight fight. The Donegal's captain bounds out like he's meeting a long-lost friend. The two shake hands.

'Morning, Bob.'

'Good morning, James. Hell of a command you had, what what?'

'Aye. Circumnavigation, too.'

'Well, I never. How about that? You should have a medal for that alone.'

'Um. Oh well.'

'I've heard some tales, alright.'

'Probably not even a pinch of it, old boy. So then, Bob. How are we going to do this? Have you documents to sign? Can we get on with it?'

'Alas no, James.'

'No?'

'No, you will have to do this properly, over yonder in the Town Hall. Orders from above.'

'Right.'

'Get your lads aboard, and we'll treat them to rum while you take care of your business. It's fit and proper to get them pissed.'

'That is very kind of you, James. They had better go below as they'll catch their death up here.'

'You're too used to sunnier climes to a man.'

'Thank you, Bob. Your kindness is making this altogether easier.'

'Think nothing of it. The whisper I heard was that we damn nearly joined you. Imagine what that would have been like. The Yanks wouldn't have stood a chance. Pity, eh?'

Master Irvine joins Waddell's side as a landing craft is prepared. 'Your choice, son. You coming with or staying here for a few?'

'My brother would chide me if I wasn't present at the end, Captain,' says Irvine, 'He's a dour fellow.'

'So I hear.' The landing party is ready. 'Come on, then.'

It was Irvine who received the news of the capitulation of Richmond from HMS Barracouta while they were still in the Pacific. Since then, they have been running scared of a piracy charge under maritime law owing to their activities after Lee surrendered. At least, now, they get to become part of the official history with no mention of the vulgar 'p' word, but it remains a bitter pill. Fears of getting strung up by the Yankees like Captain Kidd have mercifully abated.

Waddell takes one look back at his blessed sloop, the best he will ever command. Poseidon drew together the finest ship and crew for him. Upon the shore, there isn't a soul to welcome them, unlike the rapturous crowds they experienced in Melbourne harbour, another place that embraced the Confederate story like it was their own. There is solace to him that this tale will endure and inspire future generations. Who knows, one day?

Well, it had seemed like there was no one here, but he spots a gaggle upon the landing as they approach and the pilot moors. It is a man of advancing years in a Union uniform, whom he recognises as Thomas Haines Dudley, flanked by a tiny African woman, and a woman that matches a description in despatches: a contemptible traitor and spy here in Liverpool. Irvine had mentioned them from his brother's letters. What sick mischief is this, some manner of jibe from the Federals? Technically, they are still at War until he signs the last surrender. He could shoot her for a bit of sport, one last victory.

As he scales the steps up and onto the boardwalk, she stands in his path, as does the African, goading him that extra inch. 'Madam, gangway if you please.' Waddell glances at the other. 'And whatever you are.'

'Careful you don't fall back in,' grunts the Union spy in a Louisiana drawl. Yes, that must be her, infamy in her very demeanour. These are the steps the Yankees took to win the war, recruiting women to do their dirty work. Cowards.

'Peculiar creatures. I have business.'

'If only you knew,' says the old duffer in the blue uniform.

'You must be Haines Dudley.'

'That I am.'

'Then you will back away, sir. Our agreement was with the British, not you. Even this conversation is illegal.'

'What you going to do, Waddell? Take me to court?'

Waddell pushes him back, but the woman is upon him now. 'Gangway, please, ma'am, sir,' grunts Irvine. One of the Royal Navy tars accompanying them pushes through and they proceed. This was not the reception he expected in this so-called friendly port.

A carriage waits for them by the dock for the short journey up Water Street. Waddell feels her eyes burning into him, and he wonders just how that brave comrade of his put up with such savage behaviour from a woman he was good enough to marry.

'This damned world is going to pot, Irvine.'

The Town Hall is as resplendent as ever. Waddell and Irvine depart the carriage and clamber up the red carpet of the steps. This represents the only ceremony they will receive against the bustle of a city-town that carries on regardless, relentless in its commercial process and progress. This is all they get: a footnote. The rancour is stoked again, now at the bitter end.

From inside the ornate lobby step Charles Prioleau and James Bulloch, the two stalwarts who he knew would be here to ensure a smooth process. A thick-set man in tweeds with a splint upon his nose and a rather irascible-looking female stand by. Surely they can't be the Mayor and Lady Mayoress? And if not, who are they? Surely not who he suspects they are. This day gets odder and odder.

The Bulloch brothers are reunited without as much as a handshake. Prioleau steps forward with a pen. A parchment sits upon a table in the middle of the vestibule. 'Hello brother,' says Irvine. His brother doesn't even acknowledge him, like he's done something wrong. Lost the war, perhaps.

Waddell takes the pen and dips it in the ink well. 'I must say that I had higher expectations, Charles. A civic reception. A spot of afternoon tea, at least.'

Prioleau glances back towards the two interlopers. 'We were under orders. No fuss.'

Waddell sneers back at them, finally getting it. 'Very well.' He scribbles his signature upon the document and the American Civil War is over.

#28 – THE PATH TO SALVATION

New York City, December 24th, 1865

'From the moment we first lost sight of the American shore, till we landed at Liverpool, our gallant steamship was the theatre of an almost constant discussion of the subject of slavery, commencing cool but growing hotter every moment as it advanced... the truth was being told and having its legitimate effect on the ears of those who heard it... the slave-holders, convinced that reason, morality, common honesty, humanity and Christianity, were all against them, and that argument was no longer any means of defence... they actually got up a mob – a real, American, republican, democratic, Christian mob and that too, on the deck of a British steamer...'

The bill poster for the inaugural event at the Steinway Rooms, East Fourteenth Street, announces: *OUR COMPOSITE NATION, A KEYNOTE ADDRESS BY MR FREDERICK DOUGLASS, ORATOR AND ADVISER TO PRESIDENT LINCOLN*. Pat has made his way to the front, jostling to find the optimum spot in a crowd of liberal, mainly white artisans, well-meaning to a man and woman. Do they connect with Mr Douglass in the way he connects with Pat? The speaker is a prolific and best-selling author, but since Pat is making painfully slow progress in learning how to read, this is the only way that he can absorb the great man's words, in person and as a sober listener. No priest or politician has affected him in this way, as if they would bother with his kind of rabble. But Mr Douglass, well, he is magnificent, he transcends the dogma and hate, he speaks directly to every person in every hall. He speaks directly to Pat from Cavan.

A sturdy table is brought onto the stage and a stack of books is set upon it. Mr Douglass sips water and then sits down with his prints, pen ready in hand. An orderly queue is formed of keen readers, pleased to have the opportunity to connect with the man himself and to purchase his work with his very own signature, in exchange for just one greenback per copy. A bargain for such a litany of great thinking.

'Excuse please. Excuse me, please.'

'Sir, you are jumping your place.'

'I'm sorry, like. I have to get home to my kids and wife. They're starvin' like.'

'Then what on earth are you doing here? Can you even read?'

'No. I'll just budge past if I can so, though. Thanks a million, like.'

'Illiterate Irish oaf. How rude.'

'Don't antagonise him, Edmund. He may be violent.'

'Who let him in here?'

'Sorry, like. Not sorry at all. Fuck you very much, like.'

'Ouch! My toes!'

'Sorry.'

'What did he just say?'

'You just trod on my foot, you imbecile!'

It hasn't escaped the attention of Mr Douglass as he signs copies. Pat squirms his way up the queue and finds himself in front of the great man. He clutches his cap and puts down his dollar. Mr Douglass' eyes fill with amusement at the reaction Pat has caused among the people behind him.

'Here,' he says, 'This one's on me.' Mr Douglass slides the dollar back to Pat. Pat slides it back.

'No sir, I'm good for it. Honest. Charity be damned.'

'Have we met?'

'Liverpool, sir. I got carried out and thrown on me arse. My own fault, mind. Stupid arse drunk, I was. But no longer, no more.'

'Yes.' A broad smile and Mr Douglass picks up his pen. Pat has no doubt that Mr Douglass does recall him, even from the thousands who have attended his rallies. 'Who do I dedicate this to?'

'Sarah, please.'

He scribbles her name and his signature. 'Sarah. A fine woman, no doubt.'

'Me son will read it to us. Mr Douglass?'

'Yes, sir?'

'Can I ask you something, like?'

'Surely?'

'What are you doing for your tea?'

'Goddamn it, move on will you? Damn paddywhack,' grunts Edmund behind him.

By Bronx standards, it is a luxury home. Neighbours told her that New York winters are notoriously cold and their first one lives up to the billing. Sarah sits by the fire darning the stockings, ready to fill with fruit for the children to enjoy on Christmas morning. It is one of her favourite feasts and she feels blessed this evening, if a little worried that Pat is out so late. Please God, he doesn't fall back into drink. Trust him as she does these days, hard won as that was, it is always at the back of her mind when the clock moves past nine and he's still out cleaning windows in the deathly cold. Surely they don't need the money? More than anything, though, tonight she is altogether so excited about his return that she could burst, but for another reason than just Christmas.

She darns and knits, fingers working dexterously in and out of the thread, although she could readily have gone to that nice Lord & Taylor on Fifth Avenue to buy new ones. It is in much the same way that they can look into buying a house in a nicer neighbourhood, although neither really want to leave the Bronx as the people here are more decent than uptown, no matter what them there knobs all say. They tried living that way back in Liverpool and nearly ended up back in a court house.

'Can I get you more tea?' she offers her guest.

'No thank you. I'm fine.'

The door in the hallway opens and shuts. 'Hi love. Have ye still got any of that stew on the stove left, like?' yells Pat, footsteps clumping. 'It's awful, perishing cold out there so.'

Pat appears in the doorway to the parlour. 'Have mercy the kids are in bed. Making all this noise at this late hour,' Sarah chides him, but she is immediately relieved to see that he is sober. Pat beams back at her and waves a book at her. 'What have ye got that for, pillock? You can't even read.'

Her husband steps back and a tall, exquisitely handsome black man in his fifties enters the room, stove pipe hat in his gloved hands. Sarah immediately blushes and wipes her apron. He offers a handshake and she accepts, unable to stop herself curtsying like he's royalty. Well, in this house he practically is so.

'Ma'am, your husband here tells me that you have stew?'

'Aye, sir. Hot stew. There's plenty.'

'He has some amazing stories. I'd like to hear more.'

'Mr Douglass has one or two of his own,' says Pat. Then he notices the other figure. She has been in the armchair opposite the fire, warming herself all the time. 'Harry?'

Harriet Farrell slowly gets to her feet. Baba is asleep in her arms, snoozing face nestled into her chest. She presses a finger to her lips. She pushes past Pat, winking at him. Mr Douglass nods at her. 'Most pleased to meet you, sir. A welcome surprise, for a change.'

'You too, ma'am. You must be the subject of these tales.'

'Howyer, Pat.'

'Howyer, Harry.'

Pat's eyes are wide and moist. He can't quite take it all in. Sarah approaches him and kisses his cheek. 'Happy Christmas, love.'

'What a happy home it is, so,' says Pat, beaming.

'Harry? Harriet Farrell? *The* Harriet Farrell? Now it all makes sense.' Harriet is struck with the immediate familiarity of this famous, elegant gentleman as he b-lines to her. It masquerades like he knows her as well as she knows him. Still, reputation or not, she still presses a finger to her lips to get him to lower his voice. He accedes in a fast whisper. 'Oh, forgive my excitement. Well, the very Heroine of Liverpool, come to New York City. I am honoured and humbled to meet you, brave lady. This evening really is a happy opportunity.'

'Your eye is equally sharp as your writing, sir. Alas, I am only passing through, bound for California. Tomorrow.'

'Tomorrow?' grunts Pat. Sarah presses a finger to her lips and bids Mr Douglass to sit at their table. It is almost too small for him. Harriet follows him, clinging infant at her breast.

'You are instantly recognisable from your photograph, ma'am.'

'Who has been taking my photograph, sir?'

Pat starts to get nervous. 'Let's not talk shop here on tonight of all nights, eh? It is so good to see you, Harry. So good.'

Suddenly, all she sees is Mr Douglass. Pat knows that face. He gurns in derision.

'I am curious, is all. It is my business not to be seen, Mr Douglass. So pray tell.'

'Ah well, as the most photographed man in America, I should learn from you.'

'It is necessary that you are photographed, sir. As much as it is necessary that I am not.'

Hot stew is placed in front of Douglass. 'Well this looks most appetising.'

'Who is the owner of my image?'

'Ms Farrell, I see things and I know people, uncommon to the general public. That has been important to my very survival on this mortal coil for as long as I care to remember.'

'Ditto, sir. You knew Mr Lincoln?'

'I did.'

'You advised him?'

'Perhaps. Befriended more. His was a lonely job. How I wish that he was able to finish his work.'

'Then you will know that not all of his enemies wore grey uniforms.'

'Yes.'

'Snakes among us.' Her eyes darken for a moment, then she remembers her company.

'Still among us, ma'am. Present company in this fine house excluded.'

'Who is the owner of my image, Mr Douglass?'

'Please do not fret at all. Your identity is in good hands.'

'If you say so. Nevertheless, I would like to know *whose* good hands.'

Pat squirms. His hero is being interrogated by his best friend over stew. This is not how he envisaged the evening. 'Come now, Harry. This is all behind you now. California awaits. Tell us where? San Francisco?'

'If you work for Ben Butler, it is never behind you, Pat. You of all people should know that.'

'He's gone, Harry. Let it go.'

'Says who? You?' Harriet's firm retort makes Baba stir.

'For fuck's sake, like.' Pat receives a hard elbow in the ribs from Sarah for his language. 'Five minutes she's been here and she's already causing trouble.'

'I have faced sterner inquisitions, Pat,' says Mr Douglass, still as light and gentle as they come.

Harriet continues her line. 'Good sir, you are a man of unmatched integrity. So, I would beseech you to tell me.'

He tastes the stew and savours it. 'I cannot divulge. It was imprudent of me to mention it. My apologies.'

Nothing this man does is imprudent. She can't pin him down because there are so few, if any, like him, but she will. Harriet checks the eyes of Pat and Sarah upon her, worried. Mr Douglass remains gentle, kind, and implacable. 'I am a long way from Liverpool now, sir, but the place has a way of changing oneself, sticking to one's person like indelible mud. Perhaps it is you that should forgive me.'

'That city may as well be attached at the hip to Charleston, for all the Southern favour it curries. If it ever was English, I am not so sure what it is now. Mmm, delicious stew, ma'am.'

'Not everyone there supports them Confederates,' mutters Sarah, as if it should matter to her. But then, she didn't leave Liverpool out of choice.

'Well sir, I have no plans to return soon,' says Harriet, still keen to quiz Mr Douglass on just how she became famous in his circles without her knowledge. If she bides her time, she will discover. Still, time to shed the aggressive tack.

But then he leans in, face suddenly straight and stern. 'With your good standing, ma'am, you may have no choice but to return there soon in the service of your country, if what I know comes to pass.'

Everyone stops eating. Baba coos back to sleep. Harriet's veins run stone cold.

Pat interjects. 'But the war is over, sir. Like, really over.'

'At least when you are at war, you know where you stand, Patrick. History tells us that the aftermath can be equally perilous. Disastrous, even.'

'The study of history is a fool's errand when you know the reality, sir.'

'I concur, Miss Farrell.'

'Which is why I have no intention of being remembered. Not now, nor in a hundred years.'

'That would be a dreadful shame, ma'am. All we ever become are stories after we pass.'

Harriet has yet to touch her food. It is high time she put Baba to bed, though she is loath to let her away from her bosom having finally been reunited this evening. 'And what do you know, Mr Douglass? Why should I get back to where I once belonged? You have not an iota of an idea of how difficult that place was to leave, for all the trouble.'

'Indubitably.' Douglass' eyes dart around the room, then he returns to his pleasant countenance, twiddling his spoon. He offers Harriet a warm smile before turning to Sarah. 'Ma'am, I must congratulate you on this magnificent stew. I shall pinch the recipe, if it pleases you. Or is that a state secret?'

'Mr Douglass?'

'I am so glad that I ran into you this evening, Harriet Farrell. On the other hand, you might not be as pleased, when you hear what I have to tell you.'

All In Your Head: What Happens When Your Doctor Doesn't Believe You?

All In Your Head is about what happens when your doctor doesn't believe that you're ill. When they think you are imagining a serious ailment, or worse, faking it.

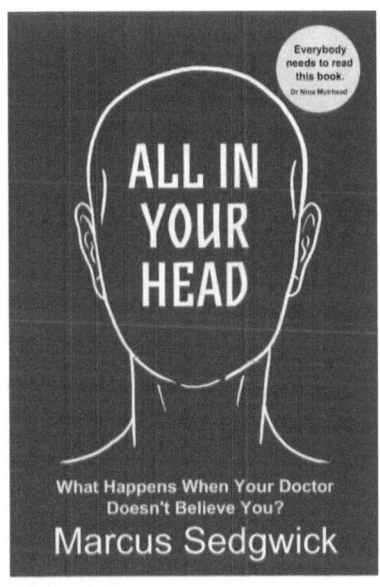

It's the story of the stigma that goes with invisible illness, and of the strange places that chronic illness takes you. It's the tale of bizarre treatments, and above all, the damage that's created through other people's doubts and indifference.

Yet, there is an epidemic of undiagnosed, hard-to-explain, and misunderstood illnesses in today's world, with new illnesses such as long-COVID steadily emerging. It is often up to individuals to drive their *own* search for recognition and a diagnosis, a task that can prove challenging due to establishment scepticism and disinterest.

With honesty, and at times, dark humour, *All In Your Head* – from multiple award-winning author Marcus Sedgwick – explores how four simple words can make you question your sense of reality.

Are We Still Rolling? Studios, Drugs and Rock 'n' Roll – One Man's Journey Recording Classic Albums

Phill Brown is the sound engineer and producer who – over an illustrious 50-year career – has worked with many of the biggest names in rock and roll.

In this reissued and updated version of his 2011 memoir, Phill describes the ups and downs of a professional recording studio, working on sessions for The Rolling Stones, Jimi Hendrix, and Joe Cocker at the famed Olympic Sound Studios in London. As a young sound engineer, Phill learned the ropes from experienced engineers and producers such as Glyn Johns and Eddie Kramer, and soon worked his way up the ladder, engineering sessions and producing albums. His remarkable roll call includes Steve Winwood, David Bowie, Led Zeppelin, The Rolling Stones, Jeff Beck, Pink Floyd, Bob Marley, Talk Talk, Roxy Music, Go West, Dido, and many other legendary rockers.

With a foreword by Robert Palmer, *Are We Still Rolling?* is more than a recollection of treasured music-making over 50 years. It is one man's journey through a life where drug abuse, chaos, rampant egos, greed, lies and the increasingly invasive record business all took their toll. It's also a cautionary tale, where long workdays and what once seemed like harmless indulgences had sinister consequences.

www.ingramcontent.com/pod-product-compliance
Lightning Source LLC
Chambersburg PA
CBHW022157260626
47155CB00019B/3082